THE ONLY

FE

THING TO

AR

BY CAROLINE TUNG RICHMOND

SCHOLASTIC INC.

Copyright © 2014 by Caroline Tung Richmond

This book was originally published in hardcover by Scholastic Press in 2014.

All rights reserved. Published by Scholastic Inc., *Publishers since 1920*. SCHOLASTIC and associated logos are trademarks and/or registered trademarks of Scholastic Inc.

The publisher does not have any control over and does not assume any responsibility for author or third-party websites or their content.

ISBN 978-0-545-87214-0

10 9 8 7 6 5 4 3 2   17 18 19 20

Printed in the U.S.A.   40
First printing 2016

Book design by Phil Falco

For Justin,
who urged me to chase this dream

1

The Nazis always arrived on schedule.

Today would be no exception.

At four o'clock sharp, Zara St. James gripped the sides of her canteen, her dark eyes fixed on the Sentinel flying toward her. He soared across the cloud-ridden sky, zipping through the breeze with his arms locked in front of him, like a superhero from an old comic.

But there was nothing heroic about him.

As the Sentinel neared the fields, he dipped down so low that Zara could see the rifle looped over his shoulder and the fist-size swastika on his olive-green uniform. His golden hair flapped in the chilly April wind, cementing the look of the prized Aryan soldier: sturdy frame, snowy skin. Adolf Hitler's shining legacy.

"Not you again," Zara whispered. The corners of her mouth tightened with worry. Twice this week she had noticed him patrolling the farm, always around four o'clock. One visit was routine. Two, a bit alarming. A third could mean trouble. Possibly an interrogation.

Or worse.

Zara's worry sank deeper as the Sentinel headed straight for the farm. He skimmed over the Shenandoah hills, which were bursting with fresh spring leaves. Then his gaze swept over the St. James land, scanning the worn-looking house and the decades-old barn and finally settling on Zara, who stood at the edge of the rain-soaked fields.

He slowed to a stop. *"Heil Hitler!"* he shouted in crisp German, hovering thirty feet above her head.

Zara's heartbeat clattered, but she stretched out her arm in the proper salute, just as her mother had taught her years ago. *"Heil Hitler,"* she replied. Her own German was passable due to the mandatory classes in primary school, but her accent had always been atrocious, which didn't bother her in the least. On most days she rather enjoyed offending the Germans' delicate ears — one of the few crimes they couldn't beat her for — but now she made sure to enunciate each syllable. She didn't want any trouble.

The Sentinel saluted in return. *"Ein Volk, ein Reich, ein Führer,"* he barked out. The Nazi motto. *One people, one Empire, one leader.*

Her breaths grew tight. At this distance, Zara could see the three lightning bolts printed on the side of his helmet, the symbol of the German Anomaly Division — the most elite, and most frightening, branch of the Nazi military. The division had been the brainchild of Führer Adolf Hitler's, an entire regiment composed of genetically altered soldiers who could crush their enemies with their superpowered fists. And those fists had changed the world.

Zara's gaze slunk toward the farmhouse, still unsure why the Sentinel had stopped by. *Please don't be here for a search*, she thought desperately. She wished she could warn her uncle somehow — *Hide the radio*, she'd tell him — but then the Sentinel landed on the field, his boots flattening an onion sprout, blocking the house from her view.

"Your name, girl?" he demanded.

She forced herself to look up at him. "Zara St. James, *mein Herr.*"

"Age?"

"Sixteen."

"And where are you *from*?"

Zara grimaced. She had heard that question enough times to know that he wasn't asking where she had been born, which was right here in the Shenandoah Valley. He wanted to know her *lineage*, where she had gotten her black hair and sable eyes in this rural mountain town.

"I'm English on my mother's side," Zara said slowly. Her chest squeezed at the mention of her mom, and she wondered where his questioning was leading. "And Japanese on my father's."

"The Empire of Japan, hmm?" His eyes skimmed over her sun-darkened skin, loitering over her sweaty, secondhand shirt and drifting toward her hips. His mouth curved into a smile.

A sour taste bloomed on Zara's tongue. She knew that smile and what it meant. Most Germans sniffed at her "half-breed" stock. She was an *Untermensch* — a subhuman — like the Polish and blacks and any mixed-race persons, only fit for factory and farm work. But not everyone scorned the color of her skin. There were a few townspeople — always men, it seemed — whose gazes lingered on the shape of her eyes and at the slight curve of her hungry waist. Like the Sentinel was doing now.

Zara's thoughts hit a tailspin. She could use her fists as a weapon, but that wouldn't be much against the Sentinel. Or she could scream, but there were acres between her and her uncle. Only the cows would hear her from here.

That left her with one last option, but Uncle Red's warning drilled through her head: *No one can know about what you can do*, he had told her countless times. *If the Nazis found out, they'd haul you off to one of their labs or a labor camp. Or a grave.*

The Sentinel stepped forward, that smile of his arching. Zara's fingers tightened around her canteen, ready to swing at his head, but then he pulled out a stack of papers from his pocket instead. He tossed one in the dirt.

"An announcement from Fort Goering," he said, referring to the Nazi citadel a few miles up the road, where thousands of soldiers were stationed. "Pick it up."

Eyes wary, Zara retrieved the paper and ignored his grin at her obedience. The fort's soldiers must have been ordered to distribute these flyers across the township; and unfortunately for Zara, the Sentinel had decided to hand-deliver hers. She scanned the paper's contents:

> **FROM THE OFFICE OF COMMAND**
> **FORT GOERING, SHENANDOAH DIVISION**
> **EASTERN AMERICAN TERRITORIES**
>
> At 1700 hours EST, all residents of the Greenfield Township are required at the Courthouse Square. An announcement will be made shortly thereafter, broadcasted live from Berlin. Attendance is mandatory.

A dozen questions ripped through Zara's mind. Most announcements from Berlin — treaties signed, battles won — were aired on the evening news reports or printed in the state-run newspaper. Only a handful merited a live broadcast, let alone mandatory attendance.

Zara still remembered the first announcement she had attended, back when her mother was alive. All of Greenfield had met in the square to celebrate the birth of Johann Hitler, the son of the current Führer, Dieter Hitler. The entire Nazi Empire, from Berlin to Brussels, from the American coast to the North African shores, was forced to salute the newest addition to the Hitler dynasty, the great-great-grandson of Adolf himself. Zara's mother had saluted dutifully, too, but a soldier struck her anyway for wearing muddy boots to such a sacred event. She had apologized immediately, but she never flinched from the hit. Years later, that memory still stuck with Zara: her mother standing tall, the bravest woman in all of Greenfield. The ache of missing her never went away.

Zara wondered what this new announcement would bring. Perhaps Dieter's wife had squeezed out another child? Or maybe the Führer had taken over the Italian Dakotas? The Italian economy had teetered on the brink of collapse since Prime Minister Benito Mussolini III came into power a decade ago. He may have sold the Dakotas, along with the Canadian lands, for a desperate price.

"Why are you still standing here, little *Mischling*?" the Sentinel said, cutting into her thoughts.

Zara tacked on a polite smile. "My apologies, *mein Herr.*"

His jewel-blue eyes looked her up and down. "See to it that you aren't late. I'll be watching."

Her cheeks burned, but she daren't say a word. Instead, she quickly turned on her heel while the Sentinel launched into the clouds. Only then did Zara shudder.

"*Mischling?*" she muttered. It was a German term for *mixed-blood*, usually used like a slur, but the Sentinel hadn't made it sound that way. Her fingers had itched to slap him, but an *Untermensch* like her would get jailed for that. Or sent to the Front Royal labor camp thirty miles east.

With another shudder, Zara hurried to the house, abandoning the onions for tomorrow. She leapt over the infant rows of corn and ran past the faded barn that her great-great-grandparents had built before the war. In the early '40s, the old United States had been a beacon of hope — of freedom so vast it could swallow you whole — but that America had long been destroyed, its cities flattened by the German Anomaly Division. After President Roosevelt was executed in early 1944, the Axis powers had cut the country like a giant birthday cake. The Nazis had claimed the fertile lands east of the Mississippi River while the Japanese took over the West, leaving the Italians with the Dakota plains, a consolation prize for their anemic role in the fighting. Decades had passed since then and the Germans still held a tight rein over the Territories, but Zara yearned for more than a life of hard labor and *Heil Hitlers*.

One day, she thought, clutching the paper in her hand. One day, her uncle would let her join the Revolutionary Alliance, an underground resistance group that had fought the Empire for decades. It was originally formed by the last remnants of the US military, who had escaped Washington, DC, after Roosevelt's execution. Back then, its members had numbered in the millions, many of them former soldiers, but with the US military long disbanded the Alliance now relied on civilian recruits, like Uncle Red. And hopefully Zara.

If only she could join the rebels, then she could help push the Nazis back to Germany or, even better, crush the regime altogether. Maybe then, finally, her mother's death would have justice.

As her lungs puffed, Zara burst through the kitchen door of the run-down farmhouse to find her uncle underneath the kitchen sink, a foot-long wrench in his hand. A water pipe had burst that morning (the second one that month), and he had stayed behind to fix it. Otherwise he would've been out in the fields as usual, planting eggplant and digging holes for the cabbage.

"What happened?" said Uncle Red. He set the wrench on the floor and pulled himself up. "Did the cow get sick again?"

Zara peered up into his bearded face. Her uncle wasn't very tall, but she stood a whole head shorter than him. "The cow's fine. Here, look at this." She handed him the notice.

His green eyes, the same color as Zara's mother's, flared wide. "An *announcement*? Now?"

"Do you know what this is about?" Her voice dropped low out of habit. They never knew who could be watching them. "Maybe the Alliance sent you a message?"

"No, we haven't gotten a thing since last week."

"This has to be serious if attendance is mandatory."

Uncle Red ran a tense hand through his thinning auburn hair. As he neared forty, he seemed to be losing more of it each year. "I know. Remember to stick close to me. The square will be swarming with soldiers. You can't lose control, do you understand?"

Zara bristled. "I haven't had an episode in years."

"It doesn't hurt to be cautious."

"I'm always cautious."

He looked doubtful, but said nothing more about it. "Grab the keys. We don't want to keep the Führer waiting."

2

They climbed into Uncle Red's ancient truck, a red Volkswagen with an engine like a foghorn. Key in ignition, the truck let out a roar and they rumbled down the mud-caked road, lumbering past acres of corn and leafy beans that the Nazis would later seize to feed the troops at Fort Goering. Every farmer was required to pay a land tax to the Empire, which made Zara's blood simmer at every harvest. After months of her and her uncle's hard work, the Germans would take the very best crops and leave them with cornhusks and bug-eaten cabbage. She *hated* cabbage.

Uncle Red cracked open his window, and the faint scent of cow manure wafted into the cab. "Who gave you the announcement? One of the town magistrates?"

"A sentinel." The fresh memory of his visit made Zara's skin crawl. That leering smile of his . . . "The one who can fly."

"He's new, isn't he? Sentinel Achen, I think. We better move the radio to be safe."

Zara nodded. For years, they had hidden a small transistor radio inside their henhouse, tucked under the floorboards along with her great-great-grandfather's rifle and pistol. Every week or two, Uncle Red would use the radio to speak with the Alliance through coded messages. It was the only reliable method of communication they had found to skirt the Nazis' watchful eyes.

"We should've checked the radio before we left," said Zara as the truck hit a bump. "The Alliance could've figured out what this announcement is about."

"We'll find out soon enough."

A thought struck her. "Do you think the Soviets have something to do with this? Maybe they broke the pact." Back in 1939, Hitler and Stalin had signed the Nazi-Soviet Nonaggression Pact, which had kept the two countries in a tenuous peace for decades. But in recent years Comrade Premier Volkov had seemed keen on expanding into the borderlands that separated Germany from the Reds. The Alliance believed that a few of those border nations, like Latvia and Estonia, could be sympathetic to the communist cause.

"Volkov wouldn't act so rashly," said Uncle Red as he turned onto the gravel lane leading into town. "His own Anomaly soldiers are strong, but they can't compete against the German Anomaly Division just yet."

Zara sighed, slightly deflated, and stared out her window at the rolling hills passing by. Her uncle had a penchant for poking holes in her theories, and as much as she hated to admit it, he was right about this one. During the war the Nazis had led the race to create the first super-powered soldier, at the behest of Führer Adolf. Known as the Dresden Study, the German geneticists had plucked test subjects from concentration camps, mostly Jews and gypsies. By 1941 they had unleashed a battalion of bulletproof Anomalies onto the streets of London. In mere weeks, that single battalion had killed off a third of Parliament and flattened half of the British capital before their genes destabilized from the wartime experiments. Nearly all of those first Anomalies fell into comas and died — the Nazi scientists still had their work cut out for them — but the soldiers had completed their mission. Churchill surrendered a month later.

After England fell, the rest of the world had scrambled to their own laboratories. Japan had had an early start — its military had been experimenting on Chinese and Russian prisoners since the 1930s — and its first Anomaly troops, dubbed the Ronin Elite, debuted in 1942. The Soviets followed suit a year later. But the Americans opted to focus on their top-secret Manhattan Project, hoping to fight the Anomalies with an atomic bomb. Their gamble, however, went sour. Before the United States could test their secret weapon, the Nazis attacked the American East Coast while Japan struck from the west. Thousands upon thousands of Anomaly troops flooded the country, crushing the United States under the Axis's polished boot.

Uncle Red rolled up his window, his jaw visibly tense. "Remember what I told you at the house. Be careful at the square."

Zara sighed. *This again?* "I *know*, Uncle Red."

A mile later, the truck entered the Greenfield town limits, and the small, sagging houses gave way to redbrick town homes, proudly standing over cobblestone streets. Iron gas lamps lit the clean sidewalks and flower boxes dangled from the windows, popping with pink tulips and cheery daffodils. Zara frowned at the picture-perfect sight.

Only the wealthy could live here. Only the Nazis.

The truck puttered down a side road and halted outside the offices of the old *Virginian Post-Observer*, long abandoned after the Nazis destroyed its presses. Next door to it, Zara saw the remnants of the synagogue that had been burned long before. It was strange to think about the Jews who had once worshipped there, who had made Greenfield their home. Almost all of them had been shot during the postwar cleansings, although a few had managed to survive by going into hiding or assuming new identities.

Zara's hand gripped the door handle as she thought about her best friend, Molly Burns, whom she met back in primary school. Molly had been the only one who didn't care about Zara's Japanese side. In the hot Shenandoah summers they would spend hours at the Burns pond, and during the fall they would fill their stomachs with fat red plums. But Molly disappeared just after the girls turned thirteen. Her whole family had vanished along with her.

Uncle Red was the one who broke the news to Zara — that years before Molly was born, the Burnses had once been the Birnbaums. Molly's great-great-grandparents had converted to Protestantism before the war, but the Nazis had discovered their Jewish heritage and shot them all dead, burning their bodies until the smoke cluttered the pale morning sky. Thinking about that day still brought a lump to Zara's throat. The Empire had killed so many people she had loved. Her best friend, her own mother. Far, far too many.

Turning her head from the synagogue, Zara hopped out of the truck and started for the square, but her uncle caught her by the elbow.

"Keep your chin down," he said.

His head was cocked toward a half-dozen soldiers patrolling the street for the announcement. They each wore a green helmet and cradled a standard-issue Heckler & Koch rifle. As they drew closer, Uncle Red tilted his chin downward and motioned for Zara to do the same, but she stole a glance at the soldiers anyway. She couldn't help noticing that some of them were Japanese, proven by the little red sun flags on their armbands. Only full-blooded Japanese were given honorary Aryan status in the German Empire, a nod to the long-standing alliance between Germany and Japan. These soldiers must be stationed at Fort Goering on a military exchange program, a goodwill gesture between the two allies.

Years ago, Zara's father had been one of these soldiers, too. She didn't know much about him, aside from the fact that he had filed for an immediate transfer once the girl he had been secretly seeing — Zara's mother — told him she was pregnant.

One of the soldiers caught Zara's eye, but she swiftly looked across the street. When she was little and didn't know any better, she had wandered up to a Japanese captain and asked if he knew her father, Corporal Tanaka. The soldier had taken one look at Zara and said, *Why would I know anything about your father or his trash?* When he started laughing, she had run away, tears swimming down her cheeks. She realized then how her father must have viewed her. Trash. Litter. Garbage to be thrown away, just as he had thrown away her mom.

"You all right? You're pale." Uncle Red looped an arm around her shoulder.

Zara shrugged and sank against him, his hug reminding her that not everyone had abandoned her. As much as Uncle Red frustrated her, as much as she wanted to box his ears sometimes, he was the only father she had known and the only one she needed.

As they neared the town center, they zigzagged through the crowd of farmers in their sweat-soaked shirts and the iron miners in their dusty coveralls, who had been let out early for the announcement. Zara followed her uncle into a wide, bricked courtyard, commonly known as the square. The Greenfield Courthouse lay ahead of them, a centuries-old building that had once been the pride of the town, with its white pillars and handsome bell tower. But now it was used for official Nazi business, complete with a portrait of Führer Dieter hanging above its doors. Everyone was expected to salute the painting whenever they walked under it, and Zara had always done so obediently, but that didn't stop her belly from twisting every time. She hated looking into Dieter's plump face and his ridiculous rectangle of a mustache, the same mustache that his great-grandfather had favored.

"Where's the painting of Reichsmarschall Faust?" Uncle Red said. He nodded to the blank space next to the Führer's portrait where a likeness of Reichsmarschall Faust, the cousin of the Führer and the head commander of the Territories, usually hung.

"Maybe they're putting up a new one."

"Maybe," Uncle Red said, although his eyes narrowed and he didn't look convinced.

Zara pushed deeper into the crowd, murmuring a quick "Pardon me" to the German housewives she bumped into. As usual, the *Hausfrauen* were dressed in the latest fashions from Berlin: leather riding boots, wide-legged trousers, and delicate blouses patterned with tiny silver swastikas. The women had brought their broods along for the show: stair-step children with cornhusk hair. Since the war, the Nazis had encouraged women to bear large families to spread the Aryan line, and now it was a common sight to see a German mother with five, six, or seven children in tow. They reminded Zara of her neighbor's brood mares: popping out child after child until their bodies could take no more.

"Redmond! Over here!"

Zara's head swiveled to find Mrs. Talley, a dear family friend and another member of the Alliance, waving a wrinkled hand in their direction. The old woman stood at the far corner of the square with her gray hair tucked into a bun and a red shawl draped around her shoulders. She leaned against a lamppost to relieve her aching right hip. Uncle Red threaded toward her.

"Hello, my sweet girl." Mrs. Talley greeted Zara with a warm hug and a peck on the cheek, a ritual left over from when Zara was little. "You wouldn't happen to know what this is all about, would you?"

"I thought it could be the Soviets, but he shot that idea down," said Zara, gesturing at her uncle.

Uncle Red tensed. "Let's keep our voices down."

Mrs. Talley only smiled. "It's all right. I'm sure no one heard us with all of this chatter around us."

"It doesn't hurt to be careful," said Uncle Red, staring straight at Zara.

Zara folded her arms, but she nodded. Her uncle's paranoia often chewed on her last nerve, but she couldn't exactly begrudge him for it. After all, he had weathered his share of Nazi interrogations because his father — Zara's grandfather — had been imprisoned for possessing an Alliance pamphlet. The Nazis had sent Louis St. James straight to a labor camp, where he succumbed to pneumonia six months later. Not long after his death, the Nazis started sniffing around the St. James farm more and more, although that hadn't stopped Zara's mother and Uncle Red from joining the Alliance.

The crowd hushed as three armored SUVs rolled down the street from Fort Goering. Rising on her tiptoes, Zara watched the vehicles stop. A dozen soldiers spilled out from their doors, including Sentinel Achen. Seeing him again made Zara grimace, wishing she could scrub her skin clean.

The soldiers fanned around a long stage that had been erected on the eastern edge of the square, rising six feet above the ground.

Behind the stage, a large white screen the size of a movie theater display had been assembled for the broadcast.

A Nazi officer stepped out of the last SUV and the soldiers snapped to attention; Zara's mouth screwed tight at the sight of him. It was Colonel Eckhart, the commanding officer of Fort Goering, marching onto the stage with his silver hair slicked back and his boots gleaming like a mirror. A bleached-white smile occupied his face, the same smile he wore whenever he ordered a public beating or an execution. At the sight of that grin, Zara fought off a scowl. Colonel Eckhart may have possessed the good looks of a Munich cinema star, but his heart was black as tar underneath. He had no problem ordering his soldiers to kill communists, Jews, or homosexuals. Not that there were many of them left nowadays. The Nazis had exterminated an untold number of "undesirables" during the postwar cleansings, and any survivors had learned to live in hiding long ago. But as much as the Colonel enjoyed killing a Soviet sympathizer or a closeted homosexual, nothing made him happier than catching an Alliance rebel — his personal favorite.

"Citizens of Greenfield!" Colonel Eckhart held up a megaphone, and his tenor voice blared like a ringmaster welcoming a fresh group of onlookers. His right arm snapped up. *Heil Hitler! Sieg heil!*

The crowd returned the salute. *"Sieg heil!"* they chanted, a popular rallying cry. *Hail victory.*

"I am pleased today to bring you a message from our beloved leader, Führer Dieter Hitler. Without further ado." The Colonel motioned toward the white screen and nodded at one of his soldiers, whose hands fluttered over a box of controls.

A few seconds ticked by before the broadcast began. A Nazi flag waved against a bright blue sky, accompanied by a cheery recording of the Nazi national anthem. When the music ended on a high F note, the flag was replaced with a live feed of the Führer, who sat behind a heavy oak desk in his Berlin palace. Behind him, the floor-to-ceiling windows offered a panoramic view of the Berlin skyline, filled with hundred-floor condominiums and shiny skyscrapers that boasted of the city's wealth.

The Führer was dressed in full military regalia, even though he had never stepped foot on a battlefield. He wore a trim olive-green uniform with broad epaulets on each shoulder and a blinding array of medals hung over his breast pocket. To the right of him, Dieter's beautiful wife, Anke, and their nine-year-old son, Johann, smiled at the camera, their pale hair combed to perfection. They were the picture of the idyllic Aryan family, but that picture was incomplete. At their Parisian summer home four years earlier, Dieter and Anke's twin girls had been killed in a bombing attack orchestrated by French rebels. Dieter and Johann had escaped unharmed, but Anke had been in a coma for a month and was now rumored to be barren.

Zara's gaze drifted to the back of the screen, her eyes drawn to the four soldiers lined up behind the Führer. The Corps of Four. A shiver wormed its way down her spine. All four of them were Dual Anomalies, the rarest of Anomalies who possessed not one but two powers, caused by a genetic glitch that the Nazi scientists couldn't re-create in their laboratories. Only a few dozen were known worldwide, and they were all extensively trained in the art of killing. Zara had no doubt that they could destroy her in a hundred different ways, each one more gruesome than the next.

The camera panned briefly over the Corps' faces. Zara could never remember their names, but she certainly remembered their abilities. At the very left stood the Medic, who could absorb his patients' pain and mend flesh wounds with a brush of his hand. To his right, there was the Mind Controller, who could plant ideas in people's thoughts and knock people unconscious with a flick of the wrist. Then there was the Protector — the youngest of the four, who wore her platinum hair in two plaits — who could conjure fireballs from her fingertips and hurl icicles from her palms. Last, there was the Monster, standing over seven feet tall, who could withstand bullets with his impenetrable skin and strangle an eighteen-hand stallion with his super-strength. Apparently, he wrestled grizzly bears for training.

Zara shivered again. With the Corps of Four at his side, it was no wonder the Führer had survived multiple assassination attempts over the past fifteen years. Only a year ago, an unnamed group — rumored to be financed by the Soviets — had tried to bomb Dieter's limousine, but the Monster had pushed the vehicle to safety while the Protector burnt the terrorists to a char. As long as the Corps was nearby, Dieter was practically invincible.

The crowd fell into an empty silence as the Führer sat forward in his leather chair. No one dared make a sound.

"Greetings, my citizens," Dieter said in German. His voice boomed as strong as his father, Anselm's, who had ruled the Nazi Empire for a decade before succumbing to a cancer that his doctors couldn't treat. "It is not often that I address my subjects in the Territories, but today is a fortunate one, for I bring good tidings to you."

The camera panned out as Dieter's wife and the Corps of Four broke into polite applause. Even Johann clapped his chubby hands together, eliciting a proud smile from his mother.

So young and so brainwashed, Zara thought. If Molly were here, they would glance at each other and resist the urge to roll their eyes.

"After three years of service, Reichsmarschall Faust, the commander of the Eastern American Territories, is entering retirement. We wish him well." Dieter's words were flat and rough as sandpaper, as if he didn't wish Faust well at all.

Zara's eyes flickered toward her uncle. This move made little sense. Reichsmarschall Faust was only in his early fifties, far too early to retire. Besides, Faust had been eager to command the Territories ever since he and Dieter had graduated from military school together. Why would he give up this plum assignment after only a few years? And why was this good news?

Dieter continued, "Now, as for who will oversee the Territories in Reichsmarschall Faust's absence, I have appointed General Emmerich Baldur to the job." He appeared much sunnier as he motioned off-camera. A second later, a barrel-chested man walked onto the screen, his beard neatly trimmed and his chin tipped high in that arrogant Nazi way. "General Baldur, soon to be Reichsmarschall Baldur, has spent twelve years in the North African Colonies, overseeing our troops there. Prior to that, he also served in the French Territorial State and the British Isles."

General Baldur stepped forward, a nicotine-stained smile glowing from beneath his mustache. He saluted the Führer with a heady *"Heil Hitler!"*

Dieter nodded and looked back at the camera. "Reichsmarschall Baldur will arrive in the Territories tomorrow. To my subjects there, I ask that you give him a warm welcome. *Guten Tag.*"

The feed returned to the waving Nazi flag, and Zara blinked at the movie screen. That was it? The entire announcement had lasted mere minutes. The Führer could easily have presented this news in the papers, but he had called a worldwide broadcast instead. Zara wondered if there was something happening behind the scenes. Why hadn't Faust attended the announcement? Had he and the Führer had a falling-out? Maybe the Alliance knew more about this. She'd have to nudge her uncle to ask them for details.

As the screen fell dark, Colonel Eckhart swept back onto the stage and clapped his hands furiously, forcing everyone else to follow suit. The miners merely tapped their hands together, but the *Hausfrauen* gave a rousing bout of applause, as if Adolf Hitler himself had risen from his crypt.

"Long live the Führer! Long live General Baldur!" Colonel Eckhart said into his megaphone.

The masses echoed back the chant, but Zara heard one voice shouting something else entirely.

"Long live the murderer! Long live the slaughterer of children!"

Zara went still. Did that person want a death sentence? Her gaze snaked through the square until she found the man saying such treasonous things, and she cringed when she found him — it was old Mr. Kerry, one of her neighbors. He was sympathetic to the Alliance, although he had never joined. However, his two sons had, but they perished in Mission Metzger nine years ago, an Alliance attack that had sought to take over Fort Metzger in central Maryland and steal its long-range missiles. But the mission had ended in misery. Tens of thousands of rebels were killed, including Mrs. Talley's husband and Zara's mother. Their lives were lost thanks to a cunning Nazi major who had tortured an Alliance rebel until she revealed the secret mission plans. After the battle was over, the major had been promoted and given command of his own fort. He now stood on the stage in front of Zara — Major Eckhart. *Colonel* Eckhart to be exact.

"Long live Dieter Hitler, the great oppressor!" Mr. Kerry slurred.

He had perched himself by the courthouse entrance, waving his arms over his head. The people standing near him hurried down the steps, hoping to distance themselves.

"That poor man," Mrs. Talley whispered. "I delivered both of his sons."

"He's been drinking again," Zara murmured. "He has no idea what he's saying."

"There's nothing we can do for him now," Uncle Red said grimly.

Zara ached to do something anyway. Mr. Kerry was one of the few townspeople who never frowned at the color of her skin. He brought her soup when she was sick and had read her stories after her mother died, even though he was grieving for his own children, too. If she was standing near the courthouse, she could try to get him to quiet down before the Nazis saw him.

But Colonel Eckhart had already spotted him. "Bring that man to me," he shouted to Sentinel Achen.

"Yes, sir," the Sentinel said with that grin of his. It didn't take long for him to fly to the steps and hoist Mr. Kerry back to the stage, where he shoved the old man onto his knees.

Colonel Eckhart paced the stage, circling Mr. Kerry. "It appears you have a strong opinion of our Führer." There was a lightness in his tone that made Zara cringe, like he was playing with his prey before he devoured it. "Our Führer is an 'oppressor,' I take it? Perhaps you forget about his charitable work in the Territories. Every month he provides food for the poor and orphaned, in case you've forgotten." The Colonel's nose scrunched as he glanced at Mr. Kerry's vomit-stained shirt. "Or perhaps you're angry that Dieter doesn't offer free liquor?"

The Nazi guards smirked, but Mr. Kerry's shoulders shook with a sob. "He murdered my children. My sons!"

"Oh? The Führer himself did such a thing? All the way from Berlin?"

Laughter erupted from the German onlookers. Near the stage, a group of young Nazi cadets, their hair spiked with gel, sniggered like jackals and shouted names at Mr. Kerry. Only one of them didn't participate in the heckling: a tall boy with a flop of messy blond curls, a couple of years older than Zara. He stood at the periphery of the group, his face blank.

Zara squinted at him. Then frowned. It was Bastian Eckhart, the Colonel's son. Rumor had it that he was a first-class snob, that his father's high status had gone to his head. But apparently Bastian hadn't inherited his father's glee at shaming peasants, or *Kleinbauern*, as they were disdainfully called.

"Scoff all you want, but America will rise again!" Mr. Kerry said. "You Nazis think you've trodden us down, but we'll come for you one day. The Alliance will come for you!" He staggered to his feet and tried to lunge at the Colonel, but the soldiers fell upon him.

The first strike hit Mr. Kerry's arm, smacking the bone with a skin-splitting crack. The second hit his head. Blood shot out of his nose, or maybe his mouth. Zara wasn't sure. She had buried her face against her uncle's shoulder, too sickened to watch. Mr. Kerry was a seventy-year-old man, but the Nazis were beating him like a piece of leather.

Mrs. Talley curled a thin arm around Zara. "It'll be over soon."

Not soon enough.

Mr. Kerry lay in a bloody heap on the stage, whimpering. Colonel Eckhart finally looked satisfied. "Take him to the camp," he said to his guards. They grabbed the old man by the arms and tossed him into the back of a truck.

Zara's fists knotted at her sides. She didn't want to stand here doing nothing. Her mother would have done something, wouldn't she? But there were Nazis all around her, in the square, on the streets.

"Let this be a lesson to you *Kleinbauern*," Colonel Eckhart said to the throng. "I will not tolerate — and Reichsmarschall Baldur will not tolerate — any defamation of our Führer. After everything he has done for us, is this the way we thank him?" He paused, but no one said a word. With a curt nod, he said, *"Ein Volk, ein Reich, ein Führer!"*

Zara gave a limp salute before the crowd broke apart, and they headed back to the truck. Mrs. Talley squeezed her hand, something that had always made Zara's heart lighten, but she only felt heavy today. Around them, the *Hausfrauen* babbled about how handsome Johann was becoming while the cadets threw bottles at the SUV that was hauling Mr. Kerry away. Disgust rolled through Zara; she wanted to tear those bottles from them, but she forced her hands to remain at her sides.

Stay calm, her uncle would tell her. *You can't cause a scene.* But Zara was so sick of these beatings and those heckling cadets. She wanted to fight back. She was ready for it, like her mom had once been.

But she couldn't do a thing. Not when the Nazis had bullets and guns, not when they outnumbered her a hundred to one. If she tried to help Mr. Kerry, they would throw her into a camp — and maybe they'd beat her uncle and then make her watch him scream. She would expect nothing less from them.

Zara broke into a run. Uncle Red and Mrs. Talley called out for her, but she didn't stop until she reached the vehicle, her breaths heavy. She had been forced to watch over a dozen public beatings, but this one had been different. Mr. Kerry wasn't a nameless face. He was a good man, a good neighbor — but now the Nazis had taken him, just as they had taken Molly, just as they had taken her mother.

Uncle Red reached the truck just behind her and pushed her in before he got into the driver's seat. "Are you having an episode? Zara, look at me."

"I'm fine," she said, irritated that he was treating her like a child again. "I just had to get out of there."

He leaned back in his seat, relieved. "You scared me."

"Do you think Mr. Kerry is . . . ?"

"He's tough. The chances are good that he'll live."

"But he won't survive long in the camp."

Uncle Red said nothing. He didn't have to. The Front Royal labor camp was a nightmare. Her grandfather had been a much younger man than Mr. Kerry when he was sent there, and he hadn't survived past six months.

"I wish . . ." Zara started and stopped. She knew that there was nothing they could have done. And yet . . . "I only wish . . ."

"I wish we could've helped him, too, but there's nothing we could have done." He started up the engine.

"If Mom were alive, she might have done something," Zara said quietly.

Frustration flashed over Uncle Red's features. "Even Annie wouldn't have been that reckless."

Zara hugged her knees to her chest. Maybe her uncle was right; maybe her mother would have done nothing at the square. But then again, Zara could easily see her mom staying up late in the kitchen, diagramming ways to break Mr. Kerry out of the labor camp. Back then, her uncle would have joined in, too — he had once been the best shot in the Shenandoah Valley — but that was before Mission

Metzger. Now his actions were always measured, always careful. Zara's mom wouldn't have recognized this man.

A marble-thick silence settled inside the car as Uncle Red put the truck in gear. Outside, dozens of farmers and miners filled the sidewalks to get back to work, but Zara didn't notice them. She only saw Mr. Kerry, getting beaten and thrown into the truck.

"Stop thinking about it," Uncle Red said. "It'll only upset you more."

"Couldn't we contact the Alliance?"

"There's nothing they could do, either." His hands tightened over the steering wheel. "I'm sorry you had to watch that beating, but this is the world we live in. The Nazis make the rules, and we have to follow them. It's as simple as that."

Zara hugged herself tighter. When did he become this callous? Uncle Red never would have said these things before Mission Metzger. Being cautious was one thing, but accepting Nazi rules was something else entirely.

"Do you understand what I'm saying?" he said.

She said nothing.

"Answer me, Zara." His eyes bored into her, and she knew she had to reply.

"I understand," she said.

But she didn't understand at all.

3

A few mornings later, Zara awoke shivering. A layer of sweat soaked the collar of her nightshirt, pooling into the hollow of her neck. She rubbed her eyes, but the dream still clung to her mind. The beating. The blood. Mr. Kerry crying for his lost sons.

Guilt gnawed at Zara's chest. She knew deep down that her uncle was right, that there was nothing they could've done unless they wanted to get beaten themselves. But what happened at the square had only reminded her that — yet again — she was powerless. She was merely another *Kleinbauer*, unable to stand up against the Nazi regime.

If only Uncle Red would let her join the Alliance, then she could at least do *something* to help. Even if she had to sift through the Colonel's trash, that would be more than what she was doing now. But her uncle wouldn't even give her that chance.

A muffled cry came from the hallway. Zara's head snapped toward the door.

Not again.

Scrambling from her covers, she bolted down the narrow hall until she burst into her uncle's bedroom. Her feet tripped over the rough floorboards and she nearly knocked into his mammoth of a dresser, but she righted herself and knelt beside his bed.

"Uncle Red?" She clutched on to his shoulder while he thrashed in the sheets.

"No," he groaned, asleep. "No, please. Annie, run!"

"Uncle Red!"

His eyes broke open. His chest heaved. "What happened?"

"You were having that dream again. About Mom."

Uncle Red sat up straight and threw his robe over his shoulders. His gaze slid away from hers. "I'm sorry if I woke you."

"Don't apologize," Zara said softly. Her mother had been gone for years now, but her uncle still dreamed about that terrible night when she was killed. He and Zara's mom had been very close — the protective older brother and the little sister who followed him everywhere, even into the Alliance. "Are you okay?"

He waved off the question. "What time is it?"

"Six-thirty."

Uncle Red swore. He typically woke at five each morning to get started on the crops. The Nazis assigned quotas that every farmer had to meet, and Zara and her uncle were always struggling to reach theirs. Shuffling to his dresser, he turned on his decade-old television for the morning news update. "You should get going. I don't want you to be late."

Zara didn't budge. "This is the second nightmare you've had this month."

"I'm fine now. Go on and get dressed. You have to leave for school."

"For work, you mean," Zara muttered. *Kleinbauern* like them only attended school until age eight. After that, they were assigned to a farm or a factory or another form of menial labor. Zara had been given the job of a *Hausmeisterin*, a cleaning girl at the German military academy. A custodian, to put it plainly.

And it was a plain job indeed: the dust, the mops, the constant stench of bleach. Most girls would be grateful for a career indoors, but Zara could barely stand it. She'd much rather stay at the farm with her uncle, but the Nazis had assigned her this job because she was deemed too small — too weak — for laboring as a farmhand. She was given a mop and broom instead, although the strict crop quota required her to help out with the farmwork anyway.

Uncle Red threw open the moth-eaten curtains, sewn by his grandmother so many years before. "I ironed your uniform last night. It's hanging in your closet."

Zara thanked him but didn't leave the room. Instead, she fidgeted with the fraying seams of her cotton shorts. "Are you going on your mission tonight?"

He tensed. "Why do you ask?" Every couple of months, he and Mrs. Talley would sneak into Fort Goering to steal medical supplies for her midwifery practice. It was the only type of mission he would agree to now, ever since Mission Metzger had killed off most of the Greenfield Alliance. No more ambushes. No more recruiting. Only supply runs.

It hadn't always been this way, of course. Years ago, Uncle Red and Zara's mother had planned missions every week, from tainting the Nazis' water supply to recruiting new members across the Shenandoah. Zara had begged them to let her come, too, but her mother would only smile and her uncle would ruffle her hair, telling her to wait until she was older.

But now she *was* older, wasn't she?

Zara cleared her throat. "I thought you and Mrs. Talley could use an extra lookout, especially after the announcement yesterday."

"No."

"Will you just —"

"I've canceled the supply run. It's too risky right now."

Zara's jaw fell ajar. "What about Mrs. Talley? She told us last week that she was almost out of antibiotics."

"She can make do until our next run."

"That won't be for another month!" Sneaking into Fort Goering was no easy task, but Mrs. Talley had learned from a patient of hers that one of the security rotations spent their shift playing poker and drinking beer instead of patrolling the fort. The one catch was that they only worked nights once or twice a month, which severely limited the supply runs.

Uncle Red let out a battered sigh. "Do you want me to jeopardize Mrs. Talley's life over this? Or my own?"

"Of course not, but there are families depending on that medicine! The Spotswoods' daughter has been sick for weeks. Let me go with you. I can be another pair of eyes."

"Absolutely not." Uncle Red's face had turned to steel, wiped clean of his nightmares. He nodded at the door. "Get ready for work."

Zara marched back into her bedroom, her breaths turning sharp. She threw on her work uniform, buttoning the yellowing blouse and tucking the patched fabric into her knee-length pleated skirt. Why couldn't Uncle Red give her this one shot? She could help him, help the Alliance.

But he wouldn't budge.

After buckling her loafers, the nicest shoes she owned, Zara burst out the front door and onto the gravel driveway. She wished she could contact the Alliance, but Celia Farragut, the head of the resistance, deferred to local Alliance leaders when it came to recruitment. And unfortunately for her, Uncle Red was the leader of the Greenfield chapter.

That didn't seem very fair to Zara. The Alliance needed all of the recruits they could get if they wanted to drive out the Nazis. Since the German takeover after the war, the rebel numbers had dwindled steadily as the Anomaly Division spread from state to state, using their powers to root out the Alliance. These days, Farragut and her team stayed hidden in a West Virginian war bunker that was built decades ago by the American government. From their hideout, they monitored local Alliance chapters and encouraged rebel activities, launching guerilla attacks and stealing weapons, but that was hardly enough to overthrow an empire.

The setbacks the Alliance had faced hadn't deterred Zara's mother from joining them — and they wouldn't deter Zara, either. The Nazis had taken far too much from their family already. What else would the Germans take if she let them? Her home? Her uncle? Herself? If she didn't fight back, they could snatch away everything she loved. Zara glanced back at the house, iron in her narrowed eyes. Somehow, some way, she would convince her uncle to let her join the Alliance.

Four miles down the road, Zara entered the Greenfield town limits, where a slew of shops cropped up on the clean street. She passed the grocer, the post office, and the tiny movie theater that boasted the newest films from the Third Reich's production department, but her pace slowed once she reached the bakery. The smell of hot buttery bread made her stomach groan, and she realized she hadn't eaten a thing since last night's potato-peel soup. Zara peeked through the storefront, her mouth watering at the sight of the golden loaves, still steaming. But then the baker caught her staring.

"Out, out!" he yelled, waving her off with his floured hands. "Your kind isn't served here!"

Zara's appetite dried like a prune. She bolted down the sidewalk, wishing she had avoided this street altogether, with its Nazi-owned shops and snooty German patrons. Most cities in the Territories were built this way nowadays: a rich, bourgeois center filled with the descendants of Germany's postwar baby boom. Nearly a quarter of the population consisted of Germans who formed an upper crust of society that staffed the military, owned the stores, and oversaw the factories that fueled the great Nazi economy.

And below that crust, the rest of us grasp for crumbs, Zara thought, but what choice did they have? The Germans possessed an arsenal of missiles along with their troops of Anomalies. So far, no other nation had dared to fight against the German Anomaly Division, even though the division itself had diminished in number since the 1960s.

In the years following the Axis victory, thousands of the Anomalies continued to perish as their bodies rejected the genetic altering that they'd received during the war. The Nazi scientists had tried to cure their former test subjects, but they soon hit a wall. Some soldiers had simply adapted to the genetic altering, and others didn't. But the scientists did find a silver lining: these "adapted" soldiers often passed their Anomaly gene onto their daughters and sons, who would then manifest new and different powers within the first ten years of life. It wasn't long before these German children were scrutinized and studied, and the Anomalies among them became the second generation of the division. But under the Nuremberg Laws, which were now instituted in the Territories as well, only Aryans and honorary Aryans were admitted to the division. If any of the Anomaly soldiers conceived a super-powered child with an *Untermensch*, the offspring would be killed or sent to a laboratory for live dissection. Which was why non-German Anomalies were so rare.

Hurrying over the cobblestones, Zara took three side streets until she reached the gates of the Heinrich Himmler Military Academy, an elite training school for future Nazi officers. The campus consisted of a cluster of redbrick buildings surrounded by sprawling training fields where the cadets ran laps and honed their shooting skills. Zara dashed up to the main building to find two other cleaning girls sweeping the sidewalk and a group of cadets loitering by the entrance. One of the boys showed off a handheld radio-vision screen that could play music and local TV channels. Most likely he had bought it in Neuberlin, the marble-paved capital of the Territories, formerly known as Washington, DC.

Zara reached for the front door, only to have someone jog up behind her and swing it open.

"After you," said a voice in a clipped German accent.

A shiver slid down her back. The cadets rarely spoke to the cleaning girls unless they needed to report a clogged toilet or complain about the cafeteria food. Her eyes climbed upward inch by inch to find Bastian Eckhart standing next to her in his tall and lithe frame, one hand propping the door open. Aside from his amber eyes, he could have stepped out of an Aryan race handbook, with his pale skin, sun-colored hair, and square jaw. The academy's female cadets often giggled and grinned during Bastian's track meets, but Zara had never thought much about his looks. He was a Nazi, after all, and that straight nose of his just made her think of his father.

"Thank you, Herr Eckhart." Zara's gaze skittered away from his, landing on the pair of dog tags that lay gleaming on his pressed shirt. She had worked at the school long enough to know that the cadets didn't appreciate direct eye contact, not from an *Untermensch* like her. But strangely enough, for the last few months Zara had caught Bastian glancing her way whenever she mopped the halls or wiped the mustard spills off the lunch tables. He always looked away when she caught him staring, and that had puzzled her even more. But Bastian had never said a word to her. Until now.

"Fräulein." Bastian nodded at the door.

Zara had no idea why he was being so polite, or why he was back at school, for that matter. A couple of days before, Bastian had taken a leave of absence due to a death in the family. Apparently, his great-uncle had passed away. Or maybe it was his great-aunt.

Zara was about to head inside when Bastian leaned in closer, his dog tags clanking together. "May I speak to you for a moment?"

She bit back a sigh. She was already running late and didn't want to get docked pay for fraternizing with the cadet, but she couldn't refuse a Nazi, least of all an Eckhart. "Can I assist you with something? I don't have my cart with me, but —"

"There's no need to get your cart. I was wondering if we could speak in private?"

"Eh, what do you have there, Bastian?" one of the cadets called out. "Flirting with the help? How much does she cost?"

Zara's face turned a shade of bright radish. She wasn't one of *those* girls, the sort who would trade her body for a handful of reichsmarks. Is that what Bastian was hoping to "discuss"?

"I didn't mean —" Bastian said, then stopped suddenly. He looked like he wanted to say more, but he only added an abrupt, "Good day, *Fräulein.*"

The cadets crowed louder, goading him to tell them how much Zara was charging him. Her face burning, Zara knew she should bow her head and wish Bastian a good day, but her lips wouldn't move. She bolted through the door instead, away from the cadets, away from their laughter, and away from Bastian Eckhart.

4

With Bastian behind her, Zara ducked into the cramped utility room where she and the other cleaning girls stowed their belongings. She heaved a sigh once she shut the door behind her. The cadets wouldn't follow her here, even if their cackling still roared in her ears.

Two of the other cleaning girls chattered inside the dark space, readying their carts with rags and bottles of bleach. Zara glanced at them, but they ignored her like always. A slow ache wove through her heart, and she wished that Molly were here. It would have been nice to have someone to talk to, especially after her run-in with Bastian. What exactly did he want to talk to her about?

"You're late," one of the girls sniffed at Zara. "I had to pick up the dormitory sheets for you."

Zara reached for a pile of rags from a metal table. "Thanks. It won't happen again."

"Make sure that it doesn't."

The girls pushed their carts out the door, leaving Zara alone in the mildewed room. She twisted the rags in her hands until her knuckles hurt. Decades may have passed since the war, but most Eastern Americans still shook their heads at Zara's lineage. They had never forgotten — and had never forgiven — the cruelty the Japanese had dealt during and after the war: the attack on Pearl Harbor, the internment camps for captured rebels, the death marches along the American

West Coast. Even today, the Empire of Japan ruled the Western American Territories as the Nazis ruled the East — with a harsh and oppressive fist. This was why the *Kleinbauern* shunned Zara just as they had her mother, once they learned she had given birth to a half-Japanese child.

It made Zara's blood boil when she overheard the farmers warning their daughters not to become like Annie St. James. Her mother had been a lonely eighteen-year-old when she met a young Japanese soldier while cleaning the cafeteria at Fort Goering. Annie's own mother was sick with tuberculosis and her father had recently been jailed, leaving her and her brother, Redmond, to care for the farm. With so many burdens pressing in on her, Annie had lost herself in the fling, but she broke it off after her brother discovered it. But by then, she was already pregnant.

Shaking off the memories of her mother, Zara spent the next six hours in a blur of dull chores. While the cadets scaled ropes outside and debated *Mein Kampf* in the classroom, she washed the bedsheets and scrubbed the cooking pots. Most of the students lived at the academy full time, arriving at age twelve and graduating at twenty. Their application process had been rigorous, and their coursework was even more so: mathematics, war strategy, and racial sciences along with shooting, first aid, and heavy combat training. About a dozen cadets dropped out every term, but Zara was never sorry to see them go. Fewer sheets for her to wash. At least until the next semester.

By early afternoon Zara's uniform smelled of dish soap and old soup, but there was nothing she could do about it. She had to fold the tablecloths and organize a storage closet for Frau Schumann, one of the history teachers. Tugging off her apron, she dashed into Frau Schumann's classroom, darted around the desks, and squeezed into the dimly lit closet as the cadets ambled to their seats. She was about to reach for the filing cabinet when another cleaning girl hurried inside.

"Good God, what a mess!" the dark-haired girl whispered. She wedged her nearly six-foot height into the space. "When's the last time Frau Schumann cleaned out this thing? You'd think she —" Her voice stopped when Zara turned around. "Oh. I thought Lizzie would be here."

Zara swallowed her groan. "Hello to you, too."

The girl didn't return the greeting. Instead, she tackled a pile of papers on the floor, pretending she was the only one there.

Zara yanked open the file drawer, her fingers dredged in dust. She had hoped for a quiet afternoon, but now she would have to share this musty closet with Kristy Coulter, of all people. Most of the cleaning girls simply ignored Zara, which wasn't so bad after she had gotten used to it, but Kristy could be cruel.

The bell clanged and a stale silence filled the storage room, only broken by the sound of shuffling papers and the sharpness of Frau Schumann's voice. Zara tried to tune out the lecture, but the words drilled into her eardrums anyway.

"Quiet, please!" Frau Schumann said in German. She was a petite woman, only five two, but she possessed the voice of a general. "Fräulein Huber, sit down. Herr Dresner, open a few windows. It's too warm in here. Now then, let's get started on your history reports. Herr Zimmermann, I believe you volunteered to go first."

The reports ticked by in a parade of Nazi pride. Herr Zimmermann spent ten minutes lauding the Anomaly war hero Lukas Ansel, or the "Jewel of the Third Reich" as he was known, who destroyed eight American cities with his ability to create mile-wide explosions. His "contributions" slaughtered millions and eventually led to President

Roosevelt's surrender, but Ansel only lived three years beyond the Nazis' victory. Unstable genes, the autopsy found.

Fräulein Huber went next, detailing the life of Führer Gustav, the son and heir of Adolf Hitler, who reorganized North Africa into colonial states and nearly warred with the Soviets over the Lithuanian border. After that, Herr Dresner described the history of the Corps of Four, from the very first Dual Anomalies to the current Corps, who had, to date, saved Führer Dieter from five assassination attempts.

When Herr Dresner finished, Frau Schumann studied her roll and nodded at Bastian. "Herr Eckhart? We have time for one more presentation."

From her vantage point in the storage closet, Zara peeked into the classroom and saw Bastian heading toward the teacher's desk, his head bowed. A couple of female cadets sent each other sly smiles, obviously pleased at the prospect of gazing at Bastian for his entire report. There was only a small number of female cadets at the academy. Many girls their age joined the League of German Maidens, where they prepared for their roles in Nazi society — wife, mother, homemaker — but it was getting more common to see German women in the military or finding work within offices and factory management.

"Dr. Eva Himmel was born in 1910 in Dresden, Germany," said Bastian in a quiet voice that wasn't very fitting for a colonel's son. "With an IQ of 174, she was destined for great things. She received her doctorate in genetics at the age of twenty and became the first female scientist to work in the Führer's national laboratory."

Zara scowled. *Laboratory?* It was more like a torture chamber. The Nazis may have prided themselves in creating Anomalies, but their discovery was paid for in blood. Thousands of test subjects, mainly Jews, had been subjected to experimentation. Some were even children. What was worse, the German history books had reveled in these deaths, lionizing Adolf Hitler for ridding the world of the "great Jewish filth."

Bastian's gaze remained glued to the pages of his report, never looking up once. "Dr. Himmel proved instrumental in the Dresden Study, specifically in the engineering of Subject K3, the very first Anomaly soldier who survived the testing process. Then, after the war ended, Dr. Himmel worked for years trying to solve the Anomaly genetic instability that had led to the early deaths of over fifty percent of the division."

Continuing on, Bastian described the good doctor's battle with cancer, but Zara had tuned out his report and had returned to organizing the file in her hand. She had barely made a dent in the pile today, which meant she would have to stay late to finish the job. On top of that, Uncle Red needed her help with the planting once she got home. She'd be lucky to go to bed before midnight. Heaving a tired sigh, she reached behind her for the trash basket, but her hand knocked into Kristy's stack of alphabetized files, sending the papers toppling.

"I've spent forty minutes on that!" Kristy hissed.

"I didn't mean to —"

Kristy wasn't finished. "Stupid kami."

Zara flinched before a flare of anger ignited inside her. She had heard that slur often enough — a shortened version of *kamikaze* — that she should have gotten used to it by now, but it always punched a hole in her heart.

Stupid kami.

She tried to shrug it off, but it rang inside her head.

Kami.

Zara hated that word. And she hated that Kristy had used it. For years Kristy had simply snubbed Zara like the rest of the cleaning girls, but then her father had gone to the Western American Territories to find work at a lumber mill. He only made it a few months before his Japanese employer hanged him for attending a few Freedom Resistance meetings, the rebel movement out West. Not long after that, Zara arrived at school to find her apron in the toilet and her cleaning cart knocked onto its side. That was when the name-calling started, too.

Zara crushed a piece of paper in her hands. She had never even met Mr. Coulter, but Kristy somehow blamed her for his death. Months of resentment rushed through her in a wave, and her face grew oven-hot. She forced herself to breathe. In and out, in and out. She wouldn't have an episode, not here.

Suddenly, a gust flew through the classroom windows, snatching papers from the desks and swirling them along the ceiling. The cadets laughed, but Frau Schumann clucked at them. "Settle down! Class isn't over. Remember to read chapters ten through twelve as your homework assignment."

Once the final bell chimed for the day, Zara leapt to her feet, ready to escape from the dusty room. She hurried to Frau Schumann's desk and asked for a restroom break.

"Make it a quick one," Frau Schumann said, but Zara didn't hear her.

Running into the hall, she wedged herself through the mass of uniforms and hurried to the nearest place where she could be alone. The broom closet. She shut the door and gulped down a breath, but the tears came anyway. She swiped at her eyes. She didn't know why she was crying — Kristy had called her a kami dozens of times before — but maybe the last few days had been too much for her. First Sentinel Achen's visit, then the beating, and now this. Sometimes she wanted to stand in the middle of the square and scream at everyone who had hurt her or her family. But if she did that, she would end up like poor Mr. Kerry.

A minute ticked by, and Zara tried to pull herself together. If she didn't get back to work, her pay would get docked, and she needed that money for the farm. Besides, she couldn't let Kristy get under her skin. The anger flared again, but Zara used it to make the tears stop. She took a deep breath.

Three knocks tapped against the door.

Zara jumped back. "I'm on a break!"

A pause. "Fräulein St. James?"

She froze. She knew that voice, although it was strange to hear him address her so formally again. Most cadets referred to her as *Hausmeisterin*. Some simply called her "girl."

"I need to speak with you for a moment."

Zara's nails dug into her palms. She only wanted a minute to herself, but the Nazis wouldn't allow even that. She sighed and twisted the doorknob to find Bastian standing in the emptying hallway, his warm ochre eyes peering into her dark ones. Out of habit, her gaze dropped to the tiled floor and fixed upon his leather shoes. The toes of his loafers were a little scuffed. Perhaps he wanted her to shine them for him. After the day she had had, she wouldn't have been surprised.

His head tilted to one side. "Are you ill, *Fräulein*?"

"I'm fine, Herr Eckhart," she forced out. "Do you need my assistance?"

"Frau Schumann wanted a quick word with you once your break is finished. You ran out before she could tell you herself, so I told her I'd relay the message." As he spoke, a set of dimples emerged at the corners of his mouth. Undoubtedly those dimples sent the Nazi girls sighing, but Zara never understood the appeal of them.

"Thank you for letting me know." Frankly, she was surprised that Bastian was delivering the message instead of another cleaning girl; but she urged her lips into a smile, knowing that she had to act extra politely around the Colonel's son. "My deepest condolences about your great-uncle."

Those dimples slid away. "My great-uncle?"

"He, um. I heard that he had passed away."

"Ah. You must mean my" — he clutched the dog tags around his neck — "my *Opa*."

"My apologies. I didn't realize." Zara grimaced at the mistake. Bastian had lost his *grandfather*, not a great-uncle. She waited for him to huff and storm off, but he didn't move.

"I mentioned earlier that I needed to speak with you."

Zara stiffened. There were only a few things that a Nazi would want from a cleaning girl like her, and she didn't like any of those reasons. Her mind frantically searched for an excuse to put him off, but she came up empty.

Bastian's long fingers dropped the dog tags and fidgeted instead with his red-and-yellow striped tie, the academy colors. "My mother is searching for a new housekeeper. Our previous one left quite suddenly."

Zara sighed, relieved. He wasn't offering reichsmarks for certain "services" from her. She knew what he was asking before he even said it.

"My mother needs someone to fill in while we search for a permanent replacement. I told her that I could speak to a *Hausmeisterin* at school, and so I thought I would ask you. You seem —" He played with his tie again, clearly uncomfortable with this conversation. "You seem very skilled."

Very skilled? Zara wondered if she was supposed to take that as a compliment, but it only reminded her of how these Germans viewed her: a work mule to service their needs. It was humiliating enough to scrub the Nazis' bathrooms every day, but now she had been asked to personally clean Colonel Eckhart's toilet, too.

"It's only an hour or two a day," Bastian said. "We'd compensate you, of course. Twenty reichsmarks per hour."

The amount made Zara suck in her breath. She only made half of that at the academy, and she had to grudgingly admit that she could put that money to good use at home. The stove was broken and the water heater needed to be replaced. She missed her hot showers dreadfully. But twenty reichsmarks per hour was, frankly, too much. Even the most experienced *Hausmeisterin* didn't make that. Zara gripped the edge of the doorframe, uneasiness sliding through her. And why was Bastian looking for a new housekeeper when his father's staff could've made the request? This task seemed rather beneath a cadet like him.

"Maybe you could stop by my house? We could walk together if you don't know the way," he offered.

Now that was even more baffling. A colonel's son would never be seen walking home with a cleaning girl.

"It won't take long," Bastian went on. His eyes grasped on to hers, and she saw the gold and green flecks inside them, like a mosaic. If he wasn't German, she might have thought them pretty.

Looking away from those eyes, Zara wondered what she should do. She couldn't refuse him, of course, but she couldn't shake the niggling feeling that something about this conversation was off, that he wasn't telling her the entire truth. She thought about all of those times she had caught him glancing at her — why? But the thought of twenty reichsmarks an hour was enough to put her questions aside. "I have to work tonight, but maybe tomorrow?"

"I see." He chewed his bottom lip, disappointment threading through his voice. "I have track practice until four. How about then?"

She nodded.

"Tomorrow at four." A smile flooded his lips, but it vanished so quickly that Zara wondered if she had imagined it. "Good day."

Zara headed back to the history classroom, but halfway there she glanced backward to find Bastian standing outside the broom closet, watching her leave. That prickling feeling tickled at the nape of her neck.

She sped past the lockers. She had no idea what to make of her day.

And she had no idea what to make of Bastian Eckhart.

5

Once Zara spoke with Frau Schumann and finally finished her shift, she didn't have time to think about Bastian or her potential title as "Eckhart housekeeper." When she arrived home at seven, the farm demanded all of her attention: the onions needed tilling; the horse neighed for food; and the gourds had developed a white-spotted blight that made her sigh, because they always fetched a good price in the fall. It would be a gourdless harvest this year.

With the moon rising in the darkening sky, Zara dragged her aching body to the house for a well-earned dinner. Inside the tiny kitchen, Mrs. Talley served a pan of fried onions and roasted pork, thanks to one of her patients who had paid her with a newly butchered sow. Zara dug in with gusto (she hadn't eaten pork since their Christmas ham) while Uncle Red fought to keep his eyes open. He had been working nonstop since morning, and the cuckoo clock in the living room now ticked toward ten at night.

"I received a message today," Mrs. Talley said, dishing out the last bit of onions. A smile pricked her lips. "An update from the Alliance."

Zara stopped midchew. "You did? From who?"

"Garrison Strayer."

As usual, Uncle Red frowned at the name. He had never warmed to Garrison Strayer, one of Celia Farragut's right-hand men. There were over fifty rebels at Alliance headquarters, each one assigned to oversee a handful of local Alliance chapters. Garrison had been appointed to the Shenandoah region two years ago, and Uncle Red had butted heads with him ever since — Garrison kept nudging Uncle Red to start up recruitments for Greenfield, while Uncle Red hemmed and hawed about staying cautious. Back and forth, back and forth. Zara had never met Garrison, but she liked him already. Someone had to stand up to her stubborn-as-a-mule uncle.

"What did Garrison say?" said Uncle Red, his brows furrowed.

"I radioed him after we called off the supply run. He couldn't spare us any extra medical supplies, but he did give me a bit of news." A twinkle shone in Mrs. Talley's gray eyes, making her appear twenty years younger. "He asked me to share it with you."

Zara put her fork down. "Well?"

"He has information about the Führer's recent announcement. The Alliance discovered why Faust 'retired' so suddenly." Mrs. Talley savored the news as if she were sipping a fine red wine. "It turns out he was taking bribes — from the Soviets."

"Impossible," said Uncle Red.

"You're joking. *Reichsmarschall* Faust?" said Zara, choking out each word. "Dieter's cousin? He betrayed the Hitler name for the Reds?"

"I thought the very same thing, but Premier Volkov offered him a deal he couldn't refuse," said Mrs. Talley. "If Faust kept the Soviets updated on the latest news in Berlin, they would appoint him commander of Western Europe once they conquered the Nazi Empire. It makes sense, doesn't it? Faust has always wanted to take residence at the Berlin palace, like his great-great-uncle Adolf."

Zara swigged her glass of water while she processed this information. It was certainly news that she didn't hear every day, much less every decade. Reichsmarschall Faust had been Dieter's loyal lapdog since they were teens. He was the last person she would think

44

of to become a turncoat, although his lust for power must have lured him from the Führer's grasp.

"What happened to Faust after the Nazis found him out?" Zara asked.

"He was executed along with his wife and children. It was done very quietly, but the Führer knew that he had to explain his cousin's sudden absence. So he decided to give the announcement. Make a show out of the whole thing." Mrs. Talley looked over to Uncle Red. "You haven't said much, Redmond."

"I'm surprised, that's all." Uncle Red pushed his plate away, his thoughts clearly elsewhere. "The Soviets must be up to something if they were willing to take this gamble."

"That's what the Alliance believes, too. Farragut has contacts within the Kremlin who have hinted that Premier Volkov wants to invade the borderlands," said Mrs. Talley, referring to the strip of European territory that divided the two Empires. Those lands stretched from Estonia in the north, down through Latvia and Lithuania, and into Belarus and Ukraine.

"He'd break the nonaggression pact?" said Zara. This news kept getting bigger and better. She couldn't help but grin at her uncle, although he kept his gaze on Mrs. Talley. It looked like her theory about the Reds stirring a war against the Führer wasn't so far-fetched after all.

"Volkov hasn't been happy with the pact for years," Mrs. Talley said, "so I wouldn't be surprised if he did just that."

"Do you know what this could mean for the Alliance?" said Zara. More theories burst through her. For years, the Alliance had only tackled small guerilla attacks, nothing on a national scale after Mission Metzger had decimated their numbers. Perhaps now, with the nonaggression pact potentially breaking, the Alliance could rise up again. A thrill buzzed through her veins, but it was mingled with a sad ache. Zara looked at the chair where her mother used to sit and wished her mom were here with them now. She would have devoured this news like her favorite strawberry pie.

"It might not mean much. The Soviets are half a world away from us," Uncle Red said in his usual gruff manner.

"But the Nazis at war would be weakened," Mrs. Talley countered. She had long gotten used to his gruffness. "And a weakened Empire would be a plus for the Alliance."

"I agree," Zara chimed in.

Mrs. Talley winked at Zara and gave Uncle Red a winning smile. "It appears you have been outvoted. We'll leave you to the dishes while Zara and I play a round of rummy."

Uncle Red pretended to grumble, but thanked Mrs. Talley for the meal. While he tackled the dinner pots, Zara and Mrs. Talley made it through two rounds of rummy and more conversation before Mrs. Talley's eyes drooped and she decided to call it a night.

"I'm turning into an old lady," Mrs. Talley said. The scent of her lavender perfume wafted into Zara's nose, a smell that had always calmed her. "I'll have to get dentures soon and a cane for this bad hip of mine."

"Oh, stop. You'll outlive us all," Zara said, giving her a quick hug.

With a wave good-bye, Mrs. Talley headed to her cottage a mile away while Uncle Red decided to call it a night, too, leaving half of the dishes for tomorrow. But Zara couldn't sleep, not after hearing the news Mrs. Talley had shared during dinner. Her mind hummed while she tackled the last of the cooking pans. If the Alliance contacts were right, then the Nazis and Soviets could soon go to war. A clash like that would be monumental. It could usher in World War III.

And that could certainly boost the Alliance. With the Nazis busy on their eastern border, they would have to draw some of their Territories-based troops for the fight. Fewer Nazis meant more chances at rebel-led riots, at rebellions. This was the sort of news that her mother had lived for, and this was why Zara needed to join the Alliance. She could never take the place of her mom, but she could try to fill her shoes the best she could. It was one small way to keep Annie St. James alive.

A glint of gold caught Zara's eye, and she realized Mrs. Talley had left her wedding ring on the counter. She must have taken it off to prepare the roast and forgotten all about it. Carefully, Zara picked up the band. It felt light as a penny in her hand. Narrowing her eyes, she read the worn inscription inside:

To Nell, my bride. With love, Arthur.

Mr. and Mrs. Talley had been married for thirty years when Mr. Talley was killed the same night as Zara's mom. Zara had only a few blurry memories of him, but she remembered how he would give her piggyback rides and tell her great tales of the American Revolution that his grandfather had passed on to him. Sometimes Uncle Red would join in on the storytelling, too, and his voice would hit a crescendo when he spoke of Paul Revere's midnight ride; Zara would fall asleep dreaming of rebels and revolutionaries. Those nights were some of the happiest in her childhood, along with the hot summer days when she and Molly would splash and swim in the Burns pond.

Zara's fist closed over the ring. Although she ached to climb into bed, she didn't want Mrs. Talley waking up in the morning and worrying about her missing wedding band.

Slipping on one of her mother's old sweaters, Zara headed into the chilly night with the ring tucked snugly in her trouser pocket. The sky was as clear as glass, without a cloud for miles, and the crescent moon offered enough light for her to take a shortcut through the fields. On some nights the Nazis sent out a patrol to roam the rural roads, and she didn't want to get stopped, especially if Sentinel Achen was the one doing the patrol.

Zara yawned a half-dozen times while she trekked through the acres of farmland, but it wasn't long before she spotted Mrs. Talley's chimney in the distance. The Talleys had lived in the one-story house, quaint as a jewel box, since they first married. They had even hosted a few Alliance meetings in their tiny basement, sometimes squeezing fifty or more members in there. But now most of those people were gone, most of them long dead.

She was about to approach the back of the house when she heard the front door open, then close. She froze in the vegetable patch, feeling open and exposed, then saw a shadow hurrying toward the dirt road, dressed all in black. An alarm bell blared through Zara's head, thinking the house had been robbed, but then she noticed the shadowed figure limping with every step. The gears cranked in her mind.

It was Mrs. Talley. But where was she going at this hour?

Zara was about to call out to her, but she hesitated. If she asked Mrs. Talley where she was going, Mrs. Talley would only smile and walk Zara home. There was only one conclusion: Mrs. Talley was up to something, and Zara wanted to know what it was. Rounding her shoulders, she slipped down the path after her friend, vanishing into the twinkling night.

Zara crept along the side of the road, stepping on patches of crab-grass and dandelions to muffle her boot steps. Forty yards ahead, Mrs. Talley shuffled toward town, stopping every few minutes to massage her hip or squint behind her, making sure she wasn't being followed.

What are you up to? Zara thought. Maybe Mrs. Talley was on her way to see a patient, but she was wearing a canvas rucksack instead of carrying her leather medical bag. Or maybe she was going to meet a potential Alliance recruit, although Zara doubted that, too. If Mrs. Talley had been contacted by a potential recruit, she would have spoken to Uncle Red about it first. After all, a recruit could easily turn out to be a Nazi informant. Numerous Alliance leaders had mistakenly trusted a German plant and gotten executed by the sentinels for it.

As they curved around the sleepy homes of Greenfield, Zara finally realized what her friend was doing. This road would soon lead them to Fort Goering — and to the medical supplies that her patients so desperately needed.

Mrs. Talley was going on the supply run. Alone.

Up ahead, Mrs. Talley checked her pocket watch and hastened her pace, ducking into the thicket of trees that enveloped Fort Goering in a leafy embrace. Zara hurried behind her, but the forest canopy obscured the moonlight, and she quickly lost sight of her friend.

Fear threaded through Zara's blood, something she hadn't expected. She wasn't scared of getting lost — she knew she'd find her way eventually — but she couldn't let Mrs. Talley tackle a mission on her own. On previous supply runs, Uncle Red was the one who would sneak inside the fort while Mrs. Talley acted as the lookout, ready to toss a can of tear gas in case they needed a distraction for the guards. Mrs. Talley had never stolen the supplies on her own. And with her hip like that . . .

Zara knew she had to find her.

The bright lights of Fort Goering glared ahead, and she made her way toward them. The fort itself sprawled over fifty acres and was enclosed by a twenty-foot barbed-wire fence. A constellation of buildings sat at the center of the acreage: the soldiers' barracks, the administrative structures, the hospital, and the prison. A wide swath of training fields lined the edge of the property, where the soldiers would ruck march and the Anomaly regiment would hone their superpowers. But now the fields lay empty as graveyards while the troops dozed in their bunks.

Zara had never stepped inside Fort Goering, but she had overheard enough conversations between her uncle and Mrs. Talley that would hopefully lead her in the right direction. Months ago, Mrs. Talley had mentioned a weak point in the fort's fence, right next to a trio of storage sheds not far from the old abandoned hospital. With that memory guiding her, she skirted around the fort, branches clawing her forehead, until she spotted a big block of a building with boarded windows and a crumbling façade. A new hospital had been built over a year ago, leaving this one to be demolished.

There it is, Zara thought. Her heart pumped faster when she spotted three storage sheds not far ahead. But where was Mrs. Talley? Leaves rustled far to her left, and Zara clambered up an enormous oak tree, her heart chattering at the thought that a soldier had found her. But once she balanced herself on a thick branch, she saw Mrs. Talley scurrying toward the fence, only thirty yards away.

"Mrs. Talley!" Zara whispered, afraid to raise her voice any louder. For all she knew, one of the patrols could be strolling on the other side of those sheds.

But Mrs. Talley didn't hear her. Instead, the old woman lifted a rusted corner of the fence and wormed her head through it, followed by her shoulders. She had nearly slithered onto the other side when her hips got stuck in the narrow passage.

Zara swore. She was ready to jump from the branch and pull Mrs. Talley out of trouble, but the slightest of movements caught her eye, forcing her to pause. Then she swore again.

A security camera sat on the corner of the shed's roof, its digital eye sweeping across the fort. Zara didn't remember her uncle mentioning the camera before, not along the fence. There were security devices installed at the fort's entrance, but the perimeters hadn't been guarded as well, probably because Colonel Eckhart focused his budget on new toys like weapons upgrades and new tanks. Maybe the capital had sent in more security supplies. Whatever the reason, the camera was about to catch Mrs. Talley red-handed. The bulky device turned in Mrs. Talley's direction, swiveling its neck toward her as she struggled to pull herself free.

Every hair on Zara's arms pricked up. She gauged the distance from the tree to the fence. By the time she reached Mrs. Talley, it would be too late. She stared at her hands, at the potential swirling through them. *No one can ever know*, her uncle's voice echoed.

But she couldn't lose Mrs. Talley. That wasn't even an option.

Without another thought, Zara thrust her hands toward the camera, palms up.

Listen to me, she called out in her mind.

A breeze tickled beneath her fingers, drifting sleepily around her wrists. Months had passed since Zara had manipulated the air, and she could feel how rusty she had gotten.

Come on. Faster!

She thrust all of her focus at the security camera, her uncle's caution shoved aside. An ache throbbed in her temples, like it always did whenever she let her power go fallow, but the breeze gathered strength. Leaves shivered and branches groaned as the wind whistled around her body. She didn't know if it was enough, but she was running out of time.

Release!

The wind obeyed, eager for her command. In a great whoosh, it pummeled forward and rammed against the camera, stalling its progress. Finally, Mrs. Talley slid through the fence and rolled into the shed's shadow, safe for now. Zara collapsed against the tree trunk, panting. That had been close. Too close, really.

Mrs. Talley scurried from shadow to shadow, like a mouse scouring for crumbs, until she reached a cinder block storage facility. She took a lock pick from her pocket and grasped the sturdy metal lock, fumbling with both before the door cracked open and she stumbled inside.

Zara wondered if she should follow after her — to make sure everything went smoothly — but she spotted that camera again. The Nazis could never know that Mrs. Talley was here; there couldn't be any evidence.

With one hand turned up, she called silently for the wind once again, beckoning it to her side. A thrill buzzed through her. She hadn't done this since Christmas, when a snowstorm swallowed the

Shenandoah hills and Zara had used the wind to carry her a few acres to locate their lost milking cow. Uncle Red had been livid when she came home.

You weren't far from the road! he had shouted while her boots soiled the floorboards with melted snow. *What were you thinking?*

Zara had been thinking that the cow was worth over two hundred reichsmarks and how they could never afford that sum again. Besides, she had been careful. The heavy snow had obscured her from view; otherwise she never would have gone after the animal. Still, she had apologized and promised Uncle Red she wouldn't use her power again, and she had kept that promise — until tonight.

Glancing at her palm, Zara focused on the air right above it. Her temples pulsed, but she ignored the pain and focused on one thought.

Spin.

A miniature tornado arose over her skin. At Zara's urging, it grew an inch taller, then another, until the tiny wind funnel reached half a foot. She aimed it toward the device.

Destroy, she thought. The tornado zipped toward its victim and battered against the machine until the lens cracked, sending shards of glass flying. A smile tugged at Zara's lips, but she knew Mrs. Talley wasn't out of trouble yet.

Zara leaned against the trunk again, finally letting her heartbeat catch its breath while she waited for Mrs. Talley to reappear. Her gaze roamed over Fort Goering, from the old hospital to the shiny new one, from the prison to the countless training fields, searching for any sign of the guards; but the fort was quiet that night. Far to the right of her, she noticed a big cluster of apartment buildings. The soldiers' barracks. One of the barracks appeared newer than the rest, and its walls had been painted with three bolts of lightning. The Anomaly Division.

For a split second, Zara envied them. The sentinels never had to conceal their powers, to hide what they truly were. Instead, once their abilities manifested as children, they were deemed "prized" in the eyes of the Empire and sent to special schools to hone their skills.

A shudder snuck down her spine. The threat of the Nuremberg Laws had been hanging over her head for years, and the thought of being caught by the Nazis still made her throat tighten with fear. That was why Uncle Red had forbidden Zara to use her power. *No one can ever know,* he had told her again and again. *It's for your safety, do you understand?* And for the most part, she had listened to him.

Zara had been seven when she had first manifested, only a few days after her mother's death. The grief had welled inside of her like a plugged-up drain, swirling and swirling until the air in her bedroom formed a miniature windstorm. Furniture splintered. Picture frames fell. Uncle Red had to douse her with cold water to calm her before he wrapped her in a tight hug, telling her that she was going to be all right. But she saw the fear in his eyes.

It had taken Zara months to control her new ability. Uncle Red had had to pull her out of primary school multiple times, citing grief over her mother's death. He told the teachers that Annie St. James had died from dysentery — a lie to cover up her ties to the Alliance — and fortunately they had believed him. After all, the death of a *Kleinbauer* hardly interested them.

Zara studied her hands with a sigh. She felt so free whenever she used her power: the wind whipping around her, the air carrying her high above the trees. In moments like those, she could almost forget the heavy shadow of Nazi rule. *Almost.* But the Nazis were never far from her thoughts. She wasn't only an *Untermensch*; she was an

Anomaly deviant, too, thanks to the American blood flowing through her. A freak, to be destroyed. She closed her fists tight. Her abilities were a curse. If she had never manifested, her uncle wouldn't have to worry so much about her, and they wouldn't be forced to keep this secret locked inside of them. The only other person who knew was Mrs. Talley. Even Molly had been kept in the dark. Uncle Red had made Zara promise not to say a word.

Still, Zara's power had become a part of her. It was the only useful thing her father had left her, after all. He wasn't an Anomaly himself, but he had told Zara's mom that his grandfather had served in the Ronin Elite, a mind reader, apparently. On lonely nights, Zara wondered if she should look up her father on an academy computer — she could have a whole other family out there — but she always snuffed out these thoughts by the morning. Her father would never acknowledge a half-American child like her. She was nothing but a mistake to him, the product of an affair he had probably forgotten about years ago.

Zara pushed aside the ache blooming inside her. She had Mrs. Talley and Uncle Red, and they were enough. Despite everything they had gone through, from Mission Metzger to Nazi interrogations, they had never left Zara, and she loved them for it. Although she should probably tell them that more often.

A sheet of clouds swung over the moon, cutting Zara's visibility in half. She scooted forward on the branch to get a better view of the storage facility, but a sharp piece of bark cut open her thumb.

"Nice one," Zara muttered. Yet another cut to add to the wounds and bruises she had collected on the farm. She tried to ignore the pulsing pain, but this one felt different. Like tiny needles stabbing through her veins.

Zara sat up. She had felt this strange stinging before. It had happened two months ago when she sliced her toe on a stray piece of glass, but it hadn't gotten infected, so she had shrugged it off. This had to be an odd coincidence or a strange medical condition, and she really hoped it was the former. The local hospital only treated Germans, and she couldn't afford the fees anyway.

The storage room door swung open, and Zara promptly shoved her injured thumb from her thoughts. She watched Mrs. Talley tiptoe out of the building with a full rucksack over her shoulder. She hobbled toward the fence, slipping the bag underneath it first before she scooted herself under.

Hidden in the leaves, Zara's heart sang, but she couldn't celebrate until Mrs. Talley made it home safely. She waited a long minute before she climbed down the trunk and headed for the Talleys' home. As she wove out of the forest the tree boughs scraped against her cheeks, but a smile remained stitched on Zara's lips because of what she had done.

She had completed her very first mission.

She had proven her uncle wrong.

6

At the academy the following day, Zara washed the windows and emptied the garbage pails like usual, but her thoughts remained fastened on last night's supply run. After the escape from Fort Goering, Zara had followed Mrs. Talley home, her ears perked for the shout of a Nazi soldier or the roar of a military truck, but none had come. Finally, around one in the morning, she had padded through her back door — thankfully, Uncle Red hadn't stirred — but she couldn't go to bed until her heart stopped banging so hard. She'd sat at the edge of the mattress, her limbs exhausted but her mind wide awake, when the realization finally sank in.

She and Mrs. Talley had gotten away with it.

The thrill had soared through Zara then. Their supply run had been the exact opposite of cautious — but they had done it anyway. And completed it to boot. She wondered if her mother would have been proud of her. A sad smile pricked Zara's mouth. She hoped so, at least.

The school bell chimed for last period, and Zara slipped into the science laboratory to wash the beakers. After work, she would go over to Mrs. Talley's and tell her what she had done. Mrs. Talley would probably scold her a little, but Zara would convince her that they needed to plan more runs. More missions. It was for the good of Greenfield, she would reason. And at last, Zara would be doing *something*.

With a lightness in her step, Zara headed toward the classroom's sink, careful to keep her eyes down to avoid the posters that compared the skulls of the Aryans to those of the Jews. The racial sciences were a favorite topic of Herr Zoller, the teacher who led the science labs and who had taken a particular interest in "crossbreeds" like Zara. *Die Mischlinge*, he liked to call them.

"Ah, greetings to you," Herr Zoller said to her from his desk. "Might you spare a moment for me at the end of class? For my vials, you see."

"My apologies, but Frau Schumann has requested my services," Zara said quickly. When she first arrived at the academy, she had thought Herr Zoller was the kindest of all the teachers because he was always inquiring about her health, but that was before she discovered his beloved vials, which he stocked with "genetically inferior" blood. He rather enjoyed using them for class projects to demonstrate the superiority of the Aryan race, and he often asked Zara if she could spare him some of her own blood. She had always declined politely, but secretly she wished she could smash all of his disgusting vials.

While Zara got to work, Herr Zoller called out the class roll, pacing in front of a large map of the world. The map itself offered the only bright spots of color in the beige-painted room. Zara studied it sometimes when she washed the chalkboards, wondering what the map would look like if the Allies had won the war instead of the Axis. That was the sort of world she longed for.

As the map stood now, a great swath of red represented the Nazi Empire, stretching over Western Europe, North Africa, and the Eastern American Territories. In violet, the Empire of Japan spilled over most of Asia, while the Italian Confederation was marked by dashes of orange, covering Italy proper, the Italian Dakotas, and the Mexican-Italian Protectorate. The Soviet Union came next, in kelly green, spreading from Siberia to Eastern Europe. Then a thick line of gold marked the neutral territories, like the strip of land that separated Germany from the Soviet Union, running from the Baltic Sea and down to the Mediterranean. For decades, both Empires had respected this neutral European zone, but the question always remained: for how long?

Finally, the rest of the world was painted a dull iron gray, split between land that was disputed (the South American Territories) or land that no one wanted (the North and South Poles).

"Open your textbooks to page sixty," Herr Zoller said.

As he launched into his lesson on the chemistry of combustion and rattled on about the interplay between fire and oxygen, Zara scrubbed the first batch of beakers. Usually it took her twenty minutes to finish the pile, but she couldn't stop thinking about the night before. Somehow, she would convince her uncle to let her go on missions. Mrs. Talley was getting older and Uncle Red couldn't tackle the tasks alone. But she could already hear his response in her head: *We'll talk about this when you're older. Until then, wash the dishes and shovel the horse manure, please.* A frown marred her lips. Her uncle could be stubborn as an old mule sometimes, especially with the sentinels always sniffing around the farm. One of Uncle Red's biggest fears was that the Colonel would finally realize that Zara's mother had died in the Mission Metzger attack, instead of from a disease. If that happened, both he and Zara would be jailed, maybe even killed.

But Zara knew that there had to be a way to convince her uncle. They could form a team, like him and her mom used to be. Perhaps she could —

"You there! *Mischling!*" Herr Zoller had stopped his lecture to point straight at Zara's nose. "Turn off that water. It's going to waste."

Thirty cadets swiveled in their chairs, their scornful eyes looking Zara up and down.

"Did you hear me?" said Herr Zoller. He glanced back to the rest of the class. "She may be a little hard of hearing. These mixed-breed specimens are often lacking in some way, and that is why we openly discourage the crossing of the races."

A few cadets snickered, and Zara bowed her head to hide the fury in her eyes. "I'm sorry, Herr Zoller," she mumbled. She shut off the faucet with a shaky hand and wished she could send a tornado into Herr Zoller's face — showing him how "lacking" she was — but she couldn't cause a scene. She'd probably end up in a Nazi laboratory with Herr Zoller overseeing her dissection. The thought of that made her stomach flip over.

As soon as the class ended, Zara rolled her cart into the corridor, weaving through the cadets with the wheels squeaking at each turn. Herr Zoller's words still stung, and she pushed the cart faster, hurtling around a corner — and promptly ramming into Bastian's leg. Her hand flew to her mouth.

"I'm so sorry!" she said while Bastian bent to rub his ankle. If she had injured him, she might as well wave good-bye to her paycheck. Zara groaned. Today had started off as a rare good day for her, but now she had ruined it.

Bastian straightened, shrugging it off. "It'll only bruise a little."

"Should I get the nurse?"

"Really, I'm all right. That won't be necessary."

He isn't angry? Zara thought. If she had done the same thing to his father, she was sure the Colonel would have suspended her from work. Maybe he would have sent her to the labor camp just for the fun of it. But Bastian didn't seem fazed.

"I'll see you at four o'clock today?" Bastian said.

Zara had almost forgotten about their meeting. Before she could answer him, though, two female cadets glided down the hall and stopped when they spotted Bastian. They stared at him, then at Zara.

"Bastian," one of them cooed. "Why are you talking to *her*?"

The other girl sniffed the air. "Ugh. When do you think was the last time she bathed?" Her nose crinkled and her gaze traveled over Zara's frayed uniform.

Bastian's back stiffened. "Don't you two have to catch your bus?" he said, his voice strained.

"We thought maybe you could give us a ride," said the taller cadet. She twisted her ponytail with one finger and flashed him a pretty smile.

"Not today," he said flatly.

The girls huffed, exchanged a dark glance, and quickly departed. Bastian turned back to Zara. "Sorry about that."

Zara could only stare at him for a few seconds before finding her tongue. A cadet *never* apologized to a cleaning girl. It was simply not done. "There's no need to apologize, Herr Eckhart," she managed to get out.

She had heard so many rumors about Bastian's snobbishness, how he thought he was so mighty that he didn't socialize with the other cadets, but so far he had treated her like no other Nazi had before. Politely. And with respect. He was a jigsaw puzzle that Zara couldn't quite piece together. Either he was being kind to her because he wanted something, or he was being kind to her because he was just that.

A kind Nazi? Doubt rolled through Zara like a steam engine. He must want something. . . . But what exactly?

"Can you meet me at my house after your shift?" said Bastian.

"I thought you wanted to meet here at the academy."

"There has been, ah, a change of plans."

The hairs pricked on the back of Zara's neck. None of Bastian's actions made sense: calling her *Fräulein*, chasing off the female cadets, offering to walk her to his house. She had a feeling he didn't want to talk about this housekeeping job at all, but she didn't know what else he could want to discuss with her.

Zara was about to agree to the courtyard meeting — she had no other choice but to accept it — but then she heard a flurry of chatter down the hallway. A swath of cadets had gathered by the front doors, waving slips of paper in their hands and peppering the air with words like "Nazis" and "arrest." One of Bastian's track teammates, Walther Dresner, broke free from the group and ran toward Bastian. His lip curled at Zara as he stepped in front of her to clap Bastian on the back.

"Can you believe it?" Walther said while he fiddled with his sapphire-encrusted watch. He was always accessorized in the most ridiculous Berlin fashions. Today, he favored a pair of thick-framed glasses with no lenses. It was the silliest thing Zara had ever seen, not to mention a waste of money.

"What's going on?" said Bastian.

"Haven't you heard? There's an execution today." He handed Bastian a piece of paper from his breast pocket. The flyer looked eerily familiar to Zara. "A few of the soldiers posted the announcement not too long ago."

"*Execution?*"

"The sentinels arrested a spy. Coach canceled practice, so don't bother going. I'll see you at the square, yeah?"

Zara froze, each word of his puncturing her skin. *A spy. An execution.* She tried to breathe, but the air wouldn't come fast enough. Was her uncle safe? Had he gotten arrested? He had been so cautious these last nine years, but when it came to the Nazis no one was ever truly safe.

She had to find out who the spy was.

Zara wanted to run to the square immediately, but she forced herself to wheel her cart back into the utility room. She had to act like a humble *Hausmeisterin* for another few minutes; she couldn't let anyone get suspicious. After she pulled off her apron, she found the nearest exit and broke into a sprint once the academy was behind her, passing the tea shop and the Nazi Women's Charity League, which was gathering old coats and shoes for an orphanage. Hundreds of people had lined the streets already, a sea of pale-faced men and wide-eyed women, Germans and laborers mixed together. No one had seen an execution in years.

Please, please let Uncle Red be all right, Zara thought desperately. A cloud of tears stormed into her eyes. She hadn't even waved good-bye to him that morning; she had been too fixated on the mission last night. She should have kissed him on the cheek, told her that she loved him. She urged her legs faster.

Weaving from left to right, Zara squeezed through the throng until she neared the stage in the square, the same setup as the Führer's announcement. Two dozen soldiers had spread over the stage, standing shoulder to shoulder, forming a wall of guns and muscle. Zara had to stand on her tiptoes to catch a glimpse of the spy.

Not Uncle Red. Please, not Uncle Red, she repeated over and over in her head.

She strained her neck until she saw a sliver of the spy's face. White hair. Wrinkled skin. A torn shawl over thin shoulders.

Zara's throat cinched like a belt.

It wasn't her uncle.

It was Mrs. Talley.

7

The blood drained from Zara's face.

"No," she whispered. "Oh, God, no."

This couldn't be happening. After the mission last night, Zara had made sure that they hadn't been followed. She had destroyed that security camera, too, hadn't she?

Bastian found her in the crowd — had he followed her from school? — but he stopped abruptly when he saw the stage. "Who is that poor woman?" he said so only Zara could hear.

Zara didn't answer him. Her gaze scrambled across the mass of *Kleinbauern*, searching wildly for her uncle, but she could barely see ten feet in front of her. The square was filled to capacity with onlookers on every corner and soldiers out in full force. Over a hundred guards had been positioned throughout the square, marked by their green uniforms, along with a half-dozen sentinels. One of them scaled the courthouse façade like a four-limbed spider, while Sentinel Achen flew overhead in a tight circle. A few of the German children pointed at him and clapped.

Zara focused back on the stage, filled with panic. She pushed forward. "Mrs. Talley!"

"Please, you mustn't make a scene," Bastian said into her ear. He cautiously tugged at her elbow. "There's nothing we can do to stop this."

"Don't say that!" Zara snapped before she remembered who she was speaking to. She started mumbling an apology, but Bastian interrupted it.

"Believe me, *Fräulein*" — without realizing it, he touched the dog tags around his neck — "there's nothing left to do. You'll only get arrested yourself."

Zara shook her head. She wouldn't believe that — and she couldn't understand why Bastian was looking out for her. He had hardly spoken a word to her in all of the years she worked at the academy, but now he was treating her like a friend.

Ignoring him, Zara squeezed deeper into the morass of townspeople. She might have stood by while Mr. Kerry was getting beaten, but she wouldn't repeat that mistake. Mrs. Talley was her friend, maybe her only friend after the Nazis had slaughtered Molly, and Zara refused to do nothing while the Nazis cut her to pieces.

But Bastian's warning echoed through her mind. Hundreds of people now packed the square, with Nazis in every corner. How could she and Mrs. Talley ever escape?

An armored SUV pulled up to the square, and the soldiers shouted for everyone to quiet down. Only then did Colonel Eckhart step out of the car and proceed onto the stage, with a megaphone held against his mouth. *"Heil Hitler! Sieg heil!"*

"Sieg heil," the masses chanted like drones.

"Today, I speak to the *Kleinbauern* of Greenfield," he said, sweeping his frigid gaze across the crowd. "A few days ago, as many of you witnessed, we arrested a man who spoke treason against the Führer. It troubles me greatly that many of you continue to disrespect his rule. How *ungrateful* you are."

The Germans in the square, clad in their pressed suits and tailored dresses, nodded their heads, but the tattered-clothed laborers exchanged glances with their neighbors. Yet, none of them dared raise a voice in protest.

"My soldiers have discovered a criminal in our midst. A traitor!" Colonel Eckhart pointed a long finger at Mrs. Talley. "A spy for the Alliance!"

Zara choked on her breath, still bewildered at what was unfolding in front of her. Mrs. Talley had always been so careful — maybe not to the extent of Uncle Red, but she had cautiously stowed her Alliance radio and kept her house free of treasonous documents. The Nazis must have set her up for this crime. That was the only explanation Zara could think of.

Colonel Eckhart pointed the megaphone at Mrs. Talley's face. "This woman, Nella Talley, has committed the offense of stealing from Fort Goering. Do you deny this?" He prodded Mrs. Talley, digging hard against her side.

Mrs. Talley said nothing. She fixed her gaze dead ahead, standing with her back straight despite the blood trickling from her nose. The Nazis' work, most likely. Zara tried to catch her eye, but she wasn't tall enough to see over the people in front of her.

"Do you deny the footage we recorded of you? Our security cameras don't lie." Colonel Eckhart smiled like a cat that had trapped a fat mouse. "We've hidden them throughout our properties to catch traitors like you."

Struggling to breathe, Zara braced herself against the woman next to her, who threw her a nasty scowl and backed away. Zara regained her balance, but sheer panic was rolling through her. Had she missed another camera during the supply run? No, that couldn't be it. If there had been another camera on top of a shed or the hospital, then she would be up on that stage as well. Then the realization dawned on her: The Nazis must have hidden another camera *inside* the storage shed where Mrs. Talley had taken the supplies. Zara may have destroyed one device, but she hadn't destroyed the one that counted the most.

Nausea swam through her stomach. Zara had been so sure that she and Mrs. Talley had gotten away with their mission, that they had outsmarted the Nazis. She had walked around all day with a spring in her step, so proud of what she had done — but she had been so stupid.

Colonel Eckhart shoved Mrs. Talley onto her knees and kicked her bad hip. Anguish spread over her face, but Mrs. Talley didn't cry out. He continued, "And now for the greater charges. Do you refute your involvement with the Alliance?" He waited for her to answer and slapped her when she didn't. A red mark exploded across Mrs. Talley's cheek, but she still remained silent. "We found a rebel radio during a sweep of your home. Are you going to tell me that it wasn't yours?"

Ask for mercy, Zara thought, desperate. She knew Mrs. Talley would never do so, but maybe the Colonel would take pity on a widow. There had to be a tiny kernel of compassion inside him.

The Colonel only continued his pacing. "I take your silence for acquiescence, then." His white smile spread wider, and Zara knew that there would be no mercy. There wasn't a speck of it in his Nazi bones. "The punishment for your crimes is death!"

A cry tore from Zara's throat before she could stifle it. "No! Please —" She stopped herself as a hush fell over the crowd. Her blood turned to frost as Colonel Eckhart searched the massive group, hunting for the source of the outburst. Hunting for *her*.

But then, more shouts rang through the square. Zara's cry had caught on.

"Set her free!" someone yelled.

"Release her!"

The murmurs hit a crescendo. Some people booed while others threw their shoes at the stage. Toward the back of the square, a group of miners shoved their way forward. Almost every *Kleinbauer* in Greenfield knew Mrs. Talley — she was the only midwife for thirty miles. For years, she had delivered screaming babies for factory workers and farmhands, for the poorest of the poor, who could only pay her in pennies and favors. The boos grew into a chorus.

"There will be order!" Colonel Eckhart said. He nodded at his guards.

Throughout the square, the soldiers knocked their rifle butts into the workers and pointed their muzzles at any naysayers. One of the guards marched toward Bastian and Zara, chewing a fat wad of tobacco and pointing at Zara's nose.

"You. I saw you yelling," he barked, his tone filled with bile. He swung his rifle at Zara's head and, before she could even wince, the butt of the weapon smacked against her temple.

Zara's vision flashed white, then blurred. The right side of her head exploded in agony, making her legs crumple, and she landed hard on her knees. Her hand flew to the side of her head, but there was no blood. Nothing broken. Yet the pain had knocked the breath out of her.

"Watch your mouth, *Untermensch*," the soldier said before he stalked away.

Once the soldier was out of earshot, Bastian glanced at Zara, worry in his eyes. "You should stay down. It's safer that way."

Zara refused to sit. Not until Mrs. Talley was safe. Somehow she had to get her friend off that stage before the Nazis slaughtered her.

Stumbling onto her feet, she ignored the throbbing in her head and watched as Colonel Eckhart motioned toward his SUV. A female sentinel emerged from the car. She stood over six feet tall, with blond hair that lay in neat braids down her back, reminiscent of a schoolgirl, but there was nothing girlish about her.

Zara's knees trembled again. She had seen this sentinel on television before, standing right next to the Führer as a member of his Corps of Four. What was she doing here?

"Sentinel Braun." Bastian's jaw clenched as the female sentinel — the Protector, as she was known — strode onto the stage alongside his father, her blond head tilted high. He looked just as confused as Zara. "She should be with the Führer, shouldn't she?"

The Colonel raised his megaphone as if he had heard his son's question. "I am pleased to introduce Sentinel Petra Braun, one of the most esteemed members of the German Anomaly Division. She arrived in the capital yesterday to train the sentinels there, and she was gracious enough to spare a few hours with Fort Goering's Anomaly troops. Before she departs back to Berlin, she insisted on attending this execution."

Sentinel Braun nodded and waved at the audience like she was a foreign dignitary receiving an award. Zara's head thudded all over again, and she went over her grim options. She could grab Mrs. Talley and fly them both out of the city, but the soldiers, especially Sentinel Achen, would be in close pursuit. Or she could send a gale-force wind at the stage and knock down the guards, but there were over a hundred armed Nazis in the square today. She couldn't fight all of them. And what about her uncle? If she and Mrs. Talley fled from Greenfield, Colonel Eckhart would be sure to arrest him. Despair clawed up Zara's throat. There had to be a way to save Mrs. Talley, but each idea wilted in front of her.

On the stage, Colonel Eckhart and Sentinel Braun exchanged a few words, causing the Colonel to grin gleefully. He turned back to his audience to announce, "In the name of the Führer, Sentinel Braun has asked to perform the execution herself. *Heil Hitler!*"

While the German onlookers clapped and cheered, Zara couldn't move. Sentinel Braun was a fire wielder and an ice conjurer. With powers like that, Mrs. Talley would be sure to suffer — and Braun would make the execution as painful as possible.

Sentinel Braun approached Mrs. Talley, the two plaits of her hair thumping her back with each step, and she ran a gloved finger down her victim's cheek. *"Guten Tag."*

Mrs. Talley didn't flinch. "I don't fear you. Or death."

Sentinel Braun laughed. With a terrible smile smeared on her lips, she removed her white gloves and held out her palm, commanding a pillar of flames to spring from her hand. The fire licked thirstily at her skin, lengthening until it spanned the size of a six-foot whip.

Despite her blinding headache, Zara beckoned for the wind. She knew her plan was insane, maybe suicidal, but she had to stop the execution. She couldn't lose anybody else to the Nazis. Sweat gathered on her forehead as she looked at her hands, but she could only muster a puff of breeze.

Listen to me! she screamed at the air. *Spin!*

A slight draft blew against her shoulders, but it wasn't enough. The hammer in Zara's head kept smashing against her skull, cutting her connection to the air around her. She glared at her fingers, but it was no use.

"The Empire will fall!" Mrs. Talley shouted, her voice echoing over the masses. "The Territories will be free once again!"

Sentinel Braun released the whip of fire, lashing it across Mrs. Talley's small form. A line of bright welts spread over the wrinkled skin, but the whip didn't stop there. It curled around Mrs. Talley's frail body, singeing off her hair, strangling her with smoke. Mrs. Talley shrieked.

A sob shuddered through Zara. She cried out for the wind, but it was too late. The whip coiled faster and faster until Mrs. Talley was drenched in orange flames. Her screams drowned out as the pillar burned hotter, as it towered higher.

"Arthur!" Her voice was fading. "Oh, Arthur . . ."

That was when Sentinel Braun unleashed her second power: a violent storm of ice. The foot-long icicles hammered into Mrs. Talley's weakening body until she fell silent.

A woman fainted. Schoolchildren cried. A man standing not far from Zara started screaming, but a soldier elbowed him in the stomach.

Zara's eyes clamped shut, but she couldn't hide from that smell — the stench of cooked flesh.

She clawed through the masses, fleeing from that terrible scent, but it followed her, clinging to her clothes, lingering beneath her nose. An awful taste climbed into Zara's throat, and she spilled her lunch onto the sidewalk. The people around her jumped back, but Bastian pushed through them and crouched next to her. He pulled a hand-kerchief from his pocket and pressed it into her hand.

"Here, take this," he said.

Zara stared at the kerchief, with his initials embroidered on it. Then she glanced up at him. Her hand clenched around the white cloth, but then she forced herself to drop it. She didn't want his help or his kindness. Not after what his father had done.

"Was Mrs. Talley a friend of yours?" he said softly.

"Just . . . just leave me alone."

Confusion clouded his eyes. "Pardon?"

"Just leave me alone!" Zara staggered forward, not caring about propriety. Bastian was a Nazi, born and bred, plain and simple. He was one of *them*.

Without another word, she ran.

Zara fled from the square. Around her, the screaming chaos continued — the shocked *Kleinbauern*, the wailing schoolchildren — but she ran past all of it. But no matter how fast she urged her legs to go, she couldn't get Mrs. Talley's cries out of her head. Or that smell. She wanted to scrub her mind clean of them, but she knew she would never forget.

Her knees buckled again, and her hands hit the pavement. Zara didn't get up this time. Her heart wrenched into a thousand pieces so small that she would never stitch them back together again.

Because Mrs. Talley was gone.

Zara curled into a ball right there on the street, not caring about the people who had to walk around her. The sobs came finally. Only yesterday, Mrs. Talley had bustled around the St. James house, cooking dinner and playing rummy. Now, not even a day later, Zara would never see her friend again.

Anger bubbled in Zara's chest, and the cut on her thumb from last night began to throb. The stinging started up again, the same needle pricking she had felt last night. Zara swore. She couldn't deal with an infection right now, not after what she had witnessed.

Footfalls struck the cobblestones behind her, but Zara hardly noticed. She barely looked up in time before she felt a pair of arms engulf her in a tight embrace. It took her a moment to register who it was.

"Uncle Red?" she whispered.

"Thank God, you're all right!" He looked her over and winced at the welt on her temple. "Why didn't you stop? I was calling for you."

She collapsed against him, something she hadn't done since she was little. "Did you see it? The . . . the execution?"

"Only the very end. I was over in Ingleside at the livestock auction." Each word came out more hoarse than the last. "I came as soon as I could." Minutes passed before he pulled away. "Let's get you home."

Zara gripped onto his arm, blindly stumbling next to him. Each step felt heavier than the last, like walking in tar, and Uncle Red had to help her into the truck. His face was paper white as he pulled onto the road.

"Try not to think about it," he said.

How could she not? Zara shut her eyes, but she could still see the execution, every little detail. The fire. The smoke. The smell.

Zara slammed her fists against her seat, her shock replaced with a surge of anger. "How could this happen? Mrs. Talley was so careful. She was so . . ." A hundred words rushed through her thoughts: smart, good-hearted, and she gave the very best hugs that left you smelling like lavender tea. But the Nazis had killed her anyway.

The tears came back. Zara wiped them from her eyes, only to have a new batch replace them. "They *burned* her, Uncle Red. And they stabbed her, too." White-hot fury now coursed through her every pore. She could taste the bitterness on her tongue. "I couldn't do anything. She was screaming, but I couldn't help her."

Her uncle pulled the car over and threw it into park. His arm wrapped her into another hug. "It's going to be all right."

"How can anything be all right?" She twisted free from him and huddled on her side of the cab, her heart splitting in half and then splitting again.

"This hurts for me, too," her uncle said. His eyes welled. "We have to keep going, though. That's what Nell would've wanted."

"What about the Nazis? We'll let them get away with this?"

"I know you're angry —"

"Of course I'm angry! They killed Mrs. Talley over a few stolen supplies and a radio!"

"Shh, listen to me." He tipped her chin up so she had to look at him. "We have to keep our wits about us, okay? The Nazis are going to make more arrests. They're going to arrange more interrogations. We have to be cautious."

"Cautious?" Zara seethed. "The Nazis *murdered* Mrs. Talley, and you want me to be cautious?"

"I'm trying to keep you alive. It's only the two of us now."

"But they killed her!"

He gripped her shoulders. "I told her that I'd care for you, and I'm doing my best to do that." Tears fell from his eyes, and Zara's mouth opened. He never cried. Not since Mission Metzger. "I lost her and now Nell's gone and if I lost you next . . ."

At the sight of his tears, Zara's squall of anger died down. He was talking about her mom, she realized. Her uncle never talked about her mother; it was too painful for him even all these years later. Zara's heart sank, heavy as an anchor, and she thought about the horrible cards that her uncle had been dealt in his life: losing his sister, raising a little girl on his own. It hadn't been easy. And yet, she couldn't follow him on his road of caution.

"Promise me you won't go looking for trouble," he said, his gaze fastening onto hers. "You saw what the Nazis did to Nell."

Zara swallowed. She didn't want to lie to him.

"*Promise me.*"

But she told him what he wanted to hear. "I promise."

Uncle Red breathed out. His hands slipped from her shoulders, and he started up the car again. The truck rumbled through the town's streets, passing a German family at the bakery who were sharing a slice of streusel cake. Apparently, they had felt like celebrating after the execution.

A stiff silence fell inside the vehicle, and Zara rolled her last words over her tongue.

I promise.

Her gaze fixed on her uncle. She couldn't keep this promise to him, not after what had happened today. Nine years ago, the Nazis had shot her mother dead, and six years after that they had killed her best friend. Now, they had executed one of the people she loved most.

Zara's nails drilled into her palms. She couldn't — she *wouldn't* — let the Germans get away with this.

8

A few days later, as the stars winked across the sky, Zara tiptoed toward her uncle's bedroom. She leaned her ear against the door until she heard the familiar sound. The soft fluttery snores.

Good, she thought. *He'll be out for a few hours at least.*

Tiptoeing back, Zara glanced at her clock — 9:42 p.m. — and slid on her grandfather's old wool coat. It was three sizes too big on her narrow frame, but it had ample pockets, which she would need for tonight. Even better, the coat should camouflage her figure. From far away, it would make her look like a man. Or, at the very least, a skinny boy.

With her fingers moving silently, Zara slipped a hunting knife into her right pocket and a can of spray paint into the left. She reached for the window latch, but her hand stilled when she glimpsed the photograph on her nightstand. Her fingers brushed against the frame, and the grief hit her all over again.

"Oh, Mrs. Talley," she said.

Days may have passed since the execution, but Zara's eyes had yet to dry. She stared at the wrinkled photo, one of the few she had of Mrs. Talley. It was taken right before Mission Metzger, one of the last remnants of the old Greenfield Alliance. Her thumb grazed over the faces that smiled up at her: Mrs. Talley up front, Zara's mother behind her, Uncle Red to the right, Ms. Abigail Oh in the corner, and so many more. All of them smiling. Now, nearly all of them were dead.

When the Alliance first announced its plans to take over Fort Metzger, the Greenfield chapter had volunteered immediately. Zara's mother and Uncle Red had spent months gathering weapons: Glock pistols, German rifles, and the occasional crate of C4. Zara remembered them huddled over the kitchen table at night, discussing logistics, using words she didn't understand like *high ground* and *culminating point*. Oftentimes she found them asleep at the table in the morning, with her uncle snoring and her mom's red curls a tangled mess upon her head.

They had made a good team. Uncle Red plotted the strategies while Annie drummed up new members. Together, they had grown their chapter from a mishmash of farmers to a bona fide player in the Alliance. And as a reward for their hard work, they had been given a prominent position for the attack on Fort Metzger — leading the southern charge.

But that night had ended in disaster. After Colonel Eckhart alerted the fort to the Alliance's plans, the Nazis had struck with a hard and swift fist. When it was all over, thousands of rebels had been imprisoned and thousands more executed, wiping out over half the Alliance in one night. Zara's mother had taken a bullet to the chest during the escape, but Uncle Red had managed to pull her to safety and had bribed a farmer to take them south.

The rest of their chapter hadn't been so lucky.

Two hundred had perished during the raid, including Arthur Talley and Zara's mother, who bled out on the way home. When Uncle Red arrived at the Talleys' cottage, he broke the news to Mrs. Talley first before he found Zara in the bedroom, watching a German cartoon on the ancient black-and-white television. He crouched down next to her and hugged her so tight that she thought her lungs would stop working.

Where's Mama? she had asked.

Zara couldn't think about that day without her heart hurting. She had lost her mother and, in a way, she'd lost her uncle, too. Something had broken inside of him. Something more than bone and muscle.

She felt that same way now: broken, beaten, her insides hollowed out, a dull rage thrumming through her. But she wouldn't let the Nazis defeat her, like they had defeated Uncle Red. She had to keep fighting. She couldn't let caution overtake her soul anymore.

The clock's hand hit 9:45, and Zara knew she had to be quick. She crept down the stairs and out the back door into the spring-sweetened air. The night was as black as oil, without a sliver of moon, but Zara had walked this path so many times that she only needed starlight to guide her. When she reached the town limits, she slipped through the alleyways, careful to avoid any Germans out for a stroll or a cigarette break. Fortunately, it was a Monday. Most of the residents had long since retreated to their homes to watch their Berlin television dramas or devour a second helping of cabbage rolls and fried potatoes. She was alone in the night.

The courthouse lay due north of her. Zara hid behind a broken streetlamp right before the cleaning ladies — three middle-aged women with pecan-colored skin — locked up the front doors. There were only a handful of blacks in Greenfield and nearly all of them worked at the mines, but a few of the women had landed janitorial jobs at night, long after the Nazis had headed home for the day.

The three women shuffled out of sight, and Zara pulled on a

knitted face mask that she had spent hours making the previous night. The mask was a bit too snug — she wasn't much of a knitter, like Mrs. Talley had been — but it would have to do. Now, all she needed was to run up to the courthouse, get the job done, and run back home.

It'll be simple, Zara told herself, but her pulse thumped anyway. If she wasn't careful, if anyone saw her, she would land in a jail cell, no questions asked. Perhaps she should have waited a couple more days — even her mother had spent weeks planning missions — but Zara wouldn't lose her nerve now.

Forcing her legs into a run, she gathered every speck of courage and ducked behind a row of hedges across from the courthouse. Her gaze flew upward, toward the security camera pointed at the entrance. She had spotted the camera yesterday when she was scouting the premises for her mission tonight. Maybe her uncle's caution had rubbed off on her after all.

Zara glanced over both shoulders before she conjured a tornado in her right palm, as tall as a pitcher of milk.

Destroy, she commanded. The tornado tore into the device, ripping off its lens and exposing its wires. Barely ten seconds had passed before the camera shattered into a clump of metal and glass. Satisfied, Zara repeated this process five more times, aiming for the courthouse front lights, until the entrance was plunged into darkness.

It was now or never. Holding her breath, Zara ran up the building's steps, her veins spiked with adrenaline. She called up the wind and commanded it to lift her. Her feet left the ground, raising her higher and higher until she was floating face-to-face with the Führer's portrait. At the sight of him, anger pumped through Zara, hot like a skillet, and she reached for the knife in her pocket. The Führer's oily eyes, as big as her fists, seemed to follow her as she made the first cut.

A couple of slits through those eyes. A slice through the chin. Zara's hand slashed faster, moving with a fury that matched the turmoil boiling through her.

For Mrs. Talley. Zara slit the Führer's nose.

For Molly. She cut through his ear.

And for my mom. The blade severed the mouth in half.

A scream built in Zara's throat for everyone she had lost — for all that the Führer's regime had taken away from her — but she channeled the scream into her knife, hacking at the portrait until it hung in limp ribbons. But even then, she wasn't finished. Twisting off the paint cap, she sprayed its contents over the shredded canvas, blasting Dieter's nose and the glittering medals that adorned his suit. She didn't stop until the portrait had turned into a shredded black mess.

With her breaths growing labored, Zara stared at her handiwork. The Colonel would be livid, no doubt about it. No one had vandalized the Führer's portrait in over a decade. And yet, only a hollow victory rang in her ears.

This wouldn't bring Mrs. Talley back. She would never see her friend again, no matter how many portraits she destroyed.

Zara felt defeated all over again. Landing on the steps, she sprinted down the street, wanting nothing more than to fall into bed and sleep until her heart stopped hurting. She reached for the mask, ready to tear off the scratchy thing, but then she rounded the corner and knocked into a woman in a wheelchair. The woman cried out. Zara tried to whirl away, but her foot caught on one of the wheels and she ended up sprawled on the sidewalk instead.

The woman cried louder, and the man escorting her — a young man with a headful of loose curls — tried to soothe her. He held a small telescope underneath his arm, which they must have been using to stargaze on this moonless night. That would explain why the two of them were out so late.

"It's all right, Mother. We're nearly home," he said in German. He turned to Zara. "Can I help you, sir?"

Zara looked up. *Oh no.*

Bastian's body went rigid when he saw her mask. His arms spread out to shield his mother. "We don't have money with us," he said.

Zara ignored the tweak in her ankle and took off running, her legs pumping beneath her like two machines. She waited for Bastian to shout at her, to throw threats about telling his father, but she heard nothing as she dashed through the street. She didn't stop until she left the Greenfield town limits, and when she mustered the courage to look back she only saw an empty road behind her.

She was safe.

At least, for now.

9

Zara hardly slept that night. Once she had snuck back into the house, she waited by her window for hours, jumping at any sound: a creaking floorboard, a dripping sink. Every hair on her neck stood at attention as she stared out the window, peering for a Nazi truck to come and arrest her.

Stupid, stupid, stupid, she told herself. She had tried to be so careful, but then she had to plow into Bastian and his mother on their nightly stargazing tour.

A bead of sweat rolled down Zara's forehead. What had she been thinking? She had used her power in the square *and* ruined the Führer's portrait. If she had gotten caught, she would have been thrown into prison and left there to wither. Or shot on the spot. Even worse, she would've broken her uncle's heart.

Zara's eyes fixed on the photograph on her nightstand, scanning Uncle Red's proud face and Mrs. Talley's smiling one. Her heart felt split in two. Maybe it had been a reckless thing to do, defacing the Führer's portrait. Maybe it had been rash. Dangerous.

But didn't Mrs. Talley deserve some sort of retribution?

Zara clutched the photo against her chest. She couldn't regret what she had done tonight. No, she'd had enough of her uncle's caution and his endless waiting. The Nazis had taken far too much from her — and she wouldn't let them take anything else.

Hours later, Zara jolted awake to her alarm and realized she must have drifted asleep. Hurrying to the window, she stared at the road, but she didn't see any trucks or police vehicles. Her breaths eased a little. There was no way Bastian could have recognized her last night. She had worn her mask and her grandpa's big coat. Besides, Bastian had been too preoccupied with his mother.

As Zara gathered her work uniform, she realized she had never seen Frau Eckhart up close before. When Bastian's mother first arrived in Greenfield years ago, she had busied herself as the new colonel's wife. She had organized stargazing nights for the town's German children and led the Nazi Women's Charity League; but now Frau Eckhart rarely ventured out into public aside from the occasional league function, not since the riding accident that had shattered her backbone and her mind six years ago.

It surprised Zara how much Bastian took after his mother, with that same pale hair and the same slim nose. Except Frau Eckhart resembled a faded version of her son: leeched white tresses, bony jawline, and a pretty face marred by circles under her eyes. Perhaps it was a good thing that Bastian was an only child. Frau Eckhart may not have been "blessed with children," as the Nazis called it, but another pregnancy might have done her in.

With her nerves somewhat settled, Zara chewed on a chunk of bread for breakfast and slipped out the door while her uncle was showering. She jogged toward the school, not wanting a demerit for tardiness, but her feet slowed once she neared the courthouse. Gathered out front, a small group of people stood on the front steps of the building, murmuring to one another and shaking their heads.

The portrait, Zara thought and automatically drew a few yards closer. Her neck craned to get a better view.

The painting was gone.

Zara blinked at the stretch of bright red bricks where the portrait had hung just the night before. The Nazis must have removed it early this morning. The crowd kept whispering. A few of them pointed at the roof, and one of the women gasped.

Zara, of course, looked up. She squinted at the lip of the rooftop — and the air promptly fled from her lungs. There, on the roof, the Nazis had propped up a metal cage, the size of a coffin. And inside of it there was a skeleton of blackened bones, held up by a pair of butcher's meat hooks.

Mrs. Talley.

Zara went light-headed, and she had to blink the dizziness away before she lost her balance. The Nazis had never done anything like this before. It was too cruel. Too wrong.

Slowly, Zara's gaze found its way back to the roof, and the cage entered her sight once more. She flinched and shut her eyes, but the image had been imprinted in her memory. She staggered down the sidewalk, knowing she had to keep moving or she'd collapse.

Tears huddled in her eyes as she arrived at the academy and found her way to the utility room. She sank onto the floor with her head between her knees, taking deep breaths to calm herself.

The other four cleaning girls edged toward the door as if Zara were a wounded animal. Only Kristy stepped forward.

"Shift starts in five minutes," she said coolly.

"Don't you think I know that?" Zara lashed out. She sprang to her feet, wanting Kristy to lash back at her, to call her *that* word. She was itching for a fight.

Kristy rolled her eyes and resumed tying her smock. "Go home if you're going to be sick. No one's going to clean up after you."

"I didn't ask you to!" said Zara, but Kristy was out the door already, the rest of the girls following her.

Zara sank back against the cold metal lockers. It was bad enough that she had to watch Mrs. Talley die. Now the Nazis had strung her up like a horrifying scarecrow. She knew the Colonel was sending a message to whoever had defiled the Führer's portrait. *You want to play games with us?* he seemed to be saying. *We shall play your little game.*

The bell rang to start the school day, and Zara somehow managed to work straight through lunch, until she overheard a table of cadets talking about the caged skeleton in the square. After she rinsed off every pot and dirty plate, she had a twenty-minute break for her own lunch, but instead of nibbling on some leftovers she fled for the woods beyond the academy's perimeter. She wove through the trees until she heard nothing but the puff of her breath and the breeze whispering through the soft spring leaves. Only then did Zara stop beneath a fat oak tree and brace her hands against its cracked bark. A sharp anger twisted inside her chest, stabbing its harsh blade against her heart.

Around Zara, the wind swelled. It swirled by her shoes, kicking up moss and dead leaves. Her power may have been weakened after the blow to her head, but now it was bursting inside her, begging to be unleashed.

So Zara released it. Overhead, the branches swayed and the leaves shivered, clinging to their stems against the human-made storm. She stretched out her arm, stick straight.

Spin, she demanded.

A funnel spun into existence, only four inches high.

Spin.

The funnel doubled its height. Then it grew six inches more.

Higher!

A twig snapped behind Zara. The little tornado spun away into nothing. Whipping around, Zara saw someone walking thirty yards behind her. Her anger wilted, replaced by panic.

Bastian.

She thrust her hands behind her. Had he seen the tornado? No, he was much too far away for that, but Zara's panic failed to ebb. Maybe he had recognized her last night at the courthouse — but he wouldn't have any proof of it, would he? It would be his word against hers. Zara nibbled her lip. Yet his word would carry much more clout than hers.

"Hello, *Fräulein*," Bastian said, his hands buried in his pockets. He crossed the distance between them. "I was getting a drink of water when I saw you leave. Are you all right?"

She eyed him. "I'm fine, Herr Eckhart. I was getting some fresh air, but I was about to head back to work."

He didn't seem to hear her. "There is something I must discuss with you."

"About the housekeeping job?" Her throat tightened as she thought about bumping into him and his mother last night. *Please let it be about the job.*

"No." He drew in a deep breath. "We don't need a new house-keeper. I fibbed about that because I didn't know how else to speak to you privately." The words fell out of his mouth, tripping over one another.

"Speak to me about what?" she said slowly.

"I've heard that your grandfather had ties to the Alliance," he forced out. "I was wondering if maybe your uncle was involved with them, too."

Zara's stomach dropped against her feet. She had lost Mrs. Talley, and now her uncle's life might be in danger. She had to handle this conversation very carefully, even though she wanted to flee home this instant. "My uncle is loyal to the Führer. I promise you that," she said, struggling to contain the trembling in her voice.

"You misunderstand. If it is true about your uncle's involvement —"

"Heil Hitler!" Zara's heart pedaled faster. If Bastian had any proof about her uncle's ties to the Alliance, then she didn't want to think about what would happen next. An arrest. A beating. Another execution. She told herself to breathe; she couldn't let him get any more suspicious of her or her family.

"I don't wish to get you or your uncle into trouble." Bastian's voice lowered to a whisper. "I want to *join* you."

Zara could only blink at him. She must have heard him wrong.

"I want to join the Alliance. In fact, I *must* join the Alliance."

Finally, Zara realized what he had been up to these last few days — the housekeeping job, calling her *Fräulein* instead of "girl." He was baiting her for a confession. Colonel Eckhart must have put him up to this, hoping Bastian's handsome face would loosen her lips about Uncle Red. But there was no way she would fall for their little scheme.

"My apologies, but my uncle is an upstanding citizen. We can't help you." Zara willed her voice to be steady. "We've always met our quota. We don't want any trouble."

"Please. I know how this must look, especially with my father being who he is, but I have to contact the Alliance. I've trained as a medic, both at the academy and with my grandfather. I could be an asset to them." He rattled off his reasoning like he had rehearsed it for hours.

Zara had heard enough. "I have to get back to my shift. Excuse me." She only made it a few steps before Bastian caught up to her.

"My *Opa*. I'm doing this for him." His hand clenched around his dog tags.

"I'm sorry about your grandfather's passing, but —"

"The Nazis killed him." He bit his bottom lip to collect himself before he could speak again. "For committing treason."

Treason? That made Zara pause. She looked up at Bastian as he towered over her with his six-foot height. He was breathing hard, his nostrils flared, and there was anguish in those amber eyes of his. Had his father fed him these lies and coached him for this moment? The Colonel was sorely mistaken to think that she would fall for this.

Bastian must have seen the doubt in her eyes. "*Scheiße,*" he swore in German. "This is coming out all wrong. You have to believe me. I'm not my father. I'm not a Nazi — and I never will be."

"I'm sorry, but I can't help you." Zara knew she had to deny all knowledge of the Alliance until he gave up on her. "My uncle has never been involved with the resistance."

"Give me a few minutes to explain." He continued on before she could answer him. "Opa was a communist. He was involved with the underground party in Nazi-controlled Belgium for many years before he moved to the Territories to help with my mother. But a year ago, he and my father had a falling out over my mother's care. Father cut short Opa's travel visa and that forced my grandfather to return to Brussels. That's when he — he joined the Widerstand."

"The Widerstand?" Zara coughed out. The Widerstand was the Nazi-opposition group that sprang up during the war and had survived to this day. It now spanned across Europe, much like the

Alliance, but on a greater scale. In the last year alone, its members had bombed three forts near Berlin and kidnapped five Nazi officers.

Zara wondered who had come up with this explanation. Communists *and* the Widerstand? Colonel Eckhart should have known that she would see straight through it. As much as she despised him, she had to admit that he wasn't stupid. But if the Colonel wanted this plan to work — to lull Zara into trusting Bastian — then he would have concocted a better story.

Bastian kept talking. "I know this all sounds ridiculous. I wouldn't have believed it myself if it hadn't happened to my family." His fingers raked through his curls. "But it did happen. My *Opa* was arrested during a raid and he was hanged for it." His eyes clasped shut. "My . . . my father could've stopped it, but he didn't."

He was a very good actor, Zara would give him that. His voice had turned to poison when he mentioned his father. If she were more naïve, she would have asked him what he meant by that, but she wasn't a simple farm girl. Her uncle had taught her better.

"I have to go," Zara said. She had stayed far too long already. The other cleaning girls could have reported her to the academy administration by now.

"Wait!" There was a pleading look on his face. He held up the dog tags for Zara to read. "Albert Dubois. That's my *Opa*'s name. You can check for yourself on the school computers."

"There's no need." She pulled away from him, but Bastian caught her elbow. Her breath hitched, startled that he had touched her.

"He was everything to me." Bastian's voice, usually so polite and clipped, took on a desperate edge. "He raised me. I owe this to him."

Zara hesitated. She could have spoken the very same words; she felt the very same about Mrs. Talley, but she couldn't trust Bastian, not after what his father had done to the ones she loved.

"I'm sorry," she repeated. Then she fled back to the academy.

Zara spent the rest of the workday dusting windowsills and scrubbing the gymnasium floors, but her thoughts never strayed far from Bastian. He hadn't returned to school after their talk in the woods, but that hadn't stopped him from occupying every corner of her mind. The story he had told her verged on the ridiculous. His grandfather, a communist? A rebel with the Widerstand? Surely Colonel Eckhart would have come up with something more plausible than that — so why hadn't he? He must be planning something, unless Bastian was telling her the truth.

But that couldn't be possible, either.

Zara knew she could never trust an Eckhart, but a small part of her, a tiny speck, wanted to sneak into the computer lab and look up Albert Dubois. Just to make sure. Yet she couldn't waste another minute on Bastian. A boy like him — Aryan born and Nazi raised — had been spoon-fed German doctrine since birth. Bastian was simply a pawn on his father's chessboard, and Zara needed to avoid him and his pretty face at all costs.

With her mind a jumble of questions, Zara headed home right after she washed the chalkboards, hoping a few hours on the farm would clear the mess in her head. She rounded the last bend to her house, eager to change out of her loafers and into her trusty boots, but she stopped stone-still at the sight of a Nazi SUV pulling out of her driveway.

Thoughts of Bastian and the Alliance fled from her mind. The Nazis had no reason to come to her home. . . . Unless they had found the knife she used to destroy the Führer's portrait. But she had buried the blade in the fields last night, plunging it deep within the spring-warmed soil. Still, her heartbeat refused to slow. A visit from the Nazis was never a good thing.

The SUV turned onto the road and slowed to a stop once it neared Zara. The passenger side window rolled down to reveal Colonel Eckhart sitting inside. Zara almost stumbled back. First Bastian. Now his father.

"Heil Hitler," he said pleasantly, like he had dropped by for a cup of tea.

"Heil Hitler," Zara murmured with as much gusto as she could stomach. Her eyes darted toward the backseat, and she breathed a sigh of relief. Thankfully, she didn't see her uncle sitting there, his hands in cuffs.

"I stopped by to speak to your uncle," Colonel Eckhart continued, his gaze drifting over her old blouse and fraying skirt. He sniffed. "We had a nice chat."

Zara dared a glance into those cruel blue eyes of his. This was the first time she had seen him since Mrs. Talley's execution. Hatred broke inside of her, spilling into her veins. She wanted to press her fingers against his neck, squeezing until he begged her to stop. Instead, she bowed her head to hide the scowl on her face.

"I hope you had a pleasant visit, *mein Herr,"* Zara managed to say. She tried to muster a smile but simply couldn't.

"Isn't it early for you to be home from work?"

"I walk quickly."

"I walk quickly, *mein Herr,"* he corrected harshly.

"My apologies, *mein Herr.*"

The Colonel turned to his driver, who happened to be Sentinel Achen. Zara couldn't seem to stop bumping into him or the Eckharts. "These *Kleinbauern*. How often they forget their manners."

Sentinel Achen nodded. "They should be punished accordingly, *mein Herr.*" Then he winked at Zara when the Colonel looked down to check his watch. She suppressed the urge to run home and leap into the shower.

"Come closer, girl." Colonel Eckhart crooked a finger at her, and Zara had no choice but to comply. She shuffled toward the window, her skin crawling under his watchful eyes, until his face was only a foot away from hers. "I understand you were close to that Alliance spy, Nell Talley."

"She was a casual acquaintance." Zara winced inside. She hated herself for what she had to say next — she hoped Mrs. Talley would understand. "My uncle and I were appalled by her actions."

"Hmph. In the future, I'd take more precaution with whom you associate. Or there will be consequences."

"Yes, *mein Herr.*"

He smiled again, such a bright smile, with white, even teeth, but his eyes were steely. "Tell your uncle that I'll be in touch. And remember, the harvest isn't a long way off. Be sure to fulfill your quota. I do enjoy fresh cabbage."

The window rolled up and the truck continued down the road, burping a cloud of smoke into Zara's eyes before it gunned toward Fort Goering. She watched it leave with clenched fists, wishing she could hurl a worm-rotted cabbage at the Colonel's head.

Once the SUV was out of sight, she ran back to the farmhouse and thrust open the front door. A gasp flew out of her mouth. In the living room, chairs lay broken in jagged pieces and dozens of old magazines were tumbled over the floor, their pages mashed against the rug. The damage had spread into the kitchen, too: The cupboards hung open like gaping teeth while shattered plates splattered over the countertops. At the center of the mess, Uncle Red stood with a broom in his hand, his shoulders slumped at a tired angle.

He glanced at the door. "You're home."

"The Colonel did all of this?" Zara's chest hurt as she surveyed the house — ruined china passed down from her great-grandmother, novels that her mother had cherished. The Nazis had never done this before. Sure, they had conducted interrogations and broken a piece of furniture or two, but they had never ransacked the house. Not like this.

Uncle Red's fists knotted around the broom's handle. "They've been on a rampage today, interrogating everyone about the Führer's portrait. Obviously, they found nothing here, but . . ." His eyes hardened. "I'm only going to ask this once. Did you have anything to do with that painting?"

"Of course not." Zara held his gaze, careful not to flinch or look away. Shame knotted in her stomach at the lie, but she couldn't tell him the truth. Her voice quieted. "Did you see what they did to Mrs. Talley's body?"

He rubbed the bridge of his nose, looking a decade older than he did a second before. "I heard about it this morning."

"We can't leave her up there."

"We have no choice. Not now anyway. Eckhart's breathing down our necks more than ever." His hand swept over the kitchen. "You see what he's done to our house."

"But Mrs. Talley was like family. She *was* our family. We owe her a proper burial."

Uncle Red's forehead creased into a dozen wrinkles. "Don't you think I want that, too? Do you think I like what the Nazis did to her?"

"No —"

"Nell would understand that I'm trying to protect you."

"So we'll leave her up in that cage?" Her uncle hadn't been to the square; he hadn't witnessed how cruel this act was.

"That's enough." He thrust the broom into her hands. "Get to work. I'll start upstairs in the bedrooms."

Uncle Red exited the kitchen, leaving Zara alone with the clutter at her feet. She watched him disappear up the staircase, wishing so desperately to have her old uncle back — the one before Mission Metzger, who would stop at nothing to fight the Nazis and who would never allow a friend's body to hang in a cage. Zara knew that he loved Mrs. Talley — there was no doubt about their mutual respect for each other — but the Nazis had beaten every drop of resolve out of him. And he had let them do it.

She wouldn't let the same thing happen to herself.

Shaking her head, Zara stooped down to collect the larger bits of porcelain. It would take them weeks to save up for new plates. Until then, they would have to use paper ones. With a burdened sigh, she reached for a sliver of glass underneath the kitchen table, but she yanked her hand back when it sliced into her finger. Blood streamed from the wound and onto the floor, bright red against the ivory tiles.

Zara muttered a curse and pressed a dish towel against the cut, waiting for the blood to clot before she surveyed the damage. But that strange needle-like stinging spread over the fresh wound, just like it had days before. So she lifted the cloth to find —

A flash of blue.

A spark, like the tiniest of searchlights.

Zara's eyes grew as big as copper coins. She ran to the kitchen window to take a better look at it, but she only saw blood and jagged flesh on her hand. She ran a timid finger against the cut. Nothing.

I need more sleep, she thought, her pulse still thumping wildly. She must've been seeing things, although that didn't explain the stinging in both of her cuts. Maybe she did need to see a doctor, but they could never afford a trip to the hospital. Mrs. Talley was the one who had treated their bumps and bruises, but she was gone now.

Three knocks thudded against the front door, and Zara jumped at the sound, startled. Wrapping the towel back around her hand, she hurried to the door with the memory of that spark still glued to her thoughts.

Zara swung open the door to find a young man with hazelnut skin standing on the porch. A dusty hat sat atop his head, and a brown trench coat, a few sizes too big, hung over his lean frame. Behind him, a blue truck sat in the driveway, its paint peeling over most of its rusted body.

"Can I help you?" she said, holding the towel tight around her finger. The man appeared a few years older than her, perhaps in his early twenties. Zara wondered if he was a miner looking for extra work or a migrant laborer searching for a place to sleep the night, although he didn't have that dead-weary look in his eyes that the laborers often wore.

The young man tipped his hat. "I'm looking for Redmond St. James, if you please."

Uncle Red appeared behind Zara and nudged her aside. "Hello," he said warily.

"Good evening. I'm traveling through town, looking for work. I heard that Mr. St. James might be hiring."

"I'm afraid you've been mistaken. Best of luck to you." Uncle Red went to close the door, but the man kept talking.

"That's too bad. See, I've been traveling all the way from St. Louis."

Zara shot a glance at her uncle. *St. Louis?* The city had been bombed to pieces by the Nazis years ago after its citizens had rioted for better pay in the car factories. This man had to be lying, but for some reason Uncle Red opened the door farther.

"St. Louis?" said Uncle Red. "You're from St. Louis?"

"Yes, sir. I'm from Lafayette Park. You might've heard of it?"

"I have." Uncle Red chose his next words carefully, as if he was reading lines from a play. "Wasn't it named for the Marquis de Lafayette?"

Zara blinked at him. Why would her uncle ask this worker about an obscure historical figure like the Marquis? She had read about Lafayette a few years ago in one of Mrs. Talley's contraband books, before her uncle had convinced her to get rid of them. The Marquis had been a general in the American Revolutionary War, but hardly anyone knew about him now, much less talked about him.

The man on the porch took this all in stride. "Indeed, it was named for him." His smile lit up his face. "Like I was saying, do you know where I can find Redmond St. James?"

"*I'm* Redmond St. James," said Uncle Red. "And you are?"

"Garrison Strayer." The man stuck out his hand. "It's nice to finally meet you, Redmond. The Alliance sends its greetings."

10

Zara's mouth went dry. For a moment, she thought the man was lying, but Uncle Red reached out and shook his hand. That was when Zara realized their visitor really was Garrison — her ever-so-cautious uncle never would have let the man in if he had any doubts about him.

"Come in," said Uncle Red. "This is my niece, Zara."

"It's nice to meet you," Garrison said, sticking out his hand.

Zara shook it, slowly blinking. She had spent years yearning to meet the leaders of the Alliance — but she never imagined that they could be so young. She had always thought they would be middle-aged men who spent hours hunched over their desks, mumbling about new recruits and military strategy. Yet here was Garrison, only a few years older than she was.

"It's so nice to meet you, too," Zara said finally. She flushed when she remembered the state of their house, in shambles after Colonel Eckhart's visit. She hastily overturned the fallen chairs and kicked away the debris. "Sorry about the mess. The Nazis were just here."

Garrison's whole body tensed. "Any chance they'll come back?"

"I don't think so. They conducted a thorough search," said Uncle Red. "But we'll keep an eye out on the road."

Garrison's gaze darted to the window for half a minute before he finally relaxed. He took off his hat and propped it on the back of a chair. "Did the Nazis hurt you two?" He waited for them to shake their heads before he continued. "I'm really sorry for showing up unannounced, but there are a few things we need to discuss."

"What sort of things?" Zara blurted. If Garrison had traveled all the way here, this must be important.

"Let the man take a seat. I'm sure he's tired and wouldn't mind some water." Uncle Red ushered Garrison to the tattered sofa while Zara grabbed a cup of water and a bowl of leftover cabbage stew that Garrison took with a grateful nod. She wondered how long he had been on the road. The trip from the Alliance bunker in West Virginia would have taken hours, considering that the bunker was located a hundred miles from Neuberlin and was built underneath an abandoned hotel to curb suspicion.

"Are there any other members of your chapter that you need to contact? I'd like to speak with them, too, if possible," Garrison said between bites.

"The Nazis executed one of our members only recently. Nell Talley," Uncle Red said. His tone softened when he mentioned her name. "I sent a message to the Alliance after the execution. The Nazis discovered her radio, and I didn't want any of our codes to get compromised."

"I'm sure my colleagues are looking into that while I've been gone. My condolences, by the way, about Nell. It's always hard when we lose any of our recruits." He waited a few seconds before he said, "The Greenfield chapter is just the two of you, then?"

"Just me, actually. Zara's only sixteen."

Garrison set his bowl onto the wobbly-legged coffee table that had been upended during the Colonel's visit. "We have members as young as fourteen in some chapters. If the girl wants to join, you should let her join."

The muscles around Uncle Red's jaw pulled taut. "When she's older, perhaps."

"Fair enough, but you should work on boosting recruitment, as we've discussed before. Farragut is eager to see this chapter restored to what it used to be. We both are." He sounded very much like a politician — polite, warm, and with a hint of expectation.

Uncle Red, however, wouldn't take the bait. "The Nazis in this area are breathing down our necks." He gestured to the mess in the house. "As you can see, it's not exactly the right time."

It's never the right time, Zara almost said but bit her tongue. If she wanted to impress Garrison, she couldn't act like a pouty child.

Garrison downed his water and decided to switch topics. "I'm sure you're wondering why I'm here. The Alliance has recently come across some very classified information. If it fell into the wrong hands . . . Well, Farragut thought it best if I spoke with you in person."

Zara perked up. "Is the Alliance planning something? A national mission?"

"Let him talk, Zara," Uncle Red said gruffly.

"No, it's good to hear her enthusiasm." Garrison gave Zara an approving nod before he explained further. "We've gathered a few trusted sources in Berlin over the years — members of the Widerstand and a couple of servants at the Führer's palace, that sort of thing. They've passed along information here and there, but nothing of this caliber."

Uncle Red leaned forward. Zara did the same, not wanting to miss one syllable.

"The Führer is very ill," Garrison went on, relishing each word like a prime cut of steak.

"What does he have?" said Uncle Red. "Pneumonia?"

"It's far worse than that. He has a very aggressive form of cancer."

Zara blinked once. Twice. "Cancer?" she whispered. Dieter's father had died of cancer, too, cutting his reign short at the age of fifty-two. Perhaps Dieter had inherited the same disease. "Could this mean . . . ?"

Garrison nodded. "The Führer is dying."

The room fell silent. Zara's jaw dangled at this new revelation, hanging open like the broken cupboards in the kitchen. She wondered if she had heard Garrison correctly — because Dieter's untimely death could wreck havoc in the Empire. His only son, Johann, was nine years old, far too young to assume power.

"It's lung cancer. Stage four," Garrison went on. "The Führer's doctors have tried everything in their repertoire, but they've only been able to slow the spreading. It's the same thing that happened to his father, Anselm."

Even Uncle Red couldn't hide the surprise in his eyes. "What about his Medic in the Corps of Four? Can't he do something?"

"Anomaly healers can only fix wounds that would heal on their own. Fractures. Gashes. Even concussions. But a terminal illness like cancer is beyond their ability."

Perhaps the Führer isn't so invincible after all, Zara thought. She teetered on the edge of her chair. "How long does he have?"

"They estimate two months at most. From what we've learned, he was diagnosed last November and has been deteriorating ever since. That's why he hasn't made many appearances in the last few months."

"What about the recent announcement?" said Uncle Red. "There was a live broadcast of him in our town square."

"They used a double. The Nazis created a very convincing double who has undergone a lot of surgeries to take on Dieter's likeness. Even we were fooled by it."

Zara could hardly keep up with the steady stream of information. "How long have they been using the double?"

"Probably since Christmas. The Führer obviously wants to keep up the façade that he's as strong as ever. With Johann too young to rule, Dieter knows that his death would cause chaos among his generals." Garrison's hands gestured faster as he spoke. "He hasn't kept a tight rein on them like his father did. Look what happened with Reichsmarschall Faust, getting into bed with the Soviets. Once Dieter dies, his generals will probably jostle for power, and that'll weaken the entire Empire."

"For a time, maybe," said Uncle Red, dissecting Garrison's explanation like it was one of Zara's theories. "Although the generals will eventually finish their squabbling and choose a successor. I doubt the Empire will crack because of that."

"Perhaps, but there's also the Soviets to think about," Garrison said. So far, he had matched every one of Uncle Red's points, and Zara wished he could teach her some of those tactics. "The Reds aren't stupid. They know how sick Dieter has gotten, thanks to the information they were fed by Faust. Premier Volkov has already moved troops into the borderlands."

"When?" Uncle Red asked, his face paling. "What countries?"

"Latvia and Estonia so far. Lithuania will likely go next. They've all become sympathetic to the communist cause and have welcomed the Reds with open arms. Granted, the Soviets have only *moved* in troops so far. They haven't fired a shot. But Volkov's actions look like the first step toward breaking the nonaggression pact."

Which could lead to war, Zara thought. If her mom and Mrs. Talley were here, they would have been taking notes and already plotting ways to use this information. "So you're saying —"

"What about the Japanese?" Uncle Red cut in. "They're the Führer's strongest ally. The Soviets can't be blind enough to take on both Empires and the Italians."

"The Italian economy is about to collapse, and Mussolini III is facing a coup. As for the Japanese, they have enough on their hands with the rebellions in China and the uprisings on the California coast. Let's face it: The Empire of Japan is stretched too thin. They got too greedy when the war ended. How could they rule Asia *and* the Pacific *and* the Western American Territories?"

Zara nodded. Garrison was right. Although she hated giving credit to Adolf Hitler, he had been shrewd enough to avoid Japan's current problem. Once he had conquered the United States and executed Roosevelt, he knew he couldn't colonize the massive country on his own. And so he split the Territories with the Japanese and the Italians, saving the most fertile and most developed portion for himself. That was one of the reasons why the Nazi Empire had thrived — it had conquered a manageable portion of land and had populated it with its ever-expanding population.

Garrison leaned back on the sofa, now that all of his cards were on the table. "The Führer is losing his grip on the Empire. It's as simple as that."

Goose bumps shivered across Zara's arms. The Nazi leadership could crack in the next few months, and the entire Empire might soon collapse with it. If part of the borderlands took up arms against the Führer, then others might follow suit. And then, the Territories would have its turn.

"We believe this is the right time for a full-out revolution," Garrison said. "That's why we've come up with Operation Burning Eagle."

Burning Eagle? It sounded a bit silly, Zara thought, but fitting. The eagle was a favored emblem of the Führer, dating back to the days of Adolf Hitler, who looked to the bird as a noble creature, a rightful symbol of his beloved Germany. Zara knew the bird had once been symbolic for the United States as well, but the only eagles she saw now graced her reichsmark notes and Nazi flags.

"A revolution seems hasty," Uncle Red said. He stood from his chair and paced around the debris-ridden room. "We don't want a repeat of Mission Metzger."

"Farragut and I have discussed this at length," Garrison countered. "That's why our first move is to drum up support across the Eastern American Territories. Our chapters are strong, but we're not strong enough to take on the Nazi army. If we can garner more widespread civilian backing, however, we'd give the Germans a good fight."

Uncle Red didn't stop pacing. The lines creasing his forehead made him appear only half-convinced. "You're talking about rallying farmers and factory workers. Most of them are focused on feeding their families, not joining a revolution."

"That's why we're going to take over two Nazi forts. We'll not only take their supplies, we'll show people that the Alliance is a viable force again. They'll flock to us in droves."

Uncle Red rubbed his beard. "We've tried to take camps and forts before, but that hasn't generated nationwide support. How is this plan any different?"

"The difference will be television. We're going to broadcast each attack on live TV. On the Channel Seven evening news."

Zara's heart tapped out an ever-faster beat. If the Alliance could broadcast their victories on television, then they could reach countless Eastern American households. Not thousands of people but *millions*. A shiver breathed across her back. *This* was what she had been waiting for. Even her uncle should have been elated at this news.

But Uncle Red only had more questions. "Break into Channel Seven? How, exactly?"

"One of our rebels has gained access to the station. Let's just say she has a talent for this sort of thing."

Zara wanted to ask what this "talent" could be, but Garrison had already moved on to the next subject: the forts the Alliance planned to attack. He reached into his coat pocket and dug out a folded map of the former United States, spreading it over the coffee table.

"The first fort will be in southern Pennsylvania. Camp Hammerstein. It's mainly a holding depot with guns and ammunition, and only a few hundred guards are stationed there at a time. So we'll attack the camp and take its weapons this upcoming Thursday evening. Then three days after that — we'll take that time to regroup and move south — we'll hit our next target on Sunday night. Fort Goering."

"Fort *Goering*?" both Zara and her uncle said at the same time.

Garrison knocked his knuckle on the map. "That's why I came to speak to you. You know this town better than anyone else, Red. We're going to need your expertise on local logistics — road conditions, water supplies, anything about Fort Goering that we don't already know."

Uncle Red could only blink. "You want to attack Fort Goering in less than a week?"

"We can do it, even with a shortened timeline. We have to strike now while the Empire is distracted by the Reds."

"We're talking about an all-out attack on one of the biggest forts in the Territories!" Uncle Red said incredulously. "How are we supposed to go up against tens of thousands of Nazi soldiers? Or their troop of sentinels?"

Frustration flitted across Garrison's eyes, but only for a second. "Don't forget that we have our own soldiers and weapons, and a few tricks up our sleeves. This won't be a suicide mission."

"There's no guarantee of that." Uncle Red's jaw hardened. "Look at what happened at Fort Metzger." His eyes cast downward and he added, "I lost my sister there."

"I understand — I lost people, too, that day — but we're stronger now. We're better prepared. We've got a good shot of pulling this off, but our odds would be better if you'll help us."

Zara jumped in because her uncle wouldn't. "What do you need?"

"Zara, this isn't —" Uncle Red protested.

"We need information," said Garrison. "I'll be in Greenfield until tomorrow morning. We could scout out the fort, find the weak points. That's all we're asking for. Information."

"That's not too much to ask," Zara said to her uncle. It wasn't like Garrison wanted Uncle Red to lead a charge at the fort. "We could at least give him that, couldn't we?"

Uncle Red wasn't convinced, which shouldn't have surprised Zara, but it frustrated her all the same. "What else do you plan on asking for? Do you want to use our farm as a gathering point?" Red asked gruffly.

"Right now I need hard data. That's it," replied Garrison.

Nearly a minute passed before Uncle Red had a reply. Zara was almost certain that he was going to quit the Alliance altogether, but his response surprised her. "I can tell you what I know, local topography and roads and whatnot. That's easy enough. But scouting out Fort Goering will be much harder."

"We don't have to get too close. I only need to get my bearings so I can relay the information to my colleagues." That politician's smoothness returned to his tone. "I don't think that's too much to ask of you, Redmond. The Alliance will take on all of the legwork."

"If I do this," said Uncle Red slowly, "I don't want Zara involved."

"That's *my* decision," Zara said, anger coursing through her. He was treating her like a little kid again. Sure, she wasn't a chapter leader like her uncle was, but she knew just as much about Greenfield as he did. Zara looked to Garrison for support, since she wasn't getting any from her uncle. "I can help, too. I know this town like the back of my hand. I can tell you the best places to camp, to get water."

"I appreciate that. We don't see enough of your enthusiasm in the Territories." Garrison chose his words carefully. "But I'm afraid I have to defer to your uncle on this. He's the leader of the Greenfield chapter, and he makes the calls on who goes on a mission. That's our policy."

Zara sank into her chair, stung. Here was her chance to finally join the Alliance, but even Garrison had shot her down. She didn't know what else she needed to do to become a part of the resistance — kill the Führer with her bare hands?

Garrison clapped his hands together. "I'm grateful for both of your help. I can't tell you how much it'll mean for the Alliance. And, Red, your assistance will be critical. We *need* to take over Fort Goering if we hope to launch Operation Burning Eagle."

Uncle Red raised a brow, looking as if he might renege on his agreement to help Garrison. "I thought stealing the supplies and getting on Channel Seven was the operation."

"They're precursors to the operation, but not the operation itself. No, no, we have something much bigger planned for that."

"And that is . . . ?"

"We hit the Nazis where it'll hurt them the most. We're going to march on Neuberlin." Garrison smiled wickedly. "We're going to take it back."

11

Garrison and Uncle Red spent the entire evening hunched over the kitchen table, going over the layout of Fort Goering and the terrain of Greenfield, marking up an old map that Uncle Red dug up in the barn. After a late dinner of boiled beef and cabbage — one of the few dinners Zara knew how to make — the two men slipped out the back door to scout out the fort in person. She was tempted to follow them, like she did with Mrs. Talley, but she had a hunch Uncle Red would catch her with those watchful eyes of his.

I'll talk to Garrison on my own, Zara thought. He and Farragut needed all of the recruits they could get, she reasoned. But after she thought about how to approach Garrison, Zara realized that he would probably shoo her away like Uncle Red had, albeit more diplomatically. No matter how much she wanted to join the rebels, she was getting refused at every turn.

So she decided to take matters into her own hands.

After Garrison left early the next morning, Zara set her plan into motion. As nightfall blanketed Greenfield on Wednesday evening — a day before the planned attack on Camp Hammerstein — Zara slipped out of bed to get ready for her very own mission. She scanned the sky beyond her window for any sign of Sentinel Achen. He was overdue for a weekly night patrol, but he tended to stay on base whenever it rained. Luckily for her, a thick sheet of clouds had gathered over Greenfield, pregnant with a spring storm.

Zara returned to her mattress and yanked out a stack of papers she had hidden underneath it. She had spent the night before scribbling on each sheet by hand until she reached over two hundred copies. The message was simple:

Channel Seven. Evening news. Don't miss it.

She had stolen the blank papers from school and had written everything longhand, too nervous to use the academy's copy machines. She knew it was risky to leave her handwriting for the Nazis to find, but it was a risk she had to take. Even if the Germans discovered one of these slips of papers, they would have to check everyone's penmanship in Greenfield before they discovered her.

Zara tucked the papers into an old backpack, the same one she had worn to primary school, and she was about to tiptoe out the door when her boot crunched on a sheet of newspaper. She picked it up. Earlier that day, Bastian had slipped this article to her while she was dousing the boys' locker room with bleach.

"Just read this. Please," he had said, pressing the paper into her hand. "And I'm sorry again about your friend Frau Talley." His fingers had lingered on hers before he stammered something about running late and hurried out the door. Zara watched him go, rubbing the spot where their skin had brushed. Normally, she would have shuddered at a Nazi's touch, but Bastian hadn't been rough like his father's soldiers would have been. Instead, his hand had felt soft and warm on hers. Surprisingly gentle.

Then Zara had scowled at herself for thinking such a thing.

She uncrinkled the article. Even in the dark room, she could make out the words. It had appeared in the *Brussels Post* and was dated a month prior.

GESTAPO ARRESTS RESISTANCE MEMBERS
KRISTIANE WAGNER, BRUSSELS BUREAU

In a late-night raid, the Gestapo arrested fifty members of the Widerstand, a terrorist group with a network throughout Western Europe. The criminals have been charged with thirty counts of treason and twelve acts of terrorism, including the bombing of the Düsseldorf railway in June that led to the deaths of fifty-three German citizens.

"We have been tracking activity of this particular Widerstand chapter for nearly three years," said Chief Sergeant Bernhard Backer. "This arrest will ensure the safety of the citizens of Brussels, who have been forced to live in fear since these animals arrived in our city."

Key arrests in this raid include Arthur Farber and Edith Huber, leaders of the underground Communist Party of Germany, which was banned in 1933. The Gestapo also arrested Albert Dubois, another communist sympathizer and former veteran of the Nazi Navy. Dubois's son-in-law, Colonel Erich Eckhart, released this statement upon his father-in-law's arrest: "My family denounces the actions of Herr Dubois. He has brought shame to us and to the Nazi Empire, and shall deserve any punishment he receives."

The article continued, but Zara had stopped reading. After school ended, she had slipped into the computer lab to empty its garbage pails and to do some research of her own. She had discovered half a dozen articles similar to this one, citing the traitorous Albert Dubois. Apparently, Bastian had spoken the truth about his grandfather, although she wouldn't let herself believe his story about wanting to join the Alliance. He could be using this information to gain her trust. And she was smarter than that.

Zara stuffed the article under her bed — she would burn it later — and crept out the back door with her bag slung over her shoulders, avoiding the creakiest floorboards so she wouldn't wake her uncle. The two of them hadn't spoken much since Garrison's visit. For years, she had gone along with his wishes because she thought he would one day give her a chance. But after Garrison's visit, she wondered if that "one day" would ever come. Her uncle only wanted to protect her, she knew that, but this time she couldn't listen to him.

Thunder rumbled overhead as she darted toward Greenfield and toward the cluster of shabby houses many of the miners' families called home. She crept to the tree-ridden hill overlooking the houses and removed the papers from her bag. Then she summoned a wind at her fingertips, letting it build until her hair lashed against her face and the pages rattled in her hand. She released all two hundred of them at once.

The papers whirled toward the houses, their white color like doves' wings against the black night. With a storm coming soon, Zara tried to steer the flyers under the creaky porches or windowsills to keep them dry from the rain. The miners would find the papers in the morning, and there was a chance they would just throw the slips away — but maybe their interest would get piqued and they'd spread the word across town. Then the whole township would turn to Channel Seven tomorrow night, just as she and Garrison hoped. Zara knew it wasn't much, but it was the least she could do for the Alliance under her uncle's vigilant eye.

Lightning threaded across the sky and the heavy threat of rain lingered in the air, but she didn't head home. With the papers scattered, she still needed to tackle the second part of her mission — a mission she had hoped her uncle would undertake, but her hope had drooped after yesterday's conversation. Perhaps he could put off burying Mrs. Talley, but Zara certainly couldn't. She hadn't been able to save Mrs. Talley from Sentinel Braun's powers, but she could give her a proper farewell.

With the courthouse in sight, Zara quietly passed the grocer and the drugstore, and then she donned her knitted mask. She veered a hard left to approach the small military museum that was tucked behind the courthouse. The museum had closed hours before, but Zara scouted around it anyway, although she doubted any Nazis would take a rain-soaked nightly stroll. She scaled the slippery fire escape to access the building's roof and then crept to the very edge, her gaze fixed on the courthouse that lay a hundred feet ahead.

A shiver rippled down Zara's spine, a mixture of cold and fear. The last time she was here this late, she had ripped apart the Führer's portrait, but now that seemed trivial compared to what she planned to do. Eyes squinted, Zara spotted a single soldier on the square's rooftop, dressed in an olive-green poncho. Colonel Eckhart must have assigned him to the square after Dieter's portrait was vandalized.

It was a good thing she had come prepared.

Zara gauged the distance between the two buildings and rose slowly to her feet. Her fingers snuck into her bag and she pulled out a tranquilizer needle that she had taken from the barn, needles that her uncle used to sedate their milking cow from time to time.

On the rooftop, the soldier turned away from Zara. It was now or never.

She took off from the rooftop and rocketed toward the courthouse. The wind picked up as it carried her, its sound masking her approach, and she pointed the needle at the soldier's neck. He was only twenty feet away, now ten, now five.

Zara raised her hand, ready to plunge the needle through his skin, but the soldier spun around at the last second. Crying out, he reached for his gun. Zara's feet hit the roof and she lunged at him, but the soldier knocked her hand away. The needle tumbled into a puddle, rolling out of her reach.

As the soldier fumbled for his pistol, Zara quickly threw herself on top of him, scrambling for the gun, not knowing what else to do. Her plan was crumbling to pieces in front of her.

With a grunt, the soldier rolled over and pinned Zara down. He reached for the mask. "You'll be sorry for this!" he cried in German.

Zara clawed at his arms, but he weighed twice as much as she did. His fingers nearly caught the edge of her mask before she jerked her jaw out of reach, but she couldn't dodge him forever. Once the soldier saw her face, it would all be over.

She fought back, her legs thrashing, fueled by heart-pumping fear. Her fingernails tore at any inch of exposed skin and she tried to shove the soldier off of her, but he was too heavy. Too strong.

The soldier yanked at the mask again, uncovering her jawbone. Zara's hands grew boiling hot, both of them stinging like needles. The needles traveled up her arms, and she thought she might pass out — but then the guard went limp. His eyes rolled into the back of his head and he slumped over, his limbs dead weight on top of her.

A gasp escaped out of Zara's mouth. What happened?

The heat receded from her hands, along with the prickling needles. She ripped the mask off her face, breathing hard, and tried to push the soldier off of her. But she froze when she caught movement on the roof.

There was someone else here.

A shadow fell over Zara's eyes. A hooded man crouched next to her and rolled the guard from her body. In his right hand, he held a loose brick, its edges stained with blood. He must have used it to knock the soldier unconscious.

The man dropped the brick and pulled back his hood. "*Scheiße.* Are you hurt?"

"*Bastian?*" Zara cried. He offered his hand to her, but she only blinked at him.

Raindrops splashed against his forehead "Um. Hello."

"What are you doing here?"

"M-My mother needed a prescription from the drugstore," he stuttered. "When I came out, I thought I saw you heading toward the courthouse."

"You followed me?" The blood emptied from Zara's face and plummeted toward her toes. Had he seen her flying onto the rooftop? But Bastian wasn't making any accusations.

"I was curious. I slipped into the courthouse through the back entrance. It was unlocked," Bastian went on. "I thought . . ."

"What?"

"I thought you might be doing something for the Alliance. And I thought if I joined you tonight, then I could prove that my intentions are sincere."

Zara's mouth opened, then closed. Could he be telling the truth? Her gaze found the unconscious soldier at her feet. Bastian had clobbered one of his father's men to save her, but her uncle's caution seeped through her. As far-fetched as it sounded, this could all still be part of Colonel Eckhart's plan to catch both her and her uncle.

"What were you hoping to do here? I can help," Bastian continued.

"I don't need your help," Zara said nervously. Her gaze crept toward Mrs. Talley's body, but she couldn't finish her mission now, not with Bastian watching. She had no idea how to explain what she was doing here on the roof. Taking a stroll? Stargazing? Fear clutched her heart. He could turn her in to his father right now, and there was nothing she could do.

Bastian didn't seem to be waiting for an explanation, though. He was staring at the cage instead. "Did you come to pay your respects to your friend?"

"Yeah, I did. To say good-bye," she blurted out, snatching at the excuse he offered her. She glanced at the rooftop door. She really needed to leave before Bastian asked her another question, but he kept talking.

"My father shouldn't have paraded her like this." A jolt of lightning cracked over them, illuminating their faces, and Zara saw steel in Bastian's eyes. His jaw hard, he strode toward the very edge of the roof where the cage sat and reached his arm around to open its metal door.

"What are you doing?" Zara hurried after him, her pulse frantic. Bastian's feet hugged the lip of the roof, only inches from the open air. If he fell . . .

"Taking her down. She's your friend, isn't she?"

"Yes, but you're going to fall."

He reached for the latch anyway. "The Nazis did the same thing to Opa. They dragged his body through the streets of Brussels." The steel in his eyes had burned hot.

"Get down from there!" Zara wasn't going to be responsible for the death of Colonel Eckhart's son. As lightning flashed above them, she climbed up to yank him down, but Bastian lost his footing. His arms flapped. His feet teetered. He clutched at Zara and the cage, but gravity snatched them both, along with the cage, toward the ground.

As they careened downward, they plummeted four stories before Zara's instincts took over. She gasped out a command in her mind.

Just like that, they stopped. The wind cradled them, holding them ten feet above the ground. Bastian's cry silenced in his throat. His eyes went frighteningly wide, so wide that she could see the whites of them.

That was when Zara realized what she had done.

12

Zara panicked, losing her focus, and they tumbled toward the earth below them. She hit the grass hard, twigs snapping beneath her, the air fleeing from her shocked lungs. She gasped for breath and tried to move, but her ankle crumpled. A hot pain climbed up her foot, and one searing thought burned through her mind.

Bastian knew. He *knew* about her power.

As she struggled for air, Zara heard Bastian groan and stagger out of the boxwood hedge that he had fallen into. The cage lay by his feet, its door creaking against the rattling wind. Not far from the cage, Zara's gaze fell upon Mrs. Talley's body, planted facedown in the wet grass. Anguish flooded through her at seeing Mrs. Talley so horribly disfigured — Zara wanted to grab the body and run — but then Bastian asked a question that made her go cold.

"You're . . . you're an Anomaly?" Bastian rasped.

Terror screeched through Zara's veins. She had hidden her abilities for so long, but now she had exposed them to the son of a colonel. How could she have gotten herself into such a mess? Bastian was going to serve her on a platter to his father, and she would be executed just like Mrs. Talley.

Shouts echoed from inside the courthouse, and Zara forced herself onto her feet despite the aching in her ankle. Desperate to escape, she tried to hobble away from Bastian. Any second now, he would shout at the guards to come arrest her.

Bastian, however, only took her by the arm. "We need to find cover — now!" The clatter of thunder muffled his voice, only to be followed by a sudden burst of rain, drenching them with its cold blast. "Some of the magistrates must have worked late tonight. We have to leave before they send the guards."

Zara wasn't going anywhere with him. She had to get home and wake her uncle before both of them got hunted down by the Colonel. With her heartbeat banging, she pushed Bastian away from her, but he looped her arm around his neck before she could fully break free.

"This way!" He led her toward a garbage-scented alleyway by the military museum, but Zara fought him at every step. She was about to elbow him in the stomach, but she went limp when she heard boots slapping against the pavement. Another shout echoed behind them.

Bastian pulled her behind the Dumpster. "Stay still!"

"Let me go!" She tried to knee him in the groin, but he lurched away just in time. He wrapped one arm around her waist and clamped his free hand over her mouth.

"Please," he whispered. "You'll lead them right to us if you don't stay quiet."

"You'll turn me in anyway!" Zara said, but each word came out muffled against his palm.

The shouts multiplied. Footsteps pounded. Zara squirmed against Bastian again, but his arms were like iron around her. Why wasn't he calling for his father's soldiers? He had caught an illegal Anomaly, a prize for the Colonel; but Bastian remained hunched behind the Dumpster, wincing at every sound.

Once the shouts faded, he slowly removed his hand from her lips. "You can trust me. I'm not working for my father."

Prove it, Zara wanted to say, but the words felt hollow on her tongue. Bastian had knocked a soldier unconscious for her. He had hidden her from the guards. All of his actions pointed toward one conclusion, but she still didn't know if she could accept it yet. It was too preposterous.

He was a Nazi. An Eckhart. The son of the man who had orchestrated her mother's death.

She couldn't trust him.

Could she?

"We can't stay here," Bastian went on. He peered around the Dumpster. "The guards might circle back. Can you walk?"

Zara hesitated. She couldn't stay in this alleyway, but she couldn't get very far on her ankle. Then, without warning, Bastian hoisted her into his arms and carried her down the street, hurrying until they entered the threshold of the trees. Only then did Zara remember her original plan for the night.

"Mrs. Talley!" she gasped.

"It's too dangerous to go back there," Bastian said, not daring to stop. That left Zara staring helplessly as Mrs. Talley's remains grew smaller and smaller. She had failed her friend again.

I'm so sorry, Zara thought, fighting back tears. *I tried.*

Bastian carried her over the dead leaves until the streetlights faded into jeweled specks. With his breaths labored, he finally stopped and set Zara on a bed of soggy leaves, where she scooted away from him and huddled beneath a young pine, shivering at the disaster she had gotten herself into. Not only had she botched Mrs. Talley's burial, she had revealed her power to Bastian Eckhart. And for some wild reason, he kept trying to convince her that he was on *her* side — and she was starting to believe him.

Bastian knelt by her boots. "Let me see your ankle."

"I'm fine." Zara tucked her legs underneath her, ignoring the pain that enveloped her right foot. A part of her wanted to fly away from him this instant. With the angry clouds overhead, the soldiers would never see her — but Bastian *had* seen her power, and she needed answers.

"I've treated sprains and breaks at my *Opa's* clinic," Bastian continued. "He was a doctor for many years, and I worked with him after school sometimes. I can help."

"Why didn't you turn me in back there?" Zara burst out.

His brows knitted together, taken aback. "Why would I do that?" He paused. "I wasn't interested in being arrested. Are you?"

"They wouldn't have arrested you. You're the Colonel's son."

"That doesn't matter to my father. He didn't lift a finger to help my *Opa* — why would I be any different? I'm sure he would have jailed me himself." His chest heaved as he caught his breath. "For hiding a non-German Anomaly."

Zara went completely numb. She wrapped her arms around herself, her wet shirt siphoning any trace of warmth her body produced. She felt exposed. Raw. She didn't know how to get used to the fact that Bastian knew her biggest secret.

They sat in silence for a minute before Bastian spoke again. "You hid your power very well. I never would've guessed." There was admiration in his voice.

"I didn't have much of a choice," she finally managed to say.

"You saved us back there. If you hadn't broken our fall from the courthouse . . ." He cringed and didn't finish his sentence. "Thank you."

She didn't answer him. Maybe she had saved their lives, but now she had to face the consequences of revealing her power to Bastian.

If he told anyone about her, she'd be dead in half a heartbeat. She barely knew him, and yet now her life was in his hands.

He seemed to sense her fear. "I won't tell anyone. I promise you that." His eyes locked onto hers, so wide and earnest, so unlike his father's. She wanted to believe him, but Uncle Red's voice drifted through her thoughts. *He could be baiting you*, the voice said, but the warning was dimming.

"You'd risk your father's wrath on me? I'm a *Kleinbauer*," Zara said.

"Yes, but . . . that doesn't matter."

"It would matter to most Germans."

"Maybe so, but not to me." Bastian kept his eyes trained away from hers. Instead, he fiddled with a fallen leaf in his hands.

"Why?" Zara had never heard a cadet — or a Nazi, for that matter — talk this way before. The farmers and laborers were disposable in their eyes, and they were treated as such.

"I told you before that I'm not a Nazi. I'm not working for them." He twisted the leaf's stem between his fingertips. "And I owe you."

"For breaking our fall?"

"Not only that. For what you did for me at the academy three years ago."

Zara could only blink at him. She had no idea what he was talking about.

"You don't remember?" He sounded surprised. And a bit hurt.

She shook her head. There were hundreds of cadets at the school, and she had a hard enough time keeping up with their laundry, much less what Bastian had been up to when she was twelve. "Are you sure it was me?"

"It was you. I'm sure of it. I was fourteen at the time — my father put me in a class of cadets two years ahead of me. He thought it would challenge me." His voice darkened at the mention of the Colonel, but he swallowed and continued on. "A few of the cadets didn't think I deserved to train with them. A boy named Dirk was their leader. Maybe you remember him. Dirk Kohler?"

Zara racked her memories but came up empty. She had lost Molly three years ago, and most of her memories from around that time wrapped around that one horrible event. For months, Zara had walked around in a haze, missing her friend, having nightmares about how Molly had died.

"What happened to him?" she asked.

"He was expelled."

"For what?"

"For . . . for almost killing me." Bastian's features twisted as he recounted the events. "One day Dirk got angry with me. I don't know why. He waited until most of our class had left the locker room, and then he lunged at me. He had his friends hold me down and gag me, and he beat me over and over again."

Slowly, a blurred memory floated into Zara's thoughts. "That was *you*?"

He nodded.

She did remember that day, but she hadn't known it was Bastian. His face had been hidden in blood. So much of it. She'd been collecting the dirty towels in the locker room — she had thought that the cadets had already left for lunch — when she heard a scuffle in one of the changing areas. Fights broke out fairly regularly at the academy, and the cleaning girls usually turned a blind eye to them. If they ratted out the students, they could get bullied later on, so most of them kept mum. But Zara had never seen a cadet getting beaten so badly before. She had run to find the athletics instructor, who broke up the fight and carried Bastian to the health clinic. Zara had briefly wondered who the beaten boy was, but losing Molly had clouded her head like a fog that term.

"I should've thanked you back then," Bastian said quietly.

"I was only doing my job."

"You didn't have to, though. You didn't owe me anything. After what my father has done to the *Kleinbauern* in this town, to your family, you could've looked away." He stared at the leaf in his palm, hiding his eyes from her. "I've never forgotten what you did for me. I've . . . I've admired you ever since then, Zara."

That was the first time he had used her given name, and a strange shiver inched down her spine. She ducked her chin. Had he been staring at her all of these years, and she hadn't noticed it until recently? It was possible, wasn't it? Zara often kept her eyes cast down at school, and she avoided the cadets as much as she could.

"It was nothing," she mumbled. "Besides, you got us away from the guards tonight."

"Barely." He smiled slightly. "I meant what I told you before, you know. I want to join the Alliance."

Zara could only shrug. The evidence was certainly mounting in Bastian's favor, but so much had happened that night that her mind felt like it had been wrung dry.

"What can I do or say to convince you?" said Bastian. The rain had trickled into a drizzle and the cold had set in, making their teeth chatter, but he made no attempt to leave. He waited for Zara's reply, his head cocked to one side.

"Your grandfather really was a communist?" she forced out. Maybe Bastian was telling her the truth, but she needed to fill in the gaps of his story.

"He was." The smile on his lips saddened.

"His dog tags were Nazi tags, though."

"Every Belgian has to serve in the Nazi military. It became mandatory after Adolf Hitler annexed the country, or else Opa never would have joined. That was why he was so surprised when my mother announced her engagement to my father."

The questions kept spilling out of Zara's lips. "He didn't approve?"

"He didn't like it at first, but he eventually gave his blessing for my mother's sake. She never hated Nazism like he did. The Germans she knew had always treated her kindly. It was her coloring, I think. She was an Aryan like them."

No wonder the Colonel had married Bastian's mother, then, Zara thought. As long as his new wife was Aryan blooded, he wouldn't sully his German lineage.

Bastian continued, although his tone grew soft. "After her accident, my *Opa* came to the Territories to care for her. My father wasn't pleased, but he was always gone on assignment. It became easy for him to ignore his father-in-law and his sick wife."

"He never thought about leaving your mom?" Zara tapered off, wondering if she was prodding too much into their personal life. She was surprised, though, that Colonel Eckhart hadn't. No one would have blamed him for abandoning an unstable wife — the Nazis often quietly institutionalized the Aryan mentally ill, while they euthanized the non-Aryan ones.

"Divorce? No, it wouldn't have reflected well on his career." Bitterness laced through Bastian's every word, but it ebbed once he spoke of his grandfather again. "Opa raised me. He was the one I came home to from school. He always left a piece of chocolate or licorice on the counter for me." He reached inside his soaked shirt collar to dig out the metal tags. "I found these in my mother's drawer after he was killed. I think my father tried to throw them away, but she held on to them."

"Your dad doesn't care that you wear them?"

"He doesn't like it, but they're Nazi tags, so he lets me be for now. It's one of the only things I have of Opa's."

Zara watched Bastian tuck the chain back into his shirt, and finally she understood why he wore those tags everywhere. She had done the same thing after her mother had passed, clinging on to a pair of earrings her mom had worn even though Zara's ears weren't pierced. Maybe she and Bastian weren't as different as she had thought.

"I miss him," Bastian said so softly that Zara barely heard it. "After he was killed, I didn't know what to do. I couldn't talk to anyone at home or at school. The cadets would never understand, and my father almost seemed pleased with Opa's death."

"He was *pleased*?"

His voice turned frosty cold. "With his ranking, he could have asked for leniency when Opa was arrested. I begged him for it, but he refused. He called Opa a traitor, said that he didn't deserve to live."

Zara sucked in a sharp breath. She knew firsthand how cruel Colonel Eckhart could be, but apparently his cruelty knew no bounds. He had allowed his own father-in-law to be executed — even though he had the power to save him. She shuddered. At least she could hate the Colonel from afar. Bastian had to live underneath his roof.

"This is why I can never put on a Nazi uniform," said Bastian. "My parents had wanted that life for me, so I went along with it, but when the Nazis hanged Opa . . . I knew I would never follow that path. That was when I decided to speak with you. I knew I was taking a chance, but your grandfather once had ties to the Alliance, so I thought you or your uncle might, too."

The rain finally faded. Zara chewed her lip, trying to process everything he had told her. Doubt whispered at the back of her mind, but what if Bastian was telling her the truth? She needed to know. "I read that article you gave me."

"You did?" Surprise flickered in his eyes. "I thought you might have thrown it away."

"I almost did."

He scooted a bit closer to her, but not close enough to startle her. "Do you think you can believe me, then? Ever since Opa died, I've been filled with this need to do . . ."

"Something?" she finished.

"*Anything.*"

Zara knew the feeling. Glancing up, she looked into his eyes to find a look of hard determination. She hadn't seen him like this before. At school, he had always blended in with the rest of the cadets, who turned their noses up at the *Kleinbauern* who served them. But he had saved her from the guards tonight and, if what he said was true, he had admired her for years. Zara swallowed. Slowly, ever so slowly, he was convincing her.

The silence stretched thick between them. Another minute passed, and he scooted closer again. "Can you please let me look at your ankle? I know it must be painful."

Zara was so surprised by the question that she nodded. Bastian swiftly got to work, untying her boot and gently pulling the shoe from her foot before he rubbed the anklebone with his fingertips.

"It's just a sprain." He rubbed his hands together to warm them. "You should keep off of it for a few days, though. When you get home, place a bag of ice on it to help with the swelling."

"Thank you," Zara murmured.

He nodded.

She looked down at her muddy hands. Both had turned to prunes in the rain. "I'm sorry. About your grandfather. He sounds like a good man."

"The very best." More silence passed between them, until Bastian cleared his throat and said, "We should go."

Zara nodded, eager for a change of clothes and a warm bed. She still couldn't quite grasp everything that had happened since she last stepped foot in her room. Her mission tonight had been to distribute the flyers and bury Mrs. Talley, but now here she was, talking like friends with Bastian Eckhart, the son of a Nazi. The enemy. And yet, somehow, he was none of those things.

Using a tree trunk for support, Zara tried to put a little weight on her foot. It still throbbed, but she could probably hobble on it.

Bastian reached out to her. "You won't get far like that. Here, let me help." He curled his arm around her, propping half of her body against him. Zara's eyes flew wide open as their sides pressed together.

"What are you doing?" she asked, too stunned to pull away.

"Helping."

Heat climbed up Zara's neck. Before tonight, she had never stood so close to a boy before. Bastian may have carried her from the courthouse earlier, but she had been too shocked to notice it then. But now, she *did* notice. His hand on her hip; his arm warm against her back. The smell of him surrounded her, like leather books and earth and sage.

Embarrassed, she tried to wriggle free, but nearly toppled in the process. Bastian steadied her, and their gazes caught.

"I can manage on my own," she said.

"I don't want your ankle to get any worse. And I don't mind. Really."

As much as she didn't want to admit it, Zara needed his help to get home. Flying wasn't an option now, not with the clouds breaking overhead. With a reluctant nod, she leaned against him, and they limped together slowly. His hands were gentle on her waist as he guided her down the graveled street. Step by slow step, she got used to their closeness, even though he was a cadet, even though his father was a colonel.

By the time they reached the road, Bastian's breaths had grown heavy. "I can walk from here," Zara said. "We're going in different directions anyway."

He didn't let go. "Your house is miles away. This is the least I can do."

And then, even though he didn't have to, Bastian kept her tucked at his side and walked her all the way home.

13

When they finally reached the farm, Zara's eyelids were drooping and her ankle was throbbing, but she pressed onward with her last scraps of strength. About halfway up her driveway, she stopped and looked at Bastian, who was shivering in his wet shirt and trousers.

"Maybe I should walk alone from here," she said. "In case my uncle wakes up."

"I don't think you should risk reinjuring your ankle," he said, teeth chattering.

"It's not very far, and I'm sure you want to head home yourself." Zara had to be firm about this. If her uncle awoke and saw her with Bastian, she didn't want to think about what he would say or do. To both of them.

Reluctantly, Bastian unlocked his arm from hers. "Remember to ice your ankle and elevate it if you can. It will be sore for a few days."

"All right," Zara said. Out of habit she added a quick "Herr Eckhart."

An amused look shone in his amber eyes. "After tonight, I think you can call me Bastian."

She started to shake her head. "I couldn't —"

"It's fine, really." He ran a hand through his wet hair. Above them, the clouds had broken apart, revealing enough starlight for Zara to see his cheeks flush. "I'd like it if you called me that."

Zara didn't know what to say. Since birth, she had been taught to address a German as *Herr* or *Frau* or she'd suffer the consequences of offending a Nazi. Yet Bastian actually wanted her to call him by his first name — something she had never expected from a highborn German like him. He was treating her like a peer instead of an underling, instead of an *Untermensch*. And she found herself surprisingly touched by the sentiment.

"Very well. *Bastian*," she said, testing his name aloud.

His dimples appeared. "That wasn't too bad, was it?"

This was another side of Bastian that Zara had never seen before. At the academy, he always played the part of the proper cadet, with his crisp salutes and his stony face, an expression that everyone took as snobbery. But here he was, with that easy smile and his shoulders relaxed. She wondered if she was glimpsing the real Bastian, the one hidden behind his mask.

His dimples slowly faded, and his properness returned. "I was hoping, when you felt ready, that you could speak to the Alliance for me. Or you could put me in touch with someone who could do that."

Zara didn't know how to answer him. She was starting to trust him — she had let him walk her home after all — but saying yes to his question was like a full confession of her uncle's ties to the Alliance. And that felt too dangerous. Her head was a broken puzzle of questions.

"I'll . . . I'll ask around," she said finally. Maybe she would contact Garrison to see what he thought. The Alliance was always looking for new recruits, and Bastian's medical skills could be a boon to them — not to mention his close connection to Nazi higher-ups. As the son of a colonel, he might be able to provide vital information about Fort Goering and beyond.

Bastian turned to leave but hesitated. "Thank you," he said.

Zara nodded, knowing how big those two words were in this moment.

"Elevate that ankle, okay?"

She limped the rest of the way to the house, waving him off when he asked if she needed help. Once she reached the front door, though, Zara paused. She couldn't climb the stairs with only one good leg, not if she didn't want to wake Uncle Red. Biting her bottom lip, she peered up at her bedroom. It wouldn't take her long to get up there and squeeze through the window.

Once Bastian disappeared around the bend in the road, Zara drew the wind to her side and commanded it to lift her toward the second story of the house. Thankfully, she had left her window unlocked, so she pried it open with her fingers and climbed inside the dark bedroom. She reached for a towel on the floor, ready to dry herself off and hop into bed, but then the bedside table lamp snapped on.

Zara nearly fell over. With her pulse galloping, her gaze climbed upward until she met his furious gaze.

"You have a lot of explaining to do."

"Uncle Red!" Zara gasped out. Her uncle was sitting on her bed, perched there like a hungry owl. She didn't know how long he had been waiting for her, but it was obviously long enough to make his mouth curl into a scowl.

"Where have you been?" he demanded.

She leaned on her oak dresser, holding up her ankle, while she fumbled for an excuse. "I . . . I went out for a walk. I couldn't sleep."

"You went out for a walk for over three hours? With your leg like that? When did that happen?"

"I tripped on the way home! Look, I'm sorry —"

"Don't lie to me. I saw who you were with outside."

Zara's blood turned cold. Her uncle had seen her with Bastian. There was no denying it, then. Her lips parted, fumbling for words, but she didn't know what to say.

"How long have you been sneaking around with the Eckhart boy?" His face bloomed red, from the top of his hairline to the tip of his beard. But it was his eyes — cold and harsh — that made Zara flinch the most. "Is he the reason why you're limping around? Did he hurt you?"

"No, I told you that I tripped!" Which was partially true. "He walked me home. That's it."

"The Colonel's son 'walked' you home? From where?" He leapt off the mattress. "How could you be so careless? Those German boys only want one thing, don't you realize that?"

Zara gaped up at him. Was he implying . . . ? "Nothing happened!"

"I thought you were smarter than this! I thought I'd taught you better."

"There's nothing going on between us," she said again. Although that wasn't quite true, either. Bastian knew about her power. And Zara could still remember the feel of his arm around her, even though he was only helping her home.

Fury embedded itself inside Uncle Red's eyes. "That's what your mother told me, too. She said that there was nothing going on, that there was nothing for me to worry about."

"What are you saying?" The words tore out of Zara's mouth. "That because my mom fell for my father that I'll fall for the enemy, too?"

Uncle Red stepped back, wincing. "I didn't mean it like that. I'm trying to look out for you. Your mother would want the same thing."

"Don't tell me what she would want!" In only seconds, her fear at getting caught was shoved aside and replaced with white-hot fury that flamed up her neck and spread into her fingertips. She couldn't believe what her uncle was saying — or what he was implying about her mother. "Look at what you've become! Do you think that's what Mom would want? The brother she knew would be out there with the Alliance instead of being so cautious that you don't do anything at all."

The accusation hit its mark. Anger racked Uncle Red's face. "Your mother would want you to be safe! What happens if I get involved and don't make it back? Then what? What happens to you?"

Heat rose inside Zara like a furnace. So now it was her fault that Uncle Red wasn't doing more for the Alliance? She was about to shout at him again, but then her hands blazed hot, burning like she had stepped into a pyre. Zara blinked at the sight of her fingers, at the bright pink skin that was reddening by the second. Her anger slipped away, replaced with shock.

Uncle Red reached for her again, but he pulled back as soon as he touched her, as if he had been stung. "You have to calm down."

"How am I supposed to do that?"

"Please!" He pointed at her hands. "You're glowing!"

Glowing? Zara looked at her hands again and nearly crumpled to the floor. On her left palm there was a hot ball of electricity sizzling over her skin. "Wh-What's happening to me?"

"Zara, look at me!" Uncle Red took a tentative step toward her. "You're going to be okay, but you have to calm down."

"Why do you keep saying that?" she cried out. She tried to scrape the lightning from her hands, but it flew wide, heading straight for her uncle.

"No!" Zara shouted.

It was too late.

Uncle Red backpedaled toward the hallway, but the ball rammed into his side, fanning over his body in a spidery wave. He crashed onto the floorboards, his cheek slamming against the wood.

"Uncle Red!" Zara screamed. She limped over to his body, skidding onto her knees. Tendrils of smoke steamed from his shirt.

"Uncle Red," she said again, a sob breaking her voice.

He didn't make a sound.

Zara gripped her uncle by the shoulders. She cried his name one more time, but he still didn't stir. With tears dripping down her cheeks, she pressed two fingers against his neck. Hours seemed to pass before she found the slow thump-thump. She clutched his hand, overwhelmed by relief. He was still alive. For now.

"Hold on, do you hear me?" she told him.

Leaping to her feet, she limped into the kitchen and yanked the first aid kit from under the sink. She flipped through the pamphlet inside, scouring for whatever she could find about electrocutions, because she didn't know what else to call what had happened, but its only advice was to contact the hospital. Zara threw the pamphlet back into the kit. They could never afford the medical fees and, besides, how could she explain what she had done to her uncle? Zara wished so desperately that Mrs. Talley were still alive. Mrs. Talley would take care of Uncle Red, and she'd take care of Zara, too, telling her that they would figure out all of these changes happening to her.

Zara's gaze fell upon her hands. There was no trace of the lightning that had sprung from them. Was she developing another power? The mere thought made her tremble. Dual Anomalies were rare, so very rare, that she didn't think it could be possible; but she couldn't think about that right now. She had to focus on her uncle. He needed to see a doctor. . . . Or a medic.

Then it hit her: Bastian.

He could check up on Uncle Red, couldn't he? But he must be halfway home by now, and she didn't know where he lived. Fear clawed up Zara's throat, and she was ready to drive her uncle to the hospital herself — she would deal with the fees later — but then she heard a groan from upstairs. She stumbled toward her bedroom, ignoring the pounding pain in her ankle.

"Uncle Red!" She collapsed next to him, lying sprawled on the rough floor.

He coughed and cracked open his left eye. "What happened? I feel like a truck hit me."

"You — you don't remember?"

"We were talking. No, we were fighting." He paused as the memories came back to him. "Your hands. The lightning."

"I'm sorry! I tried to stop it. I don't know what happened." Tears flooded her eyes again, both at hearing him speak and remembering what she had done to her uncle. She could've killed him.

"Were you manifesting another power?" he whispered.

She hiccupped and said, "I don't know."

Uncle Red blinked at the ceiling, his eyes cloudy and his features slack. Zara drew her knees against her chest, forming a tight ball. She knew that look on his face — that same worry-laden look he had given her when she first manifested years ago. Was he afraid of her now?

"I'm so sorry, Uncle Red. I never meant —"

"Hush, I know you didn't do it on purpose." His gaze locked onto hers, tight as a weld. "I don't want you blaming yourself for this, do you hear me?"

"Look at you. You can barely move."

"I'm a little stiff, that's all. Help me up."

Zara let out a shaky laugh, but shook her head. "I don't think you should get up yet. What if you go into shock?"

"I might do that if I keep lying on this cold floor. Come on. Give your old uncle a hand."

Reluctantly, Zara helped him onto his feet and did her best to tuck him into bed while balancing on her healthy ankle. Uncle Red's eyes fluttered shut as soon as his head hit the pillows.

"I'll get you a glass of water," she said.

"No, let me sleep for a few hours." He reached out and clasped her hand. "Zara, about that boy."

Guilt flooded over her. "There's nothing going on with him."

"I don't want you speaking to him again. Are we clear on that?"

"Perfectly." Zara fidgeted. She didn't want to lie to him, especially not when he was in this condition, but she didn't know what else to say. She couldn't tell him that Bastian wanted to join the Alliance, and she definitely couldn't say that Bastian knew about one of her powers.

"One more thing," Uncle Red said, fighting off sleep. "We have to control this new power of yours. You'll have to learn how to harness it, like you did the last time. That has to be your number one priority."

Zara's gaze plummeted to the floor. Maybe she could have been excited about her new power if she hadn't electrocuted her uncle, the only family she had left. Right now, though, the last thing she wanted was to see those lightning bolts shoot out of her hands again.

"We can't risk you having an episode," he said.

"We can talk about this later. When you're better."

Uncle Red wouldn't hear of it. "It's not going to go away. We have to get started on your training, the sooner the better. Okay?"

"Do you have to be so stubborn?"

"Of course. I'm a St. James." That made him crack a smile, although it soon vanished as he started coughing.

"You really should drink some water."

He ignored her. "Listen to me. You have to control this new power. Promise me that." He took her hand, squeezing it, and Zara knew he wouldn't let go until she agreed with him.

She swallowed. "I promise, Uncle Red."

Once her uncle fell asleep, Zara stayed in his room, curled in a blanket next to his bed with an ice pack lying across her ankle. She tried to get some rest, but she jolted awake whenever her uncle coughed or groaned. After a while, she gave up on sleeping and made sure to check his pulse every half hour, along with touching his forehead in case he had a fever, a sign of shock. His face did feel warm to the touch, not quite fever hot, but she worried about it nonetheless.

The hours stretched by, but Uncle Red didn't awaken. In the morning, Zara called in sick for work, using up one of her precious leave days, but her uncle's life was far more important than a handful of reichsmarks. She'd easily give up her annual salary for him to get better. Or at least for a doctor's visit. She thought about calling Bastian, but she didn't know his phone number, and she didn't want to risk having the Colonel pick up.

Around five in the evening, a knock on the front door jolted Zara from her worried daze. She wondered if the academy administrator had come to check on her, to see if she was really sick, but when she opened the door she found Bastian standing on the porch, still wearing his uniform and with his school bag slung over one shoulder. His eyes were red, as if he had been crying.

Zara tensed. "What's wrong?" Her frazzled nerves made her hands shake. Had someone found out about them being at the courthouse last night? She couldn't handle that right now, especially on top of her uncle's wounds.

"It's nothing," he said quickly. "I was worried about you. You didn't show up at work today, so I came as soon as practice was over." His gaze flitted past her and into the house. "Is your uncle home? I don't want to intrude."

"He's upstairs. He's . . . he's had an accident."

"Is he all right?"

"It was an electric shock. A fuse must've blown last night." Zara tucked her hands behind her back, not wanting to think about what she had done to her uncle. "Actually, I'm really glad that you came by. Can you take a look at him?"

Bastian stepped into the house. "Did you bring him to the hospital yet?"

"That wasn't an option." Bastian could probably figure out by the state of the house that Zara never would've been able to pay the medical fees. Shame coursed through her. Most of the cupboards were still broken after the Colonel's raid, and a sea of water stains swam over the ceiling like ink blots.

Bastian, however, didn't look at the cupboards or the ceiling. His eyes were fixed on her. "Have you given him any medicine?"

"Only a sleeping draft. He was tossing and turning for hours, so I thought that would be okay." Tears wet Zara's eyes as her exhaustion overtook her. She was tired to her very bones, but she couldn't sleep until she made sure her uncle would be okay. "Will you take a look at him? *Please*, Bastian."

His face seemed to soften when she said his name. "Let me get my medical bag from my car."

"Your car?" Zara peered outside past Bastian but didn't see any vehicles, aside from her uncle's truck.

Seeing the look on her face, Bastian explained, "I parked next to the barn. I didn't want anyone getting suspicious."

Immediately Zara understood. The barn would obscure Bastian's car from the road, and she felt a flood of relief at his cautiousness.

Together they headed for the barn, Zara walking with a slight hobble. The swelling had gone down since yesterday, but her foot throbbed if she put too much weight on it. Still, her ankle was nothing compared to what she had put her uncle through.

It took Bastian a few minutes to notice her limp. After they left the house, his eyes had gone all foggy again, like his head had wandered elsewhere. "You shouldn't be walking on your ankle yet," he said, frowning.

"I'm fine. I iced it last night." She glanced up. "Did something happen today? You seem . . ."

"It's nothing." His fingers reached for his dog tags, but they weren't hanging around his neck today.

"Is it about last night?"

He caught the worried look in her eye. "No, it's about my mother. She's . . . she's not well." He continued toward his car. "You should rest your ankle. I'll get my bag. It won't take long."

She matched his pace. "Is your mom okay?" When he hesitated, she mumbled a quick "Sorry, it's none of my business."

"No, I don't mind. You're the first person today to notice something was bothering me." His lips formed a sad smile, and his knuckles turned white as he gripped the straps of his backpack. "My mother wandered outside again, and it took us nearly an hour to find her. My father wants to send her to a facility."

"What sort of facility?"

"For people with brain injuries. There are a few treatments that might help her. Father found a place in Neuberlin."

"He didn't discuss this with you at all?"

"Colonel Eckhart doesn't believe in that sort of discussion. He has already packed her things." He stepped over a puddle and helped Zara jump over it. "He took Opa's dog tags, too. Told me I shouldn't wear anything that belonged to a traitor."

"What a *Schweinehund*," Zara said before she could stop herself. A look of horror crossed her face as she realized that she had called his father a swine. "I'm sorry, I shouldn't have —"

"You don't need to apologize." He shook his head slowly. "I don't know what my mother saw in him."

I don't know what my mother saw in my father, either, Zara thought. She stared at the fields ahead. They had only spent a few hours last night together, but he was confiding in her as if they had known each other for years. But it didn't feel uncomfortable, strangely enough. Bastian knew what it was like to have a father he was ashamed of, just like her.

"It feels good to say that aloud," he admitted as they reached the car. "The cadets and soldiers idolize my father, so I have to keep all of this to myself." His gaze flitted toward her. In the soft light of the setting sun, the green flecks in his eyes made his irises appear almost hazel. "And they'd never call him a *Schweinehund*."

"I shouldn't have said that. He's your father."

"A father who's a definite *Schweinehund*." He laughed, a rich buttery sound that broke through the bleakness on his face.

Bastian retrieved his medical bag from his blue BMW sedan, an old satchel made of worn leather that must have belonged to his grandfather. Once they returned to the house and Zara showed him to her uncle's bedroom, something shifted in Bastian. His shoulders straightened and a hard determination conquered his eyes, chasing away the earlier sadness. He worked like a battle-seasoned doctor, none of his usual shyness to be seen, checking Uncle Red's pulse and then his temperature and breathing. But Bastian's hands paused when he examined the red, spidery marks that snaked along Uncle Red's chest.

"Is he going to be all right?" Zara said, hovering beside the bed.

"He needs rest and plenty of fluids." Bastian's fingers fanned across the marks. "These burns should fade after a few days, too. How did he get injured again? An electric shock?"

Zara nodded.

"I've only seen these burns once before, at Opa's clinic, when a little girl was struck by lightning. They're called Lichtenberg figures."

"I — I don't know how he got those. Maybe he went outside last night. There was that storm, remember?" Zara's mind flooded with images of the ball of lightning sizzling on her hands, making her dizzy, making her clamp her eyes shut. She wouldn't have another episode. She wouldn't hurt her uncle again.

"It's all right," Bastian said, walking over to her side of the bed. "You've had a long night. Can you —"

"I did this to him," Zara blurted out. She wished she could fold up the memories of last night and toss them into a fire, but she couldn't. "I never meant to hurt him."

"What do you mean?" His voice was calm, and because of that the story tumbled out of Zara's lips.

She told him everything: about her fight with her uncle, about the strange bolts of lightning that had formed in her hands. With every word that she spoke, she waited for Bastian to flinch and back away, but he only stood there, listening.

"So you're a Dual Anomaly?" he said, looking a bit awed.

Hearing Bastian say those words — *Dual Anomaly* — finally cemented for Zara what she was. A part of her thrilled at this realization: There were only a handful of Dual Anomalies in the world, after all, but the rest of her quivered at the revelation. She never thought that she could have a second power, much less one as destructive as conjuring lightning. Her first ability usually felt so freeing — flying over the fields, feeling the breeze nibble against her skin — but this new one only reminded her of heat and fury, stinging in her bloodstream to be let out.

"Have you had another incident since last night?" said Bastian.

"No. Nothing."

They stared at each other, thinking the unspoken. How Zara's secret was now twice as deadly — and twice as likely to anger the Nazis if they found out a *Mischling* was a Dual Anomaly.

"I don't know what to do. Wind I could handle. But lightning . . ."

"Don't worry," Bastian said, his eyes bright as gold. "I think I have an idea."

14

At Bastian's insistence, they headed back to the barn, even though Zara didn't want to leave her uncle's side just yet. But Bastian wouldn't take no for an answer. Once they entered the musty old building, he shut the doors behind them, although shafts of sunlight filtered through the gaps of the wooden slats. The earthy smell of hay filled both of their noses, followed by the sharp scent of gasoline. A tired Chevy truck sat in one corner, left over from Zara's grandfather and now used for scrap.

"What's this all about?" Zara said. The two-story barn towered above both her and Bastian, and her question bounced from wall to wall.

"I thought you could try to summon your second power."

Fear pricked along the back of her neck. "You saw what happened to my uncle."

"I can sit in that old car. If the lightning gets close to me, I should be safe."

"*Should* be safe? What if I set the whole barn on fire?"

"I can't think of anywhere else we can go, not if we want to hide from the Nazis. We'll be fine." He flashed her a grin, the type of grin that lit up his entire face, making him look even more handsome than he did at the academy.

Zara's gaze plunged to her shoes. She couldn't think such a thing, not with her uncle lying sick in bed — because of her and her new power. And when did she start thinking Bastian was handsome? She had to stop those thoughts at once. Bastian may not be a Nazi, but he was still German. Besides, he would never, ever think the same thing about someone like her.

But then she thought about last night, how Bastian had helped her home. His arm had pulled her close to him, lingering there even when she could limp on her own. And hadn't he told her that he admired her?

You're being ridiculous, Zara thought. She needed to concentrate on controlling her new power and helping her uncle get better.

Bastian hopped into the ancient truck and tucked his backpack by his feet. "You can start whenever you're ready."

"What exactly am I supposed to do?" Zara said.

"How do you summon the wind? Try that with the lightning."

Easier said than done, Zara thought. Both Bastian and Uncle Red kept telling her to control this new ability of hers, but they had no idea exactly *how* she was supposed to do that. But she had to try for her uncle's sake.

She released a long breath and stared at her hands, at the spot on her palms where the lightning had formed the night before. Silently, she called for a bolt of electricity, like she always did with the wind.

Nothing.

Zara tried again, then again and another half-dozen times, but she only managed to make her hands boiling hot. After the eighth attempt, she was tempted to kick over an empty milk pail, frustrated at what she was doing wrong. The air had always been easy to manipulate, even when she first manifested. It had heeded her call even when she was seven years old, so eager to please her; but this lightning was another thing entirely. Headstrong. Pigheaded. It may have poured out of her hands the night before, but now she couldn't muster a thing.

"You have to be patient, that's all," Bastian called out.

"I don't know what I'm doing wrong. It's being so . . . stubborn." Discouraged, Zara squeezed her hands closed, not meeting Bastian's gaze. He probably thought he was wasting his time with her. "I'm sorry. You probably want to go home and see your mom, don't you?"

"I'll see her later tonight. I don't mind staying." His shyness had crept back in, pulling his shoulders forward. "Unless you'd rather try this alone?"

"No, it's not that. I only figured you'd be bored."

"Bored? You're a Dual Anomaly, Zara. I'm not bored in the least."

He had said her name again. Not *girl*. Not *Mischling*. Just Zara. A slight smile tugged at her mouth.

"I might have an idea," Bastian said. "Have you tried harnessing a spark of electricity rather than a bolt of lightning?"

"What do you mean?"

"Well, a spark would be easier to create than a full-grown lightning bolt, wouldn't it? Perhaps you should start small, then build up from there."

Zara rolled the idea through her head. Bastian had a point. When she conjured the wind, she usually did what he had said — starting with a breeze and strengthening it until it formed a tornado or a gust of wind.

"I could be off base," Bastian admitted.

"Actually, I think you might be onto something."

That smile of his returned. "Should we give it a try, then?"

While Bastian climbed back into the rusted truck, Zara studied her hands. Immediately, a breeze picked up around her wrists, eager to follow her orders, but she brushed it off.

Charge, she thought.

Nothing again.

Lips pursed, she focused on the air resting along the skin of her palms. She only needed a spark. That was it. A tiny burst of light.

Charge.

There. A tug at her palm. She urged the air to charge up like a battery, begging for it until her temples ached. A circle of heat fanned over her hand.

Then she felt it. A hum — *a seed* — of lightning. A tiny ball of particles, burning for release. With everything she had, Zara drew the seed toward her.

Charge!

Zara's lips parted at what she saw. There it was: a pebble of light bouncing on her hand.

"Bastian!" she gasped.

"I see it!" he said. "Can you try to make it larger?"

Could she?

Zara refocused on her palm. *Multiply*, she thought, concentrating every one of her cells on this lone command. The seed quivered as its white-hot tentacles stretched farther. Excitement threaded through Zara's veins, the same feeling she felt when she first summoned a gust of wind.

The lightning dwindled to nothing, but Zara didn't care. She laughed, almost giddy.

"That was excellent!" Bastian leapt out of the cab and reached her in four easy strides. He threw an arm around her shoulders. "You'll be conjuring lightning within a week. I'm sure of it."

"You helped, too." Zara grinned. "A little bit."

"Oh, only a little?" He grinned back.

His arm remained around her, and Zara's nose filled with the scents of him: soap and sage. She stepped back, scolding herself again for her silly thoughts, and Bastian's arm swiftly dropped against his side. He fidgeted with the end of his tie, as if he was embarrassed about something, but Zara didn't know why. She was the one who should be embarrassed.

"Should we try it again?" she said, trying to break the tension.

He glanced at his leather watch and mumbled a quiet "*Scheiße*." "I can't — I have to get going. I told my mother that I'd watch one of her shows with her after the news."

Zara stilled. *The news.* Suddenly, it dawned on her: the evening news!

The first Alliance attack, on Camp Hammerstein. It was happening right now. She had forgotten all about it between her new ability, her uncle's injuries, and Bastian discovering her powers.

"Is something wrong?" Bastian said.

Zara paused. She still hadn't completely revealed her ties to the Alliance to Bastian. If she told him about the attack, then she would expose herself — and Uncle Red. Her uncle's caution flared through her one more time, tightening each breath, but she nudged it aside. She trusted Bastian; she was ready to admit that now. He had saved her from the soldiers last night, and he had kept her power a secret from his father. Plus, he was here with her now, helping her harness this new ability of hers. If she couldn't trust Bastian, then whom could she trust?

She had made her choice. "We have to find a television. Right now," she said urgently.

"A television? Why?"

"There's something we have to watch."

"I might have something." Bastian retrieved his bag and pulled out his handheld radio-vision screen. "Would this work?"

Zara snatched the device from him, flipped it on, and twisted the knob until she reached Channel Seven.

"What do we have to watch?" Bastian asked.

"This. Look!"

Static crinkled on the screen, but Zara saw a cheering crowd through the fuzziness. There were hundreds of people in the throng — four hundred or five hundred — and each one had a raised fist in the air while gunshots blasted over the phone's tiny speakers. Zara's heart marched proudly at the sight, and she wondered how many people would watch this very broadcast tonight. Maybe even the Führer would be one of them.

"This can't be Channel Seven." Bastian's brows creased. "The news should be on at this hour."

"Not tonight. The Alliance broke into the broadcast. They're attacking Camp Hammerstein."

Surprise shone in Bastian's eyes. "I visited there with my father once. I met some of the soldiers. . . ."

His voice tapered off as the camera panned to a gray-haired woman who held a megaphone in her hands.

"My fellow citizens!" the woman cried, dressed in all black. "The Revolutionary Alliance sends its greetings!"

"That has to be Celia Farragut," Zara said, awed. This was the woman who had led the rebels for the last decade and who had masterminded Operation Burning Eagle. "She's the head of the Alliance."

Bastian nodded but said nothing, his gaze strapped to the screen. The rebels whooped their approval at Farragut's words, and the camera swept over their faces — most of them so young that they couldn't be much older than Zara.

"Tonight, we celebrate an Alliance victory," Farragut cried. "Camp Hammerstein now burns to ruins!"

The lens turned sharply to the right, and both Bastian and Zara sucked in their breaths. Behind the rebel crowd, Camp Hammerstein roasted in bright orange flames, spreading over its five main buildings and toward the tall trees that surrounded the property. The entire camp had crumbled to the ground, and thick plumes of smoke rose from its bones.

"They took it over," Zara whispered. The Alliance had actually taken the camp.

The lens pointed back at Farragut. "Bring me the Nazi dog!" she shouted.

Seconds later, three rebels dragged a Nazi soldier forward, his hands bound behind his back. Farragut pointed at him. "In front of me, I have a guard who has surrendered to the Alliance. A German coward!"

The crowd erupted, shouting "German coward" over and over again until they drowned out Farragut. Long seconds passed before they quieted; then Farragut placed the megaphone in front of the frightened soldier's face.

"Renounce the Führer!" she spat at him. "Renounce the Empire!"

The soldier tried to speak, but he could only stutter a pitiful "Please!" The camera zeroed in on his ghost-pale cheeks.

"Renounce the Führer!" Farragut shouted again.

"I — I renounce him!" the soldier sobbed. He looked close to Bastian's age, perhaps a bit older, maybe nineteen or twenty. "And the E-Empire. I renounce it, too!"

Farragut nodded, looking quite pleased, but that didn't stop her from pulling a pistol from her holster. Zara stared at the gun, then at the soldier, then back again. She didn't know what was going on. Would Farragut shoot the soldier? Even after he had surrendered? Farragut must have her reasons. . . .

"Will she kill him?" Bastian said, his eyes wide. "On national television?"

"But —" *But this is war. There are no rules*, Zara thought. The Nazis had slaughtered thousands of rebels, even if they surrendered, even if they begged. And even if they had children, like her mother. "Think about your *Opa*. He was arrested by Nazi soldiers like this one."

Bastian reached for the dog tags that used to hang around his neck and nodded grimly. They turned their attention back to the screen.

"Mercy!" the soldier cried. "I beg of you!"

Farragut racked the slide and aimed the gun at his temple. "Mercy?"

"Yes, mercy!" The soldier's eyes grew so wide that Zara could see the whites of them. He sobbed again. *"Mutter!"*

Mother. He was crying for his mother. Zara's heart cringed as he cried out again, but she reminded herself that he was a Nazi. He could have arrested men like her uncle or killed women like Mrs. Talley — and he could have done both with a grin on his face. She couldn't allow herself to feel a drop of sympathy for him.

"Did the Nazis show mercy when they bombed our cities?" Farragut paced around the soldier, always keeping the gun at his head. "Did the Nazis show us mercy when our children starved? When they destroyed America? Did they?" She kicked him. "Did they?"

The soldier spluttered.

"Coward," she growled.

"I surrendered! What more must I —"

Farragut pulled the trigger. Blood spurted over her clothes, dotting the camera lens, and the dead soldier slumped to the ground. Bastian winced and turned away, but Zara kept her eyes on the screen, unable to look away.

"There will be no mercy for the Empire!" Farragut shouted.

The crowd's volume rose in a great crescendo, and the same three words overtook the masses. "Freedom, or death! Freedom, or death!"

Farragut joined in.

"Freedom, or death!"

Fists rose into the air, pumping together as one. *"Freedom, or death! Freedom, or death!"*

"Join us, our fellow citizens! Our fellow Americans! For the Alliance! For the —"

Her speech cut off abruptly. The camera jostled from left to right before it focused on the crowd breaking apart, running in all directions. A few of the rebels pointed above their heads, and the lens swung upward to show three large shadows moving across the darkening sky.

"They're sending in bombers!" someone yelled. "Fall back! Fall back!"

An ear-shattering blast exploded by the fence. Another explosion detonated near the camera, sending an awful bang into Zara's ears. The picture soon turned to static, then black.

Zara went numb. She shook the device, silently begging for the feed to return, but it stayed blank. Bastian finally reached over and pried the machine from her fingers.

"The Nazis sent in bombers," Zara said, her voice lifeless. Were all of the rebels dead? What about Garrison? He said he was going to be at the attack. What happened to Farragut?

Bastian didn't reply. He only placed a hand on her shoulder.

"It wasn't supposed to happen like this!" Zara cried. Garrison had just sat in her living room, his face bright as he laid out the Alliance's plan. But now, it looked like this attack had turned into another Mission Metzger. And that made Zara's chest hurt. "This should've been our big chance."

"Chance for what?" Bastian said softly.

"To fight the Nazis. To get rid of them."

He stepped back. "It was only one raid. How would that get rid of them? Unless there's something else . . ."

Zara nodded but didn't explain further. It didn't matter anymore. Now that the mission at Camp Hammerstein had collapsed, there would be no supplies to carry out the next attack on Fort Goering. There would be no march on Neuberlin.

"We could find them," Bastian said.

Zara glanced up at him, confused.

"We could find the Alliance. We could help them, couldn't we?" That dogged look had returned to his eyes. "I can treat the wounded. You could help them with your powers."

"There might not be much of an Alliance left," she said. "Didn't you see what happened?"

"They wouldn't have sent in *all* of their forces for one mission. That's a simple rule of battle strategy. But they probably could use our help."

Zara couldn't believe he was saying these things. Bastian had told her dozens of times that he wanted to join the Alliance, but now he was talking about running away. And she couldn't believe that *she* was the one hesitating. But she had to hesitate, for Uncle Red's sake.

"I can't leave until my uncle gets better," she told him. She wondered if she would be taking up Bastian's offer if her uncle weren't sick. She had been waiting her whole life for this opportunity. Now that it was here, would she be as brave as she thought she was?

"That's right. Your uncle." The fire in Bastian's eyes receded. His shoulders slumped inward. "My mother, too."

"We could still help the Alliance from Greenfield. We could gather information. Find more recruits," Zara offered. Maybe they couldn't join the rebels right now, but they could make a difference here in their town.

"I think we could." Bastian's gaze searched hers. "Together, then?"

She nodded. "Together."

15

Before Bastian returned home, the two of them agreed to meet the next day to discuss their plans. Zara still couldn't quite wrap her head around the idea of working with Bastian — even if it was on the Alliance's behalf — but this was a chance for both of them to do something. This was their chance to fight back.

And Zara could certainly wrap her head around *that*.

After Bastian left, Zara hurried to her uncle's bedroom, the images of Camp Hammerstein flickering through her thoughts again. The bombs. The screams. She hoped Garrison and Farragut had escaped. There was no guarantee that they had fallen at Camp Hammerstein, but doubt rolled through Zara anyway, like a Nazi tank. She had seen the explosions. It would have been nearly impossible to outrun all of those. Hopelessness sank into the pit of her stomach. It had taken years for the Alliance to bounce back from Mission Metzger — how long would it take for them to recover from this one?

Finally, at nearly ten o'clock, Uncle Red stirred. "Zara," he rasped.

She sprang up toward him, resting her hand against his head. Some of the color had returned to his cheeks, and his forehead now felt cool to the touch, but he still looked so weak. "How are you feeling?"

"Good as new," he croaked, giving her a half smile. "Sleeping has helped."

"Are you thirsty?" She stood to fetch him some water, but his fingers curled around her wrist.

"What's wrong? You're pale as a sheet."

Zara didn't want to burden him with the broadcast, not when he was recovering, but the story spilled out of her anyway. She told him about the broadcast, the bombers; and Uncle Red let out a long breath.

"I guess you were right," she choked out. "They weren't ready for this mission, and now everyone is gone."

"We don't know that for certain. The Alliance may not have used all of their forces."

"You didn't see it, Uncle Red. Garrison —" She could barely finish his name.

"Let's hope for the best. Garrison is more resourceful than you think." Uncle Red scooted off his bed, wobbling on his feet before he righted himself. He waved off Zara's protests for him to lie back down. "There might be something on TV."

"I don't want to listen to what the Nazis have to say." She took him by the elbow, steadying him, wishing she hadn't told him about the broadcast. "And you really need to get back to bed."

"We need to know the fallout of the attack. I hate to say that, but we do."

He twiddled with the television knobs to find the news station, then took a seat on the windowsill until a commercial about skin-whitening cream ended.

"We now bring breaking news from Camp Hammerstein," said the newscaster. "A group of terrorists known as the Revolutionary Alliance brutally attacked the camp at 1900 hours. Over a hundred soldiers were killed, but forces from nearby Fort Wilhelm destroyed the rebels with superior air and ground power. All Alliance survivors will be justly executed if found guilty by the SS."

"*Justly*?" Zara said, but Uncle Red placed a finger over his lips, shushing her.

The newscaster continued, "In a press release from Neuberlin, Reichsmarschall Baldur denounced the raid as 'inexcusable' and then lauded the Nazi forces who struck back against the rebels. A heightened security warning has been put into place across the Eastern American Territories. The following parameters will come to pass immediately: Random checks will be performed at the discretion of local Nazi officials. If you have any information about the rebels, contact your local Nazi office immediately and you will be eligible for a reward. Lastly, persons suspected of treasonous activities will be imprisoned; and if found guilty, these persons will be executed and their families will be taken to the labor camps."

Once the newscaster moved on to a story about a failed coup to overthrow Mussolini III, Uncle Red turned off the television, but Zara blinked at the empty screen.

"They're going to imprison family members, too? Even children?" she said, fuming.

"Baldur must want to stomp out the rebellion before it gains any more ground."

"Like he hasn't done enough already." Zara waited for her uncle to begin a diatribe on how the Alliance should have been more cautious, that they hadn't been ready, but Uncle Red surprised her with what he said next.

"We'll see what happens. The Alliance may not be as damaged as the news makes it out to be. And it's clear by the Nazis' reaction that they didn't suspect the attack — and they're angry at getting caught off guard."

Zara wondered why he was being so optimistic. Maybe he wanted to put on a brave face for her sake, which somehow made her feel worse.

"Did you try to control your new ability today?" Uncle Red asked, changing the subject. "I'm sorry I couldn't be of much help." He coughed, still looking worn from the accident yesterday, and Zara felt a tug of guilt.

She was about to tell him that she was making headway on her lightning — the one bright point of her day — but her answer was interrupted by a rapid-fire knock on the front door. Her head whipped toward the sound, wondering if Bastian had returned, but he had to be smart enough not to use the front door at this hour.

They headed downstairs with Uncle Red shuffling slowly, and they had nearly reached the bottom of the steps when the front door flew open. Was *kicked* open, to be more precise. A trio of Nazi soldiers flooded into the house — two armed guards, along with Sentinel Achen — and they were followed by Colonel Eckhart.

Zara's breath locked in her throat as she met the Colonel's hard eyes, so different from his son's. Uncle Red stepped into the front entrance. "Colonel Eckhart," he said stiffly. "What's the meaning of this?"

Sentinel Achen lunged forward and slapped Uncle Red with the back of his hand. "You dare address the Colonel in that tone!"

Uncle Red stumbled back from the blow, and Zara tried to brace him, but she stumbled with her rolled ankle. The soldiers laughed at the debacle.

"You can search the house," said Uncle Red, rubbing the spot where the Sentinel had struck him. "We still don't have anything to hide."

"Oh, is that so?" Colonel Eckhart cocked his head, amused. His mouth tightened into a sly smile. "Perhaps you don't have anything to hide *here*, but we received an anonymous tip that recently puts you at Fort Goering. It appears you have a penchant for strolling around my fort, along with an accomplice."

Garrison, Zara thought. She tried to step forward and ask who this anonymous tipper could be, but Uncle Red held her back. Dread filled her stomach at the glee in the Colonel's eyes. Her uncle had always been so careful on missions, but maybe someone had spotted him and Garrison while they surveyed the fort.

"I don't know what you're talking about, *mein Herr,*" said Uncle Red. His voice was steady, but Zara saw the quivering in his hands.

Now it was Colonel Eckhart's turn to strike him, straight across the cheek. "Tsk, tsk. We've questioned our witness thoroughly."

Uncle Red's eyes flared wide, but his face remained placid. "And who is this witness, sir?"

"I won't reveal that." The Colonel grinned. "That would defeat the purpose of an 'anonymous tip,' wouldn't it? Now then. Where is the man who was with you, hmm? Your accomplice?"

Zara went still. She had no idea if Colonel Eckhart was bluffing or if this witness was indeed real, but it didn't matter now. The Colonel's hackles were raised, and he held all of the cards. Her gaze shot toward her uncle, wondering what they should do, but he kept his eyes straight on Colonel Eckhart.

"As I said, I don't know what you're talking about," said Uncle Red.

"You will not lie to me!" the Colonel burst out. He launched a fist into Uncle Red's gut.

Uncle Red doubled over, gasping from the pain. Zara reached out to help him, but he pushed her away, shaking his head. "Stay out of this," he groaned. "Please."

"Uncle Red —" Zara started, but the Colonel interrupted her.

"Arrest them!" Colonel Eckhart nodded at his guards, who leapt into motion at his command. Sentinel Achen seized Zara by the arm, restraining her, while the other soldiers cuffed Uncle Red's wrists. Frantically, Zara struggled against the Sentinel's loathsome hands, but it was no use.

"Don't you touch her!" Uncle Red shouted, but he was silenced when a soldier punched him in the jaw. Then kneed him in the stomach.

"Stop it!" Zara cried. Heat swirled on her palms as anger surged inside her. The air charged around her hands, but she fought the hungry urge to let loose her lightning at the guards. She could electrocute them all, her uncle included.

Sentinel Achen leaned down to her ear and said, "Careful, *Mischling*. I'd enjoy shooting you." His right hand roamed up from her hip toward her rib cage, then higher still. Disgust coursed through Zara, but she couldn't use her powers and she couldn't twist free from his grasp. As his hand climbed upward, she pulled her head back and spat right in the Sentinel's face.

Cruel fury twisted his features, but before he could react, one of the other soldiers was stepping forward, swinging his gun at Zara in a wide arc.

Crack.

The first strike smashed into Zara's head, splattering blood from her nose.

Crack.

The second hit underneath her chin. She crashed onto the floor.

"Zara!" She heard her uncle screaming. His voice was so racked with pain that she almost forgot her own. "Zara!"

As blood dripped into her eyes, she clenched her hand into a fist. Desperation took over. If she didn't use her powers, the Nazis would kill her anyway. The air swirled around her fingertips, but then the last strike smacked her in the forehead.

Crack.

"We're done here," said the Colonel. "Clear out."

It was the last thing she heard before sinking into darkness.

Zara opened her aching eyelids, only to shut them a second later. Her head hammered from the slightest of movements, and her nose throbbed with a stabbing pain that made her want to retch. She breathed in and out until the nausea finally retreated. Forcing her eyes open, she found herself lying on a bare mattress. Her clothes — a bloodied shirt and her work trousers — were damp with sweat. Her fingers pried at her sticky collar while her gaze traveled to the foot of the bed, where sunlight leaked through a barred window. The place was hot as a womb.

Blinking slowly, she saw eight cots spread on both sides of the bleak room, four on one side and four on the other. It was a cramped rectangle of a space, hardly large enough to fit five patients, much less eight. Zara's eyes trained on two of the beds opposite from hers that were occupied with unconscious women, both of them black. The rest of the cots were empty.

"You're awake," someone said, crouching next to her.

Zara looked up to find a familiar face. "Kristy?" she said. A million questions sprang onto her tongue, but only one word came out. "Where . . . ?"

"We're in the old hospital at Fort Goering."

It took her a moment to put together what Kristy was talking about.

"They put us here, in the mental ward. For the locked doors." Kristy nodded toward the thick door behind them, dread in her eyes. "Do you remember what happened?"

Zara closed her eyes, and a memory came to mind: the Colonel bursting into her house and arresting her and Uncle Red. Despite the roaring in her head, she hoisted herself onto her elbows, fists clenched. "Where's my uncle?"

"He's probably at the prison like everyone else. The Nazis arrested so many people that they dumped the women and the elderly in this waste of a building." She scowled at the rotting walls and the water-stained ceiling that let in a steady drip of stinking water. Most likely sewage. "You were delirious when they brought you here."

"I was?"

"You kept muttering about going to Neuberlin."

Seconds passed before Zara stitched together what Kristy was talking about. *The mission to storm Neuberlin.* The last part of the Alliance's plan. She had never meant to say that aloud, and never in front of Kristy.

"Like you said, I was delirious," Zara said, hoping Kristy wouldn't prod any further. Not that it mattered. If both Garrison and Farragut had been killed, there wouldn't be an attack on Fort Goering, much less the rest of Operation Burning Eagle. She sank back against her thin pillow, no thicker than her fingertip. Her nose stung, pounding every time she moved, and a deep anguish sank into her stomach. She could handle the pain, but she couldn't handle not knowing what had happened to her uncle. Had the Nazis hurt him? Had they ... had they killed him?

"I have to find my uncle," Zara said frantically. Dizziness shrouded her eyes, and she tried to blink it away. She had to get both Uncle Red and herself out of this place.

"Didn't you notice the bars on the windows?" Kristy said with a joyless laugh. "And believe me, my mom and I tried to pick the lock on that door yesterday. We're not getting out."

"*Yesterday*? How long have we been here?"

"Almost two days."

Two days? Zara realized that she had been unconscious for forty-eight hours — and that meant her uncle had been withering in a jail cell for just as long. Or worse. He could have been declared guilty and shot already. She had to get out of this room, but how? Her gaze flew toward the locked door and the barred window, then at the wounded women across from her.

The Nazis had taken everything she had, and there was nothing she could do. Every inch of her yearned to tear the Colonel apart with her lightning and destroy his fort with the wind at her fingertips. But every time Zara tried to sit up, a wrenching agony twisted inside her skull, leaving her breathless.

"Just stay still," Kristy huffed. "We're not getting out of here."

Zara shut her eyes, wanting to be left alone. "Why are you even talking to me?"

Kristy stiffened. "You think you'd be my first choice? Like there are so many other options."

Zara sighed and glanced at the occupied cots. "Who are they anyway?" One of the women shivered, while the other didn't move a finger. Makeshift bandages, stained with blood, covered their foreheads. No doubt they were victims of Colonel Eckhart's rampage through the city.

"I don't know their names. I think they threw a few punches when the Nazis arrested them."

"They weren't killed for that?"

Kristy's lips pursed. "It doesn't matter. They're as good as dead anyway. That woman had her ribs crushed." She glanced out the window, and Zara noticed the purple bruises that climbed from Kristy's chin to her eye. "There were seven of us at first, but they took one of the girls away for interrogation and she never came back. Then they moved another woman into a different cell."

"So there's five of us now?"

Kristy's gaze skittered toward the floor, but not before Zara saw the tremble in her eyes. "No, four. My mom tried to break us out, but it didn't work. They took her to solitary confinement." She chewed on her fingernail and headed back to her cot, but not before adding, "There's water by the door."

Mustering every last bit of strength, Zara dragged herself toward the lone bucket planted next to the room's entrance. Her right ankle felt stiff and it still bore an angry bruise, but the pain was nothing compared to the throbbing in her head. By the time she reached the water, sweat had poured down Zara's shirt, but she brought the bucket to her lips, drinking it in great gulps. The lukewarm water soothed her parched throat.

"You should thank your Nazi fling for that," Kristy said, glancing up from her bed. The fear that Zara had seen on Kristy's face only a minute earlier had already been wiped clean.

Zara wiped her mouth with her hand. "Fling?"

"The Colonel's son. He and a bunch of cadets dropped off that water. Something about the Nazi Women's Charity League."

Zara almost dropped the bucket. Frau Eckhart used to run the Nazi Women's Charity League — was Bastian behind this idea of giving water to the prisoners? If his father found out about this ... Bastian never should have stepped foot in the hospital, but her heart warmed — her first flicker of hope — at what he had done. At what he had risked.

"What did he say?" Zara said.

"The guards wouldn't let him say anything." Kristy paused. "I guess they didn't want your fling to catch any of our diseases."

Zara set the bucket down hard. "He isn't my *fling*."

"Is he more than that, then?"

"He's not my anything!" Zara snapped, which she regretted immediately, because that made her head hurt more.

"I've seen how he looks at you at school."

The accusations kept pouring from Kristy's lips, and Zara had had enough. "We're locked inside this room and that's all you can think about?"

Boots pounded against the door. "Shut up in there!" a soldier shouted at them. "Quiet!"

Kristy stormed toward the windows while Zara flipped onto her side, ignoring the sharp ache that shook through her body every time she moved. Still, the pain was worth it. At least she wouldn't have to look at Kristy anymore.

Curling into a tight ball, Zara waited for her headache to lessen, but the throbbing refused to go away, along with her questions. Was Uncle Red all right? Where had the Nazis taken him? The worry chewed at her heart, making her stomach turn all over again.

A tear slid out of Zara's eye, followed by another. The Nazis had bombed the Alliance, and they had taken her uncle away. She wished she could talk to him. Or Mrs. Talley. Or her mother.

But her mother was dead. Mrs. Talley was, too. And maybe her uncle was as well.

Zara buried her face against the mattress, huddling against a burlap blanket. It was the only thing she had, this scratchy scrap of cloth. She knew she should get up and figure out a way to break out of this room, but she pulled her knees against her chest instead, utterly spent.

Hopelessness drifted through her. This was all too much. The Nazis. Her arrest. This stifling-hot room. When sleep finally came to her, Zara succumbed to the darkness, not sure if she ever wanted to awake again.

16

The next twenty-four hours passed horribly for Zara.

She slept fitfully, waking every half hour from the same awful nightmare of her uncle getting beaten and dragged across the square, just like Mr. Kerry weeks ago. And when she awakened, things didn't get much better.

With the windows locked, the air sweltered and almost suffocated every one of Zara's breaths. She wished she could send a breeze through the room with her powers, but she couldn't take that risk right under the Nazis' noses. They could kill her anyway, of course, but why give them a reason to? The longer she stayed alive, the longer she had to find her uncle.

The stale stench of soiled bandages and days-old urine perfumed the room, making Zara's stomach curdle. There was a toilet at the corner that she and Kristy used, but their two unconscious cellmates had wet themselves overnight. Kristy had been doing her best to clean them, but the women never stirred, never even groaned. One of them, the older woman with crushed ribs, had died that morning. The soldiers had taken her body already, most likely to be incinerated.

Zara stared at the cracking ceiling, trying not to think about that poor woman, or the pounding in her nose. It had swollen like a melon overnight, and even the softest touch made her want to scream. And yet, despite her bruises, Zara knew she was probably better off than her uncle. From her barred window, she could see the entrance to the prison, a hundred yards away, all gray and grim. At least she had water, thanks to Bastian. Her uncle and the rest of the male prisoners probably had nothing.

For hours, Zara tried to figure out an escape plan, but each idea fell to pieces. There were only two routes out of the room — through the windows or out of the bolted metal door. She could muster a wind to chew through the window glass, but the air wouldn't be able to blast through the iron. As for her new lightning ability, it wouldn't be much help to her here. She could shoot a bolt at the door, but that would only electrify the metal instead of opening it.

With her nose still pulsing, she sank onto her mattress, her head bowed low. It was Sunday, she realized. The day of the planned attack on Fort Goering. But instead of helping the Alliance prepare for the mission, Zara was locked in this room and had no way of getting out — and the Alliance wasn't coming to save her, not after Camp Hammerstein. All spark of hope emptied out of Zara, leaving her only a shell of a person.

As the sun dipped below the horizon, Zara heard footsteps thudding down the hallway. Her pulse cartwheeled as the door swung open and a soldier marched inside, a box and a bucket in hand. He dropped both on the floor before turning on his heels.

"From the Nazi Women's Charity League," he sniffed. "*Scheiße*, you women stink."

After he locked the door behind him, both Zara and Kristy raced to the goods. Kristy arrived first and slurped water straight from the bucket while Zara reached for the box. She was surprised to find a bundle of food inside it: a loaf of bread, a rind of cheese, and a few green apples. Her mouth watered at the sight of it all. She hadn't eaten since her arrest.

Right before she tore off a chunk of bread, Zara remembered what the soldier had said to them. *From the Nazi Women's Charity League.* Could Bastian be behind this somehow? He could have sent a letter to the league, maybe by forging his mother's or father's signature. And if he had gone to that much trouble, he might have hidden a message for her. With frantic hands, she scoured the box, running her hands up and down its sides, searching for clues. Frustration bubbled through her when she came up empty.

"What are you looking for?" Kristy said. She snatched the bread from Zara's hand and broke it in half. "They gave us food. *Good* food. Eat up."

Zara blinked at the box. She had no idea what Bastian was trying to tell her. Or if he was telling her anything at all.

Kristy swore and spat something out. A piece of paper. "Pass the water, will you?"

Eyes wide, Zara snatched up the paper and stared at it, the gears churning in her head. Her heart thudded as she unfolded it and read the message.

Shift change 22:00. Meet at Officers' Hall 22:30.

Kristy stopped chewing. "What does that say?"

Zara didn't answer. She clutched the paper tight in her hand, silently thanking Bastian, and returned to dismantling the box again. If Bastian wanted to meet that night, he must have given her something to get out of this room. Her hands swam through the box, coming up empty, and then she reached for the other half of the bread. Hands trembling, she broke it again and something sprang out from the loaf. Something small. Something metal.

A three-inch iron key.

Both Zara and Kristy stared at it.

This was Bastian's escape plan.

Zara's fingers closed around the key and her gaze flew to the locked door. Hope bloomed inside of her, pushing aside the misery of the past few days — and she owed it all to Bastian. It couldn't have been easy finding out what room she was in and securing this key — but he had done it anyway.

"Is that a key to the door?" Kristy whispered.

Zara barely heard the question. She stared out the window instead, trying to gauge the time. The sun had dipped below the horizon, but streaks of blue and purple stretched across the sky. It would be at least another two hours before ten o'clock struck. She cursed softly.

Kristy made a grab at Zara's hand. "What are we waiting for?" she said, careful not to let the guards hear them.

"The soldiers don't change shifts until ten."

"Let me see that paper." Kristy seized it from Zara's hand. "Who sent this? Was it that Nazi? Bastian?"

"He's not a Nazi." Zara scowled. How could Kristy even say that after what he had done for them? Only weeks ago, Zara had thought the worst about Bastian, too, but he had proved her wrong over and over again.

"He's the Colonel's son. How can you trust him?"

"You can think whatever you want about Bastian, but I'm leaving at ten," Zara said coolly. She didn't need an interrogation from Kristy of all people.

"Let me see the key." She lunged for it, but Zara sidestepped her. "I only want to see it, you —"

"*Kami*?" Zara spat out, before Kristy could say the word. Memories slashed through her of how Kristy had treated her, of the name calling and the smirks, of making Zara's life more miserable than it already was. A breeze stirred at her fingers, but she curled it into her fist.

For a second, Kristy winced. "Look, I know I've called you some things —"

Boot steps thundered down the hallway toward their room, cutting Kristy off. Icicles shot down Zara's spine, and she forgot about Kristy as the door flew open. Sentinel Achen stood in the doorframe, his gaze fixed on both of them. Fear shot through Zara as she remembered how his hands had wandered over her the last time she had seen him. Had he come to finish what he had started?

"Quiet, the both of you!" Sentinel Achen barked. He stepped inside and locked the door behind him. Thinking quickly, Zara crossed her arms behind her back, tucking the key away from his prying eyes.

"We're sorry, *mein Herr*," Kristy said, her head bowed.

"What were you shouting about?" He stepped toward Zara, those watchful eyes of his searching every inch of her. The slightest of smiles played upon his mouth.

Zara trembled, squeezing the key behind her, willing her face to remain calm. If he discovered what she was holding, he could fire a round through her forehead, no questions asked. "Nothing of importance, *mein Herr*," she said. "Our apologies. It won't happen again."

"Maybe you two need a lesson in sharing." His lips arched and he pushed Zara, hard. Crying out, she stumbled backward, losing her balance — and her grasp on the key. A metal ping echoed through the room as the key hit the floor. The Sentinel froze when he saw it.

"How did you get that?" he demanded. Spittle sprayed from his mouth and he seized Zara by the wrists, shoving her back against the wall.

"I — I found it!" Zara stammered.

"Don't lie to me." He slapped her so hard that she saw stars. "Who gave this to you? Did you bribe one of the guards? What did you offer them, huh?"

Zara struggled to shove his hands off her, but he only tightened his hold on her wrists. He slammed her again and this time her head snapped back, hitting the concrete wall, dizzying her.

The Sentinel curled one hand around her throat while he turned his attention on Kristy. "Who gave you the key? Tell me!" Using his free hand, he snatched at Zara's shirt, ripping the sleeve, but Kristy jumped in and clawed at his eyes. Achen snarled and knocked an elbow into her stomach, sending Kristy to the floor, coughing. With him preoccupied, Zara smashed her hands against his chest to escape, but he yanked her by the collar so hard that she choked. He threw her on the floor next to Kristy, pinning her there.

"Where do you think you're going, little *Mischling*?" His face was only inches from hers, so close that she could smell the coffee on his breath. His hands groped at her sweaty shirt. "What else are you hiding?"

Panic raced through every inch of Zara's body. She thrashed and kicked, but the Sentinel was too heavy, his arms too strong.

She had to stop him.

She knew what he would do to her next.

As her fear spiked, she felt a marble-size bolt of lightning spring onto her hand. Next to her, Kristy gasped.

"Where should we search first?" said Achen, who hadn't seen the spark on Zara's palm. As he started to rip Zara's shirt, she released the tiny bolt, shooting it straight into his belly. It wasn't enough to knock him unconscious, but his eyes shot open, stunned. He scuttled backward, breathing heavily, his eyes clouded with confusion.

Before he could lunge at her, Zara was ready. *Charge*, she thought. Another spark jumped onto her hand, and she urged it to grow. She'd rather risk revealing her powers than find out what the Sentinel had planned for her. Both Achen and Kristy went still, their gazes locked on the fiery lightning crackling on her fingertips.

Kristy pointed at Zara's hand, speechless, while Sentinel Achen blinked at the ball of electricity.

"You're an . . . you're an . . . ," he said, fumbling for the radio on his belt buckle.

The lightning burned hotter, doubling in size and contorting out of Zara's control. "Kristy, get down!" she managed to scream before she sent the lightning at the Sentinel.

"I need backup on floor three!" With his free hand, he tried to wrest his pistol from its holster, but his fingers were trembling too much. "I am requesting —"

Sentinel Achen didn't finish his sentence.

Zara's bolt struck him straight in the neck and sent him careening into the air. His arms flailing, he soared backward and his head hit the corner of a cot frame, sending an awful crack across the room. He slumped onto the ground, legs twitching. Then he stopped moving altogether.

Zara's eyes traveled over the Sentinel's body, but they stopped when she saw his face. His eyes were blank, his mouth slack. Kristy crept toward him and shoved her fingers against his neck.

"Is he . . . ?" Zara whispered.

Kristy glanced up. "He's dead."

Zara sank against the wall, only one thought rolling through her. *I killed him. I killed the Sentinel.*

A wave of horror swept through her.

Her heart shuddered at the sight of his body. He lay only a few feet away from her, but she could still feel his hot breath against her neck and his rough hands against her body.

He can't hurt me ever again, she told herself. She dry heaved anyway.

Kristy shrank back from Zara, staring at her palms. "Your hands —"

"I had to stop him somehow!" Zara blurted. She knew there was no way to hide what she had done. Or who she was. Everything had happened so fast: the Sentinel attacking her, the lightning surging up. Now Sentinel Achen was dead, and Kristy knew about one of her powers. Zara felt dizzy just thinking about it all.

"You're an —" Kristy couldn't quite get the words out. "You're an *Anomaly*?"

"It's not something I can exactly advertise. A kami like me," Zara replied, a bitter note in her voice. Then a ripple of fear rolled through her. She didn't know how Kristy would use this information about her power, but she couldn't worry about that right now. She had to find her uncle, and they had to break out of the fort as soon as possible. They had to run before Sentinel Achen's comrades came to check on him.

Finally, Kristy tore her gaze from Zara, her eyes drifting toward the Sentinel. "You . . . you saved us."

"He didn't give me much of a choice," said Zara, not looking at the Sentinel's limp body. Seeing his eyes, both still open, made her stomach twist into a knot, but she pushed that image far away from her. She only wished she could erase that awful cracking sound from her mind, when his skull met the cot's railing.

Blinking slowly, Kristy placed her hand on Zara's shoulder. "Thank you."

Zara startled at the softness of Kristy's words, but it was a little too late for kindness. She shrugged off Kristy's hand. "We really need to go."

"What do you want me to do?" Kristy said. A tremor had entered her voice, as if Zara might shoot her with a lightning bolt at any minute.

"Find the key and get the door open."

While Kristy retrieved the key ring from Achen's belt and hurried to the door, Zara pocketed the other key that had been knocked across the room. Then she wrestled the Sentinel's pistol from its holster, her stomach heaving the entire time as she tried not to touch him. She didn't have much experience with pistols; she'd only had brief lessons where her mother taught her how to load a shotgun for hunting deer. Pistols were Uncle Red's realm of expertise, but she would have to do her best — she didn't want to reveal her abilities to anyone else unless absolutely necessary.

Kristy unlocked the door, and Zara checked the gun's ammunition. She wished she had a few minutes to sit on a cot and catch her breath, but they had to move. It was too early to meet Bastian, but she couldn't stay in this room with the Sentinel's body, especially after he had radioed the other soldiers.

"Do you know how to get out of the hospital?" said Kristy, her eyes trailing over Zara's hands.

"I'll figure it out. It's not like I have a map." Zara peered beyond the door to find an empty hallway. For now. She had to find her way to the prison to free Uncle Red. After that . . . they'd have to escape somewhere. They couldn't go home, not after Zara had killed a Sentinel. The thought of leaving their farmhouse made her heart rip in half, but the important thing now was finding her uncle — and getting them both out of the fort alive.

Zara slipped into the corridor, followed by Kristy, and a foul rotting stench flooded her nose. The hallway was in a state of decay: Water stains covered the walls, and the ceiling tiles were crumbling or were missing altogether. Two dozen doors, like the one they had escaped from, spread to Zara's right and left. Glass skylights hung over her head, revealing a black sky.

A siren blared into Zara's eardrums. Both she and Kristy froze.

The soldiers were coming.

As the alarm pulsed through her head, Zara searched for the stairwell, her ankle still unsteady and throbbing, but fortunately she could walk on it. Kristy didn't follow her this time. Instead, using the Sentinel's keys, she ran from door to door, releasing the people inside.

"Mom?" Kristy cried every time she unlocked another door. "Are you in here?"

The hall soon swelled with women and the elderly, their hair wild and their eyes like sunken craters on their wan faces. Kristy pushed through them but couldn't find her mother — the Nazis must have taken her to an isolation cell somewhere else. In one great mass, the crowd swarmed toward the end of the corridor where Zara had finally spotted a faded exit sign.

Zara dashed down the stairwell with the rest of the horde, storming down two flights of stairs until they reached the main level of the hospital. Three women at the front burst through the door, only to throw themselves onto the chipped tile floor. Screams echoed in the stairwell as gunfire sprayed from the soldiers stationed on the main level.

"Get down!" Zara shouted, but the warning came too late. Two people collapsed in front of her, their bodies erupting with blood. One of them, an old man with frost-white hair, toppled near Zara with a bullet hole gaping in his wrinkled neck.

Zara crawled toward the door and fired off her pistol until the magazine emptied. One of her rounds drilled into a soldier's shoulder, but the rest of them went wide. The guards pushed forward, their rifles pointed at the *Kleinbauern*, ordering them to surrender.

Zara was out of bullets. They had no other weapons. With a sinking feeling she realized there was only one way out of this. She had to use her powers, even if that meant revealing herself as an Anomaly to the Nazis. Fear rushed up her throat, but she tamped it down. If she didn't fight them now, they would kill her and everyone else in this hallway.

While the soldiers snaked closer, she urged her hands to charge. Sweat dribbled down her forehead, but the lightning finally came, only a spinning ball of energy at first. She commanded it to grow larger, deadlier. As soon as it swelled nearly beyond her control, she unleashed it at the guards, sending it crackling into their chests. She caught the horror on their faces before all five of them fell onto their backs, their limbs twitching.

A stark silence fell inside the stairwell. Slowly, Zara looked behind her to find dozens of people blinking at her, all of their mouths dropped open.

Kami. Traitor. She waited for the names to come, but they didn't. They only stared.

From the back of the group, Kristy stood and broke the quiet. "What are you staring at her for? Haven't you ever seen an Anomaly?"

Before anyone could respond, Zara finally found her voice. "We have to leave right now! More soldiers are probably coming. Grab any weapons you can find and run as fast as you can." She knew most of them had never held a gun before, but there was strength in numbers, and that was all they could count on right now.

Hesitantly, the *Kleinbauern* moved. A trio of middle-aged women searched the soldiers for ammunition while Kristy snatched a rifle from the floor.

"Come on, this way!" Zara said.

Urging her legs forward, she dashed out of the hospital entrance and into the cool spring night. Giant floodlights lit the fort, blanketing them in a swath of fluorescent light. Zara blinked against the harsh brightness before she spotted the military jail two hundred yards to their right. The fort's sirens blared louder.

"On our left, on our left!" Kristy said, her voice nearly lost in the noise.

Zara's gaze jerked to the side to find thirty soldiers rushing toward them. Shots fired. Some of the *Kleinbauern* dropped flat to the ground while others scattered toward the fence to escape. Kristy ducked behind a concrete bench, firing shots from her newly stolen rifle.

The gunfire blasted through Zara's senses, but there wasn't time to shrink back in fear. She summoned the lightning again. It started as it always did, only a small flare, but soon it crackled over her palms, doubling in size every second. She reined it in, even though it yearned for release, but she urged it to grow even bigger before she aimed it at the Nazis. The spidery bolt sprinted hungrily toward the soldiers, strangling their bodies with its electric fingers. Another bolt flew toward the neatly trimmed trees and climbed up its branches. Soon, all of the leaves roared in billowing flames.

"They're falling back!" Kristy said. She gave Zara a triumphant smile.

But their victory was short-lived.

Another stream of soldiers joined the fight. Five tanks rolled in behind them, their machine guns pointed straight at Zara. At the sight of them, dread shot through Zara, and the remaining sparks of lightning died in her hands. The entire weight of Fort Goering was crushing down on her, and she didn't know how much longer she could fight back — not against the fort's endless supply of soldiers and weapons. But she gritted her teeth and forced herself to think about her mother, the bravest woman she had ever known. Zara had to make her proud this night.

"Run!" Zara screamed at the others. "You have to get out!"

While Kristy and the other women stumbled to their feet, Zara gathered every last bit of strength she possessed and lifted her hands to conjure an enormous tornado, the biggest one she had ever created. She would fight to her very last breath if she had to. But before she could muster a breeze, she heard the rumble of engines clanging into her eardrums. For a second, Zara thought the Nazis had sent in more reinforcements, but then she saw a barrage of transport trucks crash into the barbed-wire fence that surrounded Fort Goering. More trucks followed suit until the fence crumpled underneath their huge tires, grinding the wire to shreds. The vehicle doors sprang open, and dozens of people spilled out of them. Most were armed with rifles, but a few carried machine guns.

They couldn't be Nazis. They were dressed in all black instead of olive-green uniforms. Zara had no idea who they were or why they had come until she heard their deafening war cry.

"Freedom, or death!"

17

Zara darted behind a concrete bench, her eyes stretched wide. This couldn't be possible. She was so sure the Alliance had called off the attack after Camp Hammerstein, but the proof was right in front of her.

Operation Burning Eagle was pushing forward.

"Freedom, or death! Freedom, or death!" the rebels shouted. Hundreds of them had poured from the trucks, followed by hundreds more from the woods. A handful of them shouted orders through megaphones to guide the rebels into battle, while others carried video cameras to capture the entire fight.

Hidden in her nook, Zara stared at them, amazed. The timing of all of this was incredible. Just when she needed the Alliance most, it had leapt in to assist her. If there wasn't gunfire surrounding her, she might have laughed at the sheer coincidence of it all.

As another line of trucks hurtled through the fence, three of the rebels entering the fight caught Zara's eye. One of them launched herself into the sky, throwing grenades at the incoming Nazis. Another lifted a tank with a mere wave of his hand, tossing it over his shoulder. And the last rebel breathed a cloud of fire at an incoming wave of troops.

They're Anomalies, Zara realized. There were others like her, fighting with the rebels.

Zara's awe was interrupted when an Alliance medic ran up to her. "Are you hurt?" the girl said quickly, ready to move on to the next patient if Zara didn't need her.

It took a few seconds for Zara's mouth to work. "How —"

"Let me take a look at your nose." Like clockwork, the medic got to work, opening her medical bag and spraying an antibacterial liquid onto Zara's face. A cooling sensation enveloped Zara's nose at once, and the pounding went away for the first time in days.

Ear-shattering shots burst around them. "The bombing at Camp Hammerstein," Zara shouted over it. "What happened?"

The medic brushed her blond hair from her face, revealing how young she was. She couldn't be much older than Zara. "The Nazis got tipped off somehow, but we only had a few fatalities. Our real push was here at Fort Goering."

"Did Garrison survive?"

The medic was already on her feet. "You're good to go!" Then she was off again, searching for another injured rebel before Zara could even say thank you.

After the medic disappeared into the battle, Zara shook away the shock of seeing the Alliance Anomalies and forced her legs toward the prison. Bolting through the jail's entrance, she found three guards lying facedown by the metal detectors, the floor slick with their blood. Zara rounded the corner, the stink of sewage and sweat blasting into her nostrils, but she pressed onward to the cells, where she found half of them already empty. The remaining prisoners shoved their arms through the bars, reaching for a *Kleinbauer* woman who had somehow managed to locate the prison keys. The woman unlocked another cell, hurling open the metal door right before the prisoners pushed themselves out. Zara was nearly knocked over by the stampede, but someone reached out for her, steadying her.

"Zara!" Uncle Red engulfed her in his arms. "Thank God!"

"Uncle Red?" she gasped out. She slumped against him, unable to hold back her tears. All of those hours of worrying, of fearing the worst, leached away into sweet relief.

"I thought they had killed you." His voice nearly broke apart as he pulled back to look at her. "How did you escape?"

"I don't have a lot of time to explain," said Zara. Thoughts of Sentinel Achen's dead eyes rose up in her head, but she shoved them aside. "The Alliance is outside! They didn't call off the mission after all. There are hundreds of them out there, maybe thousands."

The realization sank into Uncle Red's eyes. "We've been hearing the gunfire, but we didn't know what was going on."

More shots blared beyond the walls, followed by a grenade explosion that blew concrete chunks into the cells.

"Fill me in later!" Uncle Red said swiftly. "The building isn't safe. We need to get outside."

Another grenade detonated, and one of the cells caved in, shooting a cloud of dust around Zara and her uncle. Prisoners cried out, still trapped in their cells, and the woman with the key struggled to free them. Zara wanted to run to help them, but Uncle Red yanked her away.

"The building is going to crush us. We have to go!" he said.

They ran toward the main entrance, but Uncle Red stopped when he reached the fallen Nazis by the metal detectors. He stooped down to take one of their rifles, a pistol, and ammunition. With the smooth moves of a veteran soldier, he loaded the gun and tried to give her the pistol, but she refused it.

"I'll use my powers," said Zara.

"Absolutely not. We're behind enemy lines."

"It's too late for that." Her gaze ducked away from his. "I had to use them to escape the prison. But there are other Anomalies fighting for the Alliance, too. I saw them outside."

"How many Nazis saw you using your abilities?" Uncle Red swore when a third grenade shattered behind them, jarring his thoughts. "We'll deal with this later. We have to come up with a plan — where do we go from here?"

"We'll escape with the Alliance. They should have stolen the fort's weapons by now. We can't . . ." She swallowed, her thoughts overcome with their house, their farm. "We can't go home."

His lips spread into a grim line. "No, we can't." He gripped her shoulder. "The Alliance will take us in. We'll go to one of their safe houses."

With a quick kiss on her cheek, Uncle Red raced to the door and kicked it open, only to go still. Outside, they saw a full-on war.

Bombs went off like fireworks, chewing apart the fort's buildings bite by bite. More rebels swarmed into the fort by the minute, but they were met by fresh Nazi soldiers — along with the German Anomaly Division. A battle waged across the sky as a sentinel strangled the flying rebel Anomaly, although she twisted free and punched him in the throat. Another sentinel spat poison at the Alliance fighters, but the second Anomaly rebel batted him away with a massive oak that he had uprooted.

Uncle Red pushed Zara behind a statue of Führer Dieter, which already had its arms blasted off. "Don't stand in the open like that!" He aimed at two Nazis running toward them and took them out with one shot each. Zara watched the soldiers tumble onto the grass, finally understanding why her uncle had been considered the best shot in the Greenfield chapter. He didn't miss.

"You can stare at me later!" Uncle Red said. His rifle popped again and again. Both hits. "I need your help, Zara."

Snapping to attention, Zara held out her hands, urging the lightning to spring onto her skin, but then she heard something that made her blood freeze.

"Kill the Nazi! Kill Eckhart!" The chant floated above the din.

Zara's eyes jerked toward the sound. To her left, in the shadow of the Officers' Hall, Bastian was lying in a trampled flower bed, trying to fend off three prisoners. One of them held Bastian down while the others pummeled him with their fists, striking him again and again despite his attempts to throw them off. Terror poured over her — she had to stop them.

"Stay here!" she said to her uncle. "I'll be right back."

"Where do you think you're going?" he demanded.

She didn't answer him. Shaking free from her uncle's grip, Zara ran to save the Nazi cadet.

Zara gathered a flurry of wind and thrust it toward the prisoners beating Bastian. The wall of air knocked them off their feet, hurling them into a row of hedges. While the prisoners staggered out of the bushes, she reached Bastian and dragged him behind the bullet-ridden Officers' Hall. They would be safe from the barrage here, at least for a few seconds.

She rolled Bastian onto his back and shuddered at what she saw. Blood poured out of his nose, and painful scarlet marks had already formed along his jaw. "Bastian? Can you hear me?"

His left eye opened, but his right one remained swollen shut. "Zara?"

"It's me." A loud hiss jolted Zara's attention away from Bastian's injuries, and she cursed at what she saw. Thirty yards behind them, a Nazi soldier had launched a canister of tear gas, and the poison was drifting in their direction. She hurled another gust of wind toward it, but tendrils of gas snaked toward them anyway. "I need you to get up, okay?"

Woozy from his head wounds, Bastian staggered onto his feet and leaned heavily on Zara's shoulder. "What's happening out here? I got to the Officers' Hall early, but then I started hearing gunshots."

Zara couldn't tell him about the prison break or the Alliance attack with that tear gas snaking toward them. She scrambled for what they should do next. With Bastian hurt, she had to get him away from the fighting, but she didn't know where he would be safe. She couldn't take him home, either, in case his father had discovered what Bastian had done.

Before she could form a plan, though, Zara felt someone shove Bastian away from her. Images of Sentinel Achen flashed in her mind and her body went cold all over, but then her attacker showed his face.

"What are you doing?" Uncle Red asked, his pistol aimed at Bastian. "You could have gotten yourself killed! And for what? For this Nazi boy?"

"He's not a Nazi, Uncle Red!" Zara jumped between the gun and Bastian. Her worlds were colliding at the very worst moment.

Bastian stood behind her. "She's right," he said. "Mr. St. James —"

"Stay away from us, Eckhart!"

A second tear gas canister burst open by the Officers' Hall, spewing out its poisonous contents, and Zara's instincts took over. Grabbing them both by the arm, she called to the wind, hoping it would be strong enough to hold the three of them.

"Zara, no!" her uncle cried. "It's too much weight!"

She screamed for the wind to pull them up, climbing above the noxious gas and guiding them toward the dense woods surrounding the fort. But Zara's lungs huffed with each breath. She had pushed her powers to the limits tonight, and the toll of it was catching up to her fast. They wobbled midair, dropping ten feet.

"There's a field over there!" Uncle Red shouted at her, sensing she was about to collapse.

Blinking the spots from her eyes, she steered them to an empty training field that lay on the very edge of Fort Goering. Rebel bodies littered the red-stained grass, along with a few Nazis, but the fighting had moved to the center of the base, leaving the field deserted. The three of them tumbled onto the ground, arms and legs crashing against the hard earth. Zara's face smashed against a clump of weeds, and she sat up, coughing.

Bastian was the first to stand. "Zara!" He dashed over to check on her. When he saw that she was all right, he said, "Can you get up?"

At the same time, Uncle Red yanked her toward him. "I told you to stay away from her, Eckhart!"

Bastian held up his hands. "I'm not working for my father, Mr. St. James. Please, if you give me a chance —"

"Get back," Uncle Red snarled, stepping backward with Zara in tow. He kept his gun aimed at Bastian.

"Listen to me, Uncle Red!" Zara broke from his grip, panting. "Put the gun down."

"He's the Colonel's son!"

"And he's one of *us*." She placed herself between the gun and Bastian again, the only way to guarantee that her uncle wouldn't fire.

Bastian cautiously stepped up behind her. "I know this is confusing, Mr. St. James, but we better find cover soon. There's a tunnel not far from here that we can use to get out. After that, I'll answer any questions you have."

"*We?* What do you mean by 'we'?" Uncle Red's gaze stormed from Bastian to Zara. "Someone needs to explain what's going on. *Now.*"

They didn't have time for explanations, but Zara knew her stubborn uncle wouldn't budge until she answered him. "Bastian's grandfather was a member of the Widerstand, and Bastian wants to join the Alliance. You have to trust me on this, Uncle Red."

"The Widerstand?" Uncle Red gaped. "You honestly believe that?"

"I know what you must think of me," Bastian said, his hands still up in the air, "but what Zara said is true. My grandfather joined the Widerstand and was hanged for treason."

Uncle Red didn't lower his pistol.

"Bastian tried to save me from the hospital!" Zara said. "He gave me the key to escape. Why would he do that if he was a Nazi? If he was working for his father?"

The suspicion failed to ebb from Uncle Red's eyes. "We don't know where that 'escape tunnel' goes. It could be a ploy."

"It's not," said Bastian. "I'm not my father. He let my *Opa* die, and that's when I knew that enough was enough." He went on to explain his repeated attempts to gain Zara's trust and then how he had replicated the hospital key to break Zara out from the hospital. With each revelation, Uncle Red drew in a sharp breath.

When Bastian finished, Uncle Red looked ready to launch into a barrage of questions, but the sound of an approaching engine stopped him short. The three glanced frantically around the field.

"There's a truck coming this way!" Zara pointed behind her, where a Nazi supply truck rambled down the gravel path, zooming straight toward them. The soldiers must have seen Zara flying above the fort and had come to kill her.

"The tunnel is this way — follow me!" Bastian shouted.

The three of them ran, but the truck sped faster, its lights bright on their backs. Panic burst through Zara's veins. As soon as the truck was within range, the soldiers would start firing. She screamed for the wind to carry them upward, but only a tired breeze heeded her call.

Uncle Red fired at the truck's tires, but his magazine emptied out and the vehicle overtook them, swinging around to block them from the fence. Zara skidded to a stop. The soldier in the passenger seat shouted at them and waved his arms. But, strangely, he didn't carry a weapon.

Raising his pistol, Uncle Red aimed at the truck again, but the soldier held up his hands, like he was surrendering. He cried out to the driver.

"Alene, drop the disguises!"

Zara blinked at him. *Disguises?*

Both of the soldiers climbed out of the cab, never straying a few feet away from the other. "Zara, Redmond, it's me!" said the male soldier. "Don't shoot."

Bastian took Zara by the arm. "We need to go!" The opening to the tunnel lay just behind the supply truck. They could still make a run for it.

But Zara's jaw nearly unhinged at what happened next. The soldier named Alene shut her eyes, murmuring something under her breath, and the Nazis began to *transform*. The female soldier shrank in size, and her hair turned from a straw blond to a rust red. In only a few seconds, she had changed from a middle-aged soldier to a twenty-something slip of a girl.

At the same time, the male soldier shot up in height and his skin darkened from pale white to hazelnut. As his nose and chin stretched out, Zara sucked in her breath at the new face that he wore.

It couldn't be him. She was sure he had died at Camp Hammerstein. And yet, he was standing in front of her.

"Garrison?" she whispered.

18

Garrison limped forward, his hand clutching a soiled bandage on his shoulder. When he reached Zara, she saw that his clothes were wet with blood. "It's me. Alene and I had to disguise ourselves to break into the fort's weaponry."

Zara searched for words, but they wouldn't come. Her head reeled at what she had just seen. Finally, she spluttered, "You escaped the bombers at Camp Hammerstein?"

"We both did." Garrison nodded at his companion, who stared warily at Uncle Red and Bastian. "Celia Farragut didn't. One of our colleagues, Paul Murdock, is acting commander in chief for now. He's the one who carried out the attack here."

Both Uncle Red and Bastian looked as tongue-tied as Zara. "These disguises . . . how did . . . ?" said Uncle Red.

"That's thanks to Alene Silverman." Garrison gestured at the young woman next to him. "She has the ability to manipulate appearances — her own as well as others, as long as they're standing nearby. She's the one who infiltrated Channel Seven and got the Alliance attack broadcasted. We were in the armory when I got shot, and she dragged me out. She was taking me to the medics when I saw you flying over us." His eyes searched over Zara. "You didn't tell us you were an Anomaly."

"She's a Dual Anomaly," Uncle Red cut in. "And it was my call to keep her powers a secret. The fewer people who knew about it, the safer she was."

"A *Dual* Anomaly?" Garrison said, coughing. "What's your other power?"

"Lightning," Zara said tentatively. "I only just manifested that, though."

"You could've been an asset tonight if your uncle had told us —" Garrison grimaced and leaned on Alene for support.

"Time to go. Now," said Alene. Despite her small stature, her voice contained iron. "Get in the truck. We have to get him to a doctor."

"Actually, I'm a medic." Bastian took a step forward. "I can take a look at the wound."

Alene stiffened at Bastian's accent. Her eyes cooled even more. "Is this one with you?" she said sharply to Uncle Red. "This German?"

Uncle Red stared warily from Bastian to Alene and then to Zara. "He is," he said slowly. "He saved my niece's life."

"He wants to join the Alliance," Zara said to Alene. She walked toward Bastian, who was holding his breath. "He's no more a Nazi than I am."

Garrison groaned but managed to lift up his head. "We'll take him with us, Alene. Let's get into the truck."

"Exactly where are we going?" Uncle Red said. "What about the rest of the Alliance?"

"Get in and I'll explain," Garrison replied.

Relief washed over Zara, grateful that her uncle and Garrison had accepted Bastian without any bullets getting fired — at least for the moment. Four of them climbed into the back of the military truck, which was filled with black crates — weapons that Garrison and Alene must have stolen — while Alene went around to the driver's seat. Bastian helped Garrison lie down and got to work examining his shoulder, cleaning it, and sewing it with a medical kit that Alene had handed to him. When Bastian was finished, he urged his new patient not to move, but Garrison waved him off and started talking.

"We need to head out now. The mission at Fort Goering was a success," Garrison said while Zara, Bastian, and Uncle Red sat around him. "We've used ten trucks to clean out the fort's armory. That's more than we had hoped for."

"So what happens next?" said Uncle Red.

"Murdock will retreat with the rest of the rebels, but Alene and I have our own mission ahead of us."

Alene swiveled her head around. "That's classified information."

"We'll need Zara for this next mission as well. You two are the only Anomalies we have left. Kenneally is dead, and Schmidt was shot twice. And we don't know what happened to Zhang. We have no other choice."

Alene sighed but nodded. "Fill them in on what's going on, then," she said while she started the engine. Bastian pointed her toward the tunnel out of the fort, explaining how it was one of the escape routes that only his father and his officers knew about. As Alene guided the vehicle through the dark tunnel, Uncle Red turned back to Garrison.

"What does Zara have to do with this mission of yours?" said Uncle Red. "Is the Alliance still planning on storming Neuberlin?"

"Yes, but it's more than that. Murdock will lead the siege on the capital — that plan is a go. But while the rebels sweep through Neuberlin, Alene and I are going straight to the White House."

"The White House?" Uncle Red said incredulously. "You're heading straight into the Nazi hornet's nest?"

"We're doing it for good reason." Garrison coughed again but soldiered on with his explanation. "Right before the attack on Fort Goering, we got a message from one of our sources in Berlin. Apparently, the Führer is throwing a gala to celebrate the anniversary of Nazi rule in the Territories — and the gala will be held at the White House. We think this last-minute 'celebration' is another desperate attempt to throw off the Soviets. To remind them that the Empire is still strong."

"Dieter is coming to the Territories, then?" Bastian said, steadying himself as the truck bumped through the tunnel. "And what is this attack on Neuberlin?"

"I should've told you earlier, Bastian," Zara cut in, realizing that she had never filled him in on Operation Burning Eagle. She hadn't thought it was necessary after Camp Hammerstein; she had assumed the Alliance would call everything off. And so, very quickly, she explained the operation to Bastian, or at least what Garrison had told her during his first visit to the farmhouse. "But I don't know what the Alliance plans to do at the White House." She glanced at Garrison. "What's going on exactly?" *And what does it have to do with me?* she thought.

"Like I said, Dieter is throwing a gala for all of his high-ranking officers and diplomats. He has already been in Neuberlin for weeks now, in fact, ever since the Reds pushed into the borderlands. His advisers worried that Premier Volkov would try to bomb Berlin, so they sent Dieter across the ocean to where they thought he'd be safest. He has been tucked away at the White House ever since."

"Will Dieter's double be at this gala?" said Uncle Red, both of his brows knitted together.

"Yes, the double will attend the event while the real Führer is hidden in Reichsmarschall Baldur's residential wing. He's still very ill, from what our sources tell us."

"When will the gala take place? Next week?" Uncle Red asked.

"Tomorrow night, actually," said Garrison. "That's when we'll launch the biggest mission the Alliance has ever undertaken."

"And what's that?" Zara asked, the hairs on her neck prickling.

Garrison's eyes locked onto hers. "We take out the Eagle. We assassinate the Führer."

Zara drew in a sharp breath.

Beside her, Bastian froze. "You want to do *what*?"

The Alliance had never tackled something on this level before. Or with so little time to plan. Yes, they had killed Nazis and overrun two military bases, but killing the leader of the Empire? And that wasn't all. If Zara had heard Garrison correctly, he wanted her to go on this mission with him. A thrill coursed through her, followed by a stomach-twisting fear. An operation like this would be the biggest thing she had ever done in her life — and the deadliest.

"We'll kill the Führer at the gala," Garrison repeated, as if it were that simple. "We'll record the whole thing and broadcast it on national television. We need to do this if we want to start a revolution."

"But you told us yourself that Dieter has been using a double," Uncle Red said, gripping onto Zara as the truck hit a bump. "Killing the double leaves Dieter alive."

"That's why we'll take out both of them. First the double. Then we'll find Dieter himself."

Bastian hastily wiped his hands on a towel and stood up straight, despite the moving truck. "This plan is suicide! We're going to be fugitives if we go through with it."

"Sit down!" Alene said. With both hands on the steering wheel, she shot him a frosty glare. "Frankly, we don't need you on the mission tomorrow anyway." Her head snapped back toward the road. "And by the way, you're already a fugitive — and a traitor — if you haven't noticed."

"I'm not a —" Bastian's eyes flared wide, the weight of her words setting in. He didn't finish his sentence.

"Please, Bastian." Zara took him by the wrist, tugging on it until he sat on the floor again.

He raked his fingers through his hair. "We can't go back, can we?" he whispered. "To Greenfield."

"No, what if your father found out about what you've done? He would kill you."

"But my mother . . ."

Zara went numb. She hadn't thought about that. There was no way Bastian could return to his mom, not after he had openly aided the Alliance. He couldn't go home. . . . And she couldn't, either. As the truck rumbled north, it took her farther and farther away from the only home she had ever known. She had been born in that farm-house; she had worked its lands since she was a girl in plaits. Zara's throat cinched tight, but she swallowed the lump building inside of it. She had Uncle Red with her, at least. But Bastian was alone.

She reached for his hand, setting her fingers on top of his. Warmth pulsed up her arm, so different from her powers, but Bastian pulled his hand free and moved toward the end of the truck, where he sat down and drew his knees against his chest. Zara's face flamed with embarrassment.

"Leave him be," Uncle Red said, but she followed after Bastian anyway.

She sat in front of him, waiting for him to say something, but he didn't look up at her.

"I'm sorry," she said quietly. Guilt sank into the bottom of her stomach. She knew Bastian wanted to join the Alliance, but she didn't expect that choice would break him apart from his mother so soon. He probably didn't, either. Tonight, he had only thought that he was helping her escape from the hospital. Not leaving behind his entire life. "Maybe we can get a message to your mother somehow. Or we could find a phone and call her."

"That would be too dangerous. I couldn't put us at risk like that."

"Then we'll send a letter. We won't put any return address on it. That way —"

He still hadn't met her gaze. "I knew what I was doing by joining the Alliance. I knew I might have to leave her one day." Anguish overwhelmed his features. "That was the choice I made."

Zara couldn't look at him, not with her throat tightening again. If she ever had to leave her uncle behind, never to see him again . . . She couldn't do it. The mere thought of it ripped her apart inside. But for Bastian, this was his new reality.

"I wish there was something I could do or —" she started.

"It's not your fault." He was quiet for a long moment. "I just thought I'd get the chance to tell her good-bye."

From the front of the truck, Alene called out, "We're a few hours away from Neuberlin. You better get some sleep if you can."

Zara started to move away from Bastian. "I'll let you get some rest. We've all had a long night."

He caught her hand, and she froze. He had pulled away from her only a minute before, but now his fingers curled around hers, gently seeking them. "You don't have to go. I — I don't mind."

Zara could only nod, and she didn't let go of his hand. Tingles spread from her palm, climbing up her wrist and arm. "I'm sure your mom is okay. She's safe."

He squeezed her hand. "Safer than we are, at least."

19

They drove north, passing soybean farms, sagging houses, and a handful of Nazi factories that spluttered white smoke into the sky. Despite the bumps in the road, Zara managed to drift asleep, but she blinked awake at once when the truck lurched to a stop.

Eyelids heavy, she yawned in the darkness. According to the vehicle's clock, it was three in the morning. Her body, sore and tender from the battle at the fort, yearned for more rest, but Alene told everyone to move. As Zara stretched out a kink in her neck, she realized Bastian had rested his hand over hers during the ride north. Very quietly, she glanced at him. Her gaze skirted over his profile, no longer seeing the resemblance between him and his father. In the last week, she had seen courage in Bastian's eyes and heard a gentleness in his voice, traits that the Colonel could never possess. And when Bastian smiled, there was no cruelty there. It was a smile that reached deep into his eyes, a smile that made Zara's breath tighten whenever she saw it.

Bastian shifted in his sleep, and his curls fell over his forehead. Zara was tempted to brush them aside, but then she heard her uncle awaken at the other end of the truck. Flustered, she untangled her hand from Bastian's and flushed at her ridiculous thoughts. They were heading to war soon — on a mission to kill the Führer. She had to stop thinking about Bastian in *this* way. This hope in her heart, this flutter in her stomach — she had to quash it before it bloomed even bigger.

Bastian stirred next to her. His eyes opened slowly, and when he saw Zara sitting next to him, those dimples of his appeared. But then he noticed the rough canvas of the truck covering, and the dimples vanished. The memories of last night must have crashed through his mind.

"Where are we?" he said, stretching out his long legs.

Alene opened the back of the truck, and the blinking light of a lamppost filtered into Zara's eyes. Beyond the door, she saw a row of tenement buildings crumbling around them and broken sidewalks lining the road. Graffiti covered every surface in view.

"We're on the outskirts of Neuberlin," Alene said. A gold necklace peeped out from her bloodied shirt, and Zara noticed its shiny pendant — a Star of David. *She must be one of the last Jews in the Territories*, Zara thought, thinking immediately of Molly and her family. "We'll meet with one of our contacts here."

Zara followed Bastian out of the truck and noticed Alene watching every one of his moves, still wary of him. After Bastian had fallen asleep a couple of hours earlier, Zara had asked Garrison for more details about assassinating the Führer, but he had hesitated to say anything more, not with Bastian within earshot. Zara had told him and Alene repeatedly that they could trust Bastian — that he had risked his life for her — but Garrison had pointed out that Bastian remained an unknown factor. And Uncle Red had agreed with him.

"He's unproven," Uncle Red had said while the truck veered onto a side road to avoid any Nazi checkpoints. Before she could protest, he had held up his hand. "I'm not saying that I *don't* trust him, but I haven't seen enough evidence that I can."

"He *will* prove it to you. I know he will."

"You should have told me about him sooner, Zara."

She had nearly rolled her eyes. "Like that would have gone over well."

"You lied to me, and now Bastian could be a liability to us."

"He's giving up his whole life to join the Alliance!" She had wanted to shout at him, but she hadn't wanted to wake Bastian or Garrison, who had started dozing. "And Bastian checked on you after I hit you with that bolt of lightning. He *helped*."

Uncle Red had been taken aback. "You didn't tell me that."

"Because I knew you would flip out about it." She had tried to tamp down the frustration in her voice. "Both of us would still be in those cells at Fort Goering if it hadn't been for Bastian."

"I'm not saying he isn't resourceful —"

"You only see the Eckhart in him, but he's nothing like his father. Just like I'm nothing like mine."

Uncle Red had gone quiet for a long moment, his gaze scanning over Bastian's sleeping form. Then he had surprised Zara with what he said next. "No, I suppose he isn't."

"He gave up everything to come with us. His mother. His home. He didn't realize he was doing it when he came to the jail to free me, but he's accepted it. He knows he can't go back." She had swallowed hard as she thought of her own home, the house and the farm and the land her family had worked on for generations. Despite her misery, she had said, "At least we have each other."

"That's all that matters," Uncle Red had said, but Zara had heard the pain in his voice. They couldn't go back to Greenfield, either, not when they were traitors. Zara's head had felt heavy, bowed with exhaustion and a heart-twisting sadness. She had wanted to curl up in her bed, nestled in the blanket her mother had sewn for her, but she might never sleep in that bed again.

"What'll happen to the farm?" she had whispered.

"I don't know," Uncle Red had said, his voice tinged with sorrow. "I just don't know."

It could be months until they saw their land again. Years even. But Zara decided then and there that she would do anything to reclaim their home one day. If she survived the mission at the White House . . .

Uncle Red and Bastian helped Garrison out of the truck. Thankfully, Garrison's shoulder had stopped bleeding, although he grimaced whenever he moved it. Alene led them toward a two-story factory and into the shadows of a sign that read, VEGA TOBACCO AND CIGARS, EST. 1893. The factory was silent at this time of night; the workers wouldn't start their shift for hours.

"My friend Dominic owns this building," Garrison explained. "His family has been a part of the Alliance since the very start. We've been planning to rendezvous with him after the raid on Fort Goering."

"Will we be safe here?" Bastian said. He chewed his lip as he glanced at the abandoned apartments and the rubble littering the street, remnants of the long-ago war bombings. Zara doubted that he had ever stepped foot in a place like this. It wasn't his fault, of course, but a Nazi upbringing would have shielded him from this destruction, from this poverty.

"We'll be fine," Alene said curtly. "Let's get going. I don't like being out in the street."

Once they reached the factory entrance, the door opened to reveal a heavy-set Latino man with a salt-and-pepper beard that engulfed his face in a furry mask. He hurried toward Garrison with his arms outstretched, burying him in a tight hug.

"I was starting to think the worst," said the man that must have been Dominic. "Murdock contacted us after the attack and said you should have gotten here over an hour ago."

"We took the long way, just in case anyone was following us." Garrison gave Bastian a look. Turning back to Dominic, he made some quick introductions to the others. "Dominic's the one who first told us about the gala. He has been helping us organize this last attack."

Dominic ushered them into the building. "I'm sure all of you are tired and hungry. Let's head inside and I'll have someone dispose of that truck. I told my workers not to come in today, so we'll have the building for our preparations."

"Any news from Fort Goering?" said Alene.

A smile spread across Dominic's face. "A victory! We ransacked half of the fort's armory before the Nazis regrouped and Murdock ordered everyone to fall back. Communication has been spotty since then. Many of the rebels are still on the run, but a good number followed Murdock's orders and have arrived in Neuberlin. We took in some of the wounded, but everyone else is lying low for now in the safe houses around the city."

"What about the C4?" said Garrison.

"Saved and ready for the attack. Come see."

They entered the main floor of the factory, and Zara immediately felt tiny. The ceiling soared forty feet above her, making each foot-step and each word an echo. Long tables spread neatly across the factory floor, and Zara assumed this was where the workers rolled cigars by hand. Dominic beckoned them down a flight of rickety stairs to the basement below, where stacks upon stacks of dried tobacco greeted them. Beyond the last pile of sweet-scented leaves, Zara saw dozens of men and women — rebels, by the looks of it — lying on cots or blankets spread over the floor. Some had bullet wounds, while others had gashes covering their bodies. A harried-looking nurse tried to attend to all of them.

"I can help treat them. I'm a medic," said Bastian. As he looked over the wounded, something shifted in him, like when he had treated Uncle Red's burns.

Dominic's tired eyes lit up. "We'd be grateful. My cousin Sofia has been tending to the injured and hasn't slept in hours. You should get some food in you first, though."

"I can get started right away," said Bastian. "Eating can wait."

"You really should eat something," Zara protested.

"I *need* to work," he said so quietly that only she could hear. "To get my mind off of things."

Zara didn't think starving himself was a very smart idea, but Dominic brought Bastian over to meet Sofia and directed the rest of them toward the kitchen around the corner. Each of them took a bowl of hot beef stew and sat around a small foldout table. Before anyone could even take a bite, Uncle Red started asking about the assassination attempt.

"What I don't understand is why we have to kill Dieter. He'll be dead in months," Uncle Red asked, not touching his food. "What's the point of killing him now?"

"The point is the statement we'll make," Alene said between chews. "Can you imagine the support we'll receive if the Alliance takes down the leader of the Nazi Empire?"

"It's not only that." Garrison took slow slips of water. "If we take out the Führer, the Soviets are bound to go to war with the Nazis. It's the opening they've been waiting for."

"So you want to ally with the Reds?" Uncle Red said.

"No, not if we can help it, but a war between the Nazis and the Soviets would work in the Alliance's favor. It'll force the Germans to fight on both sides of the Atlantic — and that will give us a chance to take back some power."

Uncle Red took a moment to digest the information, and Zara knew Garrison had struck a chord in him. "What's the plan, then? And what does Zara have to do with it?"

Garrison and Alene exchanged glances before Garrison continued. "We'll infiltrate the gala tonight. Alene will disguise us as the Japanese ambassador Nakamura and his personal entourage. He's over eighty and is recovering from prostate cancer. That means he turns down nearly all social functions."

"There's no guarantee that he'll turn down this one," Uncle Red pointed out.

"True, but we'll take our chances. Nakamura will be our best bet, since everyone else will most likely accept the invitation."

"How exactly will Alene 'disguise' us?"

"As long as we stand very close together, I can manipulate other people's appearances. Three or four at most," said Alene.

"That's why we can only take four people on this mission," said Garrison. "Me, Alene, and two others. We had hoped to bring two more of our Anomaly fighters, but they're either dead, missing, or injured." He looked across the table at Zara. "That's where Zara comes in."

"You want to bring my niece with you," Uncle Red said flatly. He pushed his bowl of stew away from him. "To the White House."

"If they want me to go, I'll go," said Zara, her eyes drilling into her uncle's. Despite the fear coursing through her, she knew that Garrison was right. The Alliance had a chance to take out the Führer himself — and she could help them do that.

"Actually, we want both of you to come," said Garrison.

That made Uncle Red do a double take. *"Me?"*

"I know of your exploits before Mission Metzger. You know tactics and strategy. You know your way around a gun."

"There are plenty of other rebels who know the same things that I do," Uncle Red said, flustered.

"Sure, but you're the only one who has a niece with dual powers. And I doubt you'd let her come with us if you didn't tag along, too."

Uncle Red shook his head. "Zara just manifested her new power. She needs more time to control it."

"I *can* control it," Zara said. *Mostly*, she thought. There was no way she could sit this mission out. Finally, she could bring justice to her mother, to Mrs. Talley, to Molly. How could she say no to this?

Zara looked her uncle in the eye. "I'm going with them." Before he could say anything else, she added, "I want you to come with me, too. We'll do it together."

"This has to be suicide." There was so much uncertainty in Uncle Red's voice, so Zara pressed harder.

"If we don't go to the White House, the Nazis will keep coming after us. We're fugitives already. We can't go home." She swallowed as she thought about Greenfield and their farm. "We have to finish what Mom started."

"She died for what she believed in. If that happened to you, too —"

"Then come with me. I have to do this, for Mom."

Uncle Red stared blankly at the table and said nothing for an achingly long minute. His gaze traveled from Alene to Garrison and finally to Zara, where it came to rest.

"If I can't stop you, then I don't have a choice." He nodded at Garrison. "Count me in."

"Really?" Zara breathed.

"Count us both in."

Garrison explained the rest of the mission while their stew turned cold in their bowls. Apparently, getting into the White House — tricky as that was — would be the easiest part of the plan.

Once they arrived at the White House and passed through the metal detectors, they would keep a low profile until the official ceremony started at seven, at which point Dieter's double would offer a speech. At seven-fifteen, the Alliance rebels would strike from the Hofer Street entrance, due west of the White House. Using Dominic's C4 explosives, the rebels would break through the electrified fence and storm the gala, drawing attention away from the real mission: the attack on the Führer.

"That's why we told everyone to head to Neuberlin after the attack on Fort Goering," Garrison said. "There will be soldiers stationed throughout the White House grounds, over a hundred maybe, not to mention the Corps of Four. If the four of us want a fighting chance just to reach the Führer, then we need the Alliance attack to distract some of those guards."

Garrison went on to explain that once the C4 went off, Zara would use her lightning to destroy Dieter's double, which would be captured on camera by the incoming rebels. Uncle Red bristled at the suggestion, saying how he should take on that responsibility, but Garrison shook his head.

"Even if we could smuggle a gun into the White House for you — and we're working on that — there's too much of a chance that you'd miss the target," said Garrison.

"I don't think you've seen me shoot," Uncle Red countered.

"Look, I'm not doubting your abilities, but we have to maximize our chances of success, and Zara's power is our best option right now. I'll need you and Alene to protect Zara so she can take out the double."

Uncle Red didn't seem pleased with this plan, but he didn't protest it further. "What will you be doing, then?" he asked Garrison.

"I'll split off before the speeches start and head for the White House basement. During the building's renovation a few years ago, an elevator was added that leads from a linen closet in the residential wing to a safe room, in case Neuberlin came under attack. My job will be to shut off the elevator by destroying its control box in the basement. That'll trap Dieter in his room, where the rest of you will find him."

"What about your shoulder?" said Uncle Red. "That's going to slow you down."

"We've got no other choice. About a year ago, Farragut tasked me to find out everything I could about the White House after the renovations. She thought we might have to tackle a mission like this one day, so I memorized the new schematics. I'm the only one who will know my way around down there."

The rest of the plan was more straightforward. After Zara, Alene, and Uncle Red conquered the Corps of Four (which didn't sound the least bit straightforward to Zara), they would locate the Führer in

Baldur's residential wing, a key piece of intelligence passed on from one of Garrison's contacts. Finally, the three of them would coordinate the assassination of Dieter — the crowning moment of the mission — before escaping through any window or door they could find. Under Alene's disguises, they would flee to an Alliance safe house.

By the time Garrison had finished laying out the plan, his voice had gone hoarse and his eyelids were heavy with exhaustion. Zara's stomach was churning at everything he had told them. In about fifteen hours, she would be at the White House, the Führer in her sights — and the success of the mission would depend on her. On her lightning. On her wind. Alene could get them into the White House and her uncle was a great shot if Garrison managed to smuggle a gun to the ceremony, but her dual abilities had to carry them through it. Fear jackknifed through her. What if she failed? What if she couldn't protect Uncle Red?

"Hey, look at me," her uncle said to her. They were alone at the table now. Garrison had left to rebandage his wound while Alene went to greet a new batch of rebels who had arrived. "It's going to be a long and tough night. The toughest we'll ever go through, I'm sure."

"I know," she said. She wondered if he was going to talk her out of the mission. After all, it would be the least cautious thing that they had ever done.

"There'll be gunfire and bombs. Every Nazi in that building is going to try to kill us. But you know what?"

He was only making her feel worse, so Zara only shrugged.

"We've already survived that yesterday. So now, we'll do it again, and I'll be with you every step of the way. We're going to do this together."

Overwhelmed, tears clung to Zara's eyes as he pulled her into a hug. "I know you don't want me to go."

"No, I don't — and I think I'm a little insane for even agreeing to this — but this could be our chance to take down the Nazis. And even I don't think we can pass that up." He released her but kept a hand on her shoulder. "Now we both better get some sleep. I don't want you passing out during the Führer's speech."

She smiled as she wiped her eyes. "Uncle *Red*."

While Uncle Red searched for a couple of cots for them to lie down on, Zara filled a clean bowl with stew and retraced her steps back to the makeshift infirmary. Fatigue had filled her from her head to her toes, but she couldn't sleep until she checked on Bastian. When she reached the infirmary, she found him curled up on a cot in the corner, a blanket thrown over his shoulders, fast asleep. Not wanting to wake him, Zara left the bowl on the floor next to him.

"Zara?"

Zara glanced behind her, blinking in the dim lights of the factory. "Kristy?" she whispered. She hadn't expected to see Kristy's face again, especially not here in Neuberlin. "When did you get here?"

"My mom and I just arrived." A layer of dirt and dried blood had seeped into Kristy's clothes, and her face had taken on a ghostly pallor, but otherwise she didn't look injured. "Some of the rebels drove us out of the fort, but our truck broke down ten miles outside of the city limits. We walked the rest of the way."

"There's food in the kitchen around the back." Zara wasn't sure what else to say. She was glad that Kristy had survived the attack, but that didn't change their past. With a quick pat on Kristy's shoulder, Zara was about to go look for her uncle, but Kristy kept talking.

"I — I owe you an apology. The way I treated you at school was . . ."

Zara looked back at her, surprised. She hadn't expected this from Kristy. Not now. Probably not ever. She had dreamed about this moment for so long, but now that it was here she only wanted to sleep.

"I'm sorry," Kristy finally said in a shaky voice. Zara waited for her to say more, but evidently this was the best that Kristy could do. It was far from enough, but Zara was too tired to argue.

"Get some sleep. I'm sure you and your mom are exhausted."

Kristy wrapped her arms around herself, looking like a girl half her age. "What are we supposed to do now? We can't go back to Greenfield."

"Stay with the Alliance. Fight with us. I can't tell you what to do, but I'm sure you'll figure it out." Her answer was cold, perhaps, but it was the best that Zara could do — and it would have to be enough. "Good luck."

And she meant it.

As the assassination ticked closer, the hours blurred together. Zara managed to sneak in a few hours of sleep before Garrison roused her to train in an empty section of the factory. With Uncle Red's help, she worked most of the day on harnessing her lightning, controlling its growth, and steering its release until her uncle was satisfied.

After an early dinner of onion soup and hard bread, Alene steered Zara to the women's locker room to give her their mission uniform. The clothes and gear were laid out on a bench: a slim black shirt and cargo pants, combat boots and a bulletproof vest, and a hand-held video camera to tape the assassination.

"Dominic found the gear for us," said Alene, who had already changed. Her clothing was identical to Zara's, except she had a pistol holstered on her belt. "Try it on."

Zara's brow furrowed. "I doubt we can get close to the White House dressed like this."

A ghost of a smile trailed on Alene's lips. She narrowed her eyes and, in only a second, her T-shirt and cargo pants transformed into a silky blue gown with glittering rhinestones dotting the straps. "How about like this? Think they'll let us in now?"

Zara had seen Alene transform once before but witnessing it again made her head spin a little. "Can you really do that for all of us?"

"If we stay close."

"You mean we have to touch one another?"

"No, not touching. Just standing close together, about three feet apart at the very max." Her smile erased as quickly as it appeared. "That's the key. We can't drift too far away from one another until the rebels invade the White House and we can blend in with them. Otherwise our cover will get blown in seconds."

Stay close to Alene, Zara repeated in her mind. It would be her mantra at the gala; she shuddered to think what would happen if she forgot it.

"What about the vest and your pistol?" said Zara. "Doesn't the White House have metal detectors?"

"The vest has ceramic plates, so we'll get through just fine. As for the pistol, it's for your uncle and I've got it handled," Alene said. "Now, quick, quick. We have to move out."

Zara got dressed in the gear, grateful to change out of her sweaty hospital clothes, and she followed Alene out of the locker room for one last briefing with Garrison. But when they passed the infirmary,

Bastian hurried toward them, calling out Zara's name. Alene frowned at his intrusion, but she glanced at Zara and said, "Five minutes. Find us in the kitchen."

"Are you leaving for the gala soon?" Bastian asked Zara when he reached her. Bags hung under his eyes, dark and hollow, as if he had been living in a war zone. In a way, he had. "I've been hoping to find you all day."

He's been looking for me? Zara thought. Despite the weariness in her bones, she brightened a little at his words. Ever since they had arrived at the factory, she had been overwhelmed with training and adrenaline and a chest-knotting fear that refused to go away, but hearing him say that made her heart a little less heavy.

"We leave in an hour," she told him. "How are you holding up here?"

"It has been busy, much busier than Opa's old clinic," he admitted. He fought off a yawn. "But I'm fine, really. Dominic's cousin Sofia relieved me for a couple hours so I could sleep."

Zara figured he was putting on a brave face for her. This factory was a far stretch from what Bastian was used to: a comfortable home, his very own car, hired help to take care of every last worry. But in the last twenty-four hours, his life had transformed into something unrecognizable — and Zara could see it in the dazed look in his eyes, the slump of his shoulders.

"I'm much more worried about you," Bastian went on. He stepped closer to her, and Zara could smell the antiseptic on his jacket. "The White House, this attack."

"We'll be fine," Zara said, even though her hands wouldn't stop shaking. She knew the chances were against her tonight — the odds of success must have been one in a million — but she wouldn't back out of it now. Not with the Führer at her fingertips. Now it

212

was her turn to put on a brave face for Bastian. "I'm a Dual Anomaly, remember?"

Despite her attempt to lighten the mood, the worry didn't retreat from Bastian's face. "I could go with you. With my training —"

"No, you have to stay at the infirmary. They need you here." Zara knew that Bastian couldn't go with them — Alene would never even consider it — but she warmed at the thought that he was willing to go with them anyway, especially after everything he had been through.

"Is Garrison sure that the Nazis will even go through with this gala? The raid on Fort Goering just happened."

"They haven't canceled it yet," Zara said. Garrison had worried about this very same thing, but the Führer must have been more concerned about the Reds. If the gala was canceled, Premier Volkov could take that as a sign that the Nazis had a real rebellion on their hands. That the Nazis' hold on the Territories was weakening. "And we can't pass up this chance to kill the Führer."

Bastian's eyes drifted over Zara, sweeping from the top of her head to the combat boots on her feet. His face hovered above hers. For a split second she thought he was going to kiss her, but he cleared his throat instead. "You're far braver than I am, Zara St. James." Admiration glinted in his amber gaze.

Zara dipped her chin down so he wouldn't see her reddening face. Had she wanted him to kiss her? The thumping of her heart answered that question for her, but it didn't matter now. She was about to leave for the White House, for the assassination; she refused to think about an almost kiss. She needed her head in the mission, and *only* the mission.

"I better go," she said, about to turn away, but Bastian caught her by the shoulders.

"Wait a second."

Zara waited, even though she had to go. She felt Bastian's fingers dig into her shoulder, ever so gently.

"Be careful tonight. Please, Zara," he said.

"I will."

"If anything happened to you . . ."

Zara stared up at him. He had never looked at her like this before, like he was memorizing the planes of her face. Did he . . . did he really care so much?

"I'll be careful. I promise," she said.

"I'll hold you to it." Then he pulled her into him, nestled in his arms. For a second, Zara was so startled that her arms hung limply at her sides, but then she pressed against him, giving into the flutters in her stomach. Closing her eyes, she breathed in deep, inhaling the scent of him that lingered underneath the antiseptic smell. He released her, his pale cheeks a bright red.

"I'll see you when I get back," she managed to get out.

Then it was time for her to go.

20

Despite Garrison's warning to keep their heads down, Zara snuck in a few glances at the city anyway, letting her eyes feast upon the splendor of Neuberlin. She thought she would feel disgust at this brick-and-marble town, especially with the Third Reich flags flying on every building, but she couldn't peel her gaze from the shining capital.

The city was — in one word — grand. Newly paved streets ran underneath Zara's feet, smooth as fresh butter, and fifty-story buildings climbed to her left and right. As they ventured deeper into the capital, they passed department stores with names like Kaufhof and Alsterhaus that featured block-long window displays of silk ball gowns and sharp-cut suits. Cafés dotted the busy roads, too, offering delicacies like chai tea and powdered donuts with raspberry filling. The heavenly sweet scent drifted into her nose, making her taste buds clamor for one bite, even though she could never afford such extravagances.

And then there were the cars. Zara had never seen the likes of them before: red Mercedes convertibles alongside black Porsche SUVs with platinum rims. The vehicles were shined to a gloss, no dents or scratches to be seen.

So this is how the Neuberliners live, Zara thought. While she and her uncle labored on their farm, the Nazis sipped tiny cups of espresso and drove their newly washed cars.

Now the disgust rolled through her.

Soon, they entered the center of the capital. Gigantic German museums — once known as the Smithsonian — flanked Zara on both sides: the Museum of Industry, the Museum of Nazi Militaria, the Archives of the Territories. If she looked behind her, she could also see the shrine to Adolf Hitler that was built over the razed Capitol building and decorated with enormous Nazi flags waving across its entrance. *Hopefully, it won't be a shrine much longer,* Zara thought fiercely.

"We can't dawdle," Uncle Red said to her. "Alene needs you to stay close."

Zara hurried to catch up, murmuring an apology to Alene, whose brows were furrowed in concentration to keep them all disguised. Thanks to her ability, they had walked the last few miles looking like a wealthy entourage of Japanese emissaries strolling through the city. Whenever Zara caught her reflection in a store window, her eyes gaped to find herself five inches taller and her body clad in a floor-length velvet gown, the darkest of burgundies. A pair of satin heels adorned her feet as well, with a cluster of green jewels along its toe cap. The prettiest — and most impractical — shoes she had ever seen.

The rest of the group was similarly dressed: a violet silk dress for Alene, a navy suit for Garrison, and a black tuxedo for Uncle Red, who had taken on the appearance of the Japanese ambassador. Zara's eyes darted up and down the boulevard, wondering if any of the Germans could see through their disguises, but she only received polite nods from the pedestrians who passed them by.

They turned onto Schicklgruber Avenue, named for Adolf Hitler's paternal grandmother, and Zara's stomach quickly tied into a knot. A few blocks ahead, she spotted the bright green lawn of the White House, along with the electrified fence that encircled the property. The fence had been installed after a failed assassination attempt in

1975, and as they drew close to it Zara made sure to keep her distance. Every time she strayed too near the fence, she could hear the hum of the voltage.

"All right," Garrison said in a hushed tone, his lips hardly moving. "Remember, if we get separated, make your way back to Dominic's factory. If that has been compromised, head to our headquarters in West Virginia. It's ten miles south of Wardensville and built right underneath the Hotel Liberty, 150 Corona Road. Go to the lobby and tell them that 'the birds chime at midnight.' That'll get you inside the bunker."

Zara tucked away that bit of information inside her head before they shuffled toward the White House checkpoint, where a slew of armed guards scanned ID cards and ushered people through the metal detectors.

"What about our IDs?" Zara whispered.

"Alene and I have it covered," Garrison whispered back. "Stay calm."

Sweat beaded on her palms as they edged closer to the checkpoint. Chewing her lip, Zara watched the gray-haired woman in front of them — an Austrian diplomat, perhaps? — present her passport and walk through the metal detector.

Then it was their turn. Zara's fingers clenched around her uncle's arm, and she felt him suck in a deep breath.

"Identification, please," one of the guards said in German.

"Here are our passports." Alene smiled. Reaching into her pocket, she took out several tattered pieces of paper and handed them to the guard.

Zara's heart went from doing somersaults to double flips. Old pieces of paper? That was their plan? The urge to flee climbed up her legs, but the guard only nodded at Uncle Red.

"Welcome, Ambassador Nakamura," he said. "Please remove any belts or wallets or metal items from your person and place them in the bin."

Zara waited for him to scrutinize their "passports" again, but he had moved on to the next guests in line. A bit stunned, she watched Alene and Garrison pass through the detectors without a problem. Then it was Uncle Red's turn. He took off his belt, and Zara noticed that Alene had disguised his holstered pistol as a very large belt buckle. It was a risky move, but the guards merely ushered them through the detector and handed the belt back to Uncle Red. Against all odds, Alene's plan had worked.

Zara released her pent-up breath, but she knew the dangers were far from over. Along the path, she saw a dozen uniformed soldiers standing at attention, ready to spring into action if anything went awry.

Looking up from the cobbled path, Zara almost stumbled at the sight of the White House, which loomed ahead, shining like a beacon in the evening light. The house itself was enormous — the recent renovation had doubled it in size — and equally stunning, from the handsome marble pillars to the lush flower boxes in the windows and finally to the circular fountain that stood on the front lawn. The tinkle of bubbling water flowed into Zara's ears.

After the Nazis won the war and set about changing Washington, DC, to Neuberlin, Adolf Hitler originally wanted to demolish the White House and build a mansion to his liking. But once he toured the building, he became partial to its stately ceilings and fine wood floors. *It will be a fine little home,* Adolf had told his staff, who were tasked with burning all of the "filthy American artwork" and replacing it with pieces of fine art that hadn't made it into the Führermuseum he had founded in Austria.

One step at a time, they ascended the stairs to the White House and entered the grand foyer side by side. Zara's eyes widened at the stateliness of the space. High above their heads, a magnificent chandelier sparkled and shone, comprised of thousands of pieces of delicate glass. And down by her feet, her shoes were greeted by the finest white marble, polished to gleam like a mirror. She wondered how many cleaning girls had hunched over the cold stone to achieve such a shine. No doubt they had spent hours at the task only to receive a few meager coins for their work.

A waiter approached their group with a silver tray of champagne flutes in hand. Zara took a glass to be polite, but her lips didn't touch the fizzing liquid. Instead, she fixed her attention on the enormous oil painting that hung on the right wall, depicting an elderly Adolf with his wife, Eva, and with their grandson, Anselm, Dieter's father, sitting on his lap. The painter had treated his subjects very kindly — *too* kindly for Zara's tastes — with apricot cheeks and wholesome white-toothed smiles. Doting grandparents with their cherubic grandchild.

A lovely family portrait, Zara thought, holding back a scowl. Adolf Hitler had overseen the deaths of millions under his reign and yet here he sat, the picture of quaintness.

Garrison leaned in. "Let's walk to the hallway to our right. I need to head downstairs."

They strolled through the corridor, feigning interest in the portraits of Nazi royalty on the walls until the sound of party chatter faded away. Now that their group was alone, Garrison snagged an empty hors d'oeuvre platter and headed for the very last door in the corridor. The words SERVICE ENTRANCE were painted across it.

"We have to be quick," Garrison said, looking to Alene. It was time for him to head into the White House basement, where he would destroy the box that controlled the elevator to the safe room, preventing Dieter from escaping. He stepped back from the group, breaking away from the connection that kept him disguised. His crisp suit shimmered away to reveal a service uniform underneath, similar to the other workers. He hadn't worn the battle gear that the rest of their group was wearing in order to blend in with the White House staff.

"If I don't find you tonight, I'll meet you at the safe house." He touched each of them on the arm. "Good luck."

Just then, a weary blond waitress emerged from the service entrance, and Garrison quickly held the door open for her. Her blue eyes searched over their group, and her lips curled at Garrison.

"Get downstairs. They've been looking for bussers," she said to him.

"Many apologies, but the ambassador and his guests are lost. I was trying to show them the way back," Garrison said smoothly.

"I'll take care of them. Go on downstairs," she snapped.

Garrison's gaze flickered over her name tag before he bowed his head. "Yes, Frau Gottlieb." Then he reached for the door, giving Alene one last glance before he disappeared.

The waitress straightened her blouse and gave Uncle Red a sparkling smile. "The Sieg Garten is this way, Ambassador. Please walk down this hallway and turn to your right."

With polite nods, they followed the waitress to the Sieg Garten — long ago known as the Rose Garden — and stepped outside into the warm spring night. A hint of humidity hung in the air, a taste of the hot summer to come. Sweat gathered around Zara's neck, thanks to the stiff vest that clung to her. Usually, she loved these types of evenings, but she couldn't wait for this one to come to an end. Now that they had infiltrated the White House, she was even more eager to get it over with. She tried not to think about the soldiers surrounding them or the bullets in their guns, ready to tear through her bones.

What if one of us doesn't make it out? she thought. What if Uncle Red got caught in a sniper's crosshairs, like her mother? All of that blood . . . Zara's heart hammered at the possibilities, but then she felt her uncle's gaze upon her.

"I'm right here," he mouthed to her. And Zara's fear abated slightly.

"Let's find our seats," Alene said, tilting her head toward the rows of white folding chairs on the lawn. "The ceremony will be starting soon."

Skirting around the garden, they passed a long buffet table topped with a lush spread of appetizers available before the formal dinner that would take place after the speeches. Many of the ambassadors and diplomats milled around the table, nibbling on roasted rabbit with fennel stuffing, sweet potato gnocchi as soft as pillows, and platters loaded with juicy berries and the biggest red grapes Zara had ever seen. Her belly growled at the sight of the spread, all of it free for her taking, but this was the Nazis' food, the Führer's food. She'd rather let her stomach groan than partake of their fare.

They walked past the ten-piece band that played a repertoire of traditional German tunes and found a trio of empty chairs. Zara studied the podium where the Führer would soon give his speech, and then she glanced toward the guards. Each of them wore a tailored black suit that helped them blend in with the other guests, but Zara noticed the earpieces tucked into their ears and the pistols bulging inside their jackets. A shiver spread over her arms. In a few minutes, those guns would be pointed at her and her uncle.

"Is that . . . ?" Uncle Red murmured.

Zara followed his eyes toward a cluster of Nazi officers. Most of them were gray haired and thick waisted, laughing and chewing on slices of sausage. She looked them over one by one, wondering if her uncle was being paranoid, but then her gaze skidded to a stop.

There he was, chatting with the other officers and sipping a glass of golden champagne.

Colonel Eckhart.

A shiver climbed down Zara's spine, followed by a burst of anger. She was about to suggest they move seats until she remembered that they were disguised. There was no way the Colonel could recognize her or Uncle Red — as long as they stayed close to Alene — although a part of her wished that he could. The last time she had seen him, he had had her beaten and thrown into a locked room. She wouldn't mind tackling him with his very own bolt of lightning.

"Do you know one of those men?" Alene said.

Uncle Red nodded. "The one on the left. Colonel Eckhart, the commander of Fort Goering."

"*He's* the one who uncovered Mission Metzger?" said Alene. One of her hands closed into a fist.

Zara shifted in her wooden seat, figuring it would be best not to mention that Colonel Eckhart was Bastian's father, too. "We better stay focused. The mission comes first, right?"

Alene muttered a curse under her breath and nodded sullenly while Zara snuck one more glance at the Colonel. His own fort had been bombed yesterday and his only son had gone missing, but he had come to the gala anyway. Unbelievable.

"Ladies and gentlemen," a woman's voice said over the loudspeakers. "Please find your seats. The Führer's speech will begin shortly."

The White House ushers moved through the garden, gently prodding the guests to finish the last remnants of their champagne. Once everybody had found their seats, the band struck up a rousing rendition of the Nazi national anthem and the crowd rose to their feet, pressing their hands over their hearts as the song surged into a brassy crescendo.

"Your hand!" Alene elbowed Zara's side.

Zara had been so busy trying to mouth the words that she had forgotten about her hand. She hurriedly slammed her palm against her chest, just in time for the band to draw its last note. Then the same voice blared over the loudspeakers again.

"Please remain standing for his eminence, Führer Dieter Adolf Heinrich Hitler!"

Rousing applause burst through the garden, and Zara did her best to join in. Beside her, both her uncle and Alene clapped enthusiastically, and she tried to match them. Soon, the Führer's entourage emerged from the White House. First, Reichsmarschall Baldur marched into the Sieg Garten, dressed in full Nazi regalia, and strode to the far end of the stage. Next, the Corps of Four walked onto the lawn with their chins held high: the Monster, the Mind Controller, the Medic, and finally the Protector — Sentinel Braun.

Bile scratched at the back of Zara's throat. The last time she had seen Braun, the Sentinel had burned Mrs. Talley in a tower of flames. Zara's nose wrinkled at the memory of that terrible smell, and she felt the air crackle around her fingers, nibbling at her skin. Braun was so close. A few bolts of lightning would easily do her in, but Zara pushed the temptation away. No matter how much she wanted to hurt Braun, she couldn't jeopardize the mission. Although she wouldn't be sorry if someone took out the Protector that night.

The trumpets blared an upbeat melody as the guest of honor finally arrived. At last, Führer Dieter — or his double, at least — stepped onto the stage to the loudest of clapping. He saluted the audience, and they all saluted in return. Zara peered at him, amazed at the likeness that he shared with Dieter: the same round cheeks, the same thin shoulders. He even possessed the absurd smear of a mustache that every *Führer* had long favored.

The applause ended, and the double gripped the sides of the podium. "Citizens of the Eastern American Territories! *Ein Volk, ein Reich, ein Führer!*"

"*Ein Volk, ein Reich, ein Führer!*" the crowd chanted back.

"Many decades ago, my great-grandfather Adolf Hitler conquered this land that I now stand on. He claimed this nation as his own and built it into what it is today: a beacon of Nazi strength. Today, we celebrate the decades of German rule, spreading from the shores of the Chesapeake to the plantations of the South and the banks of the great Mississippi!"

The double continued with his speech, praising the years of glorious Nazi rule, but Zara's attention had slipped away. Her hands were sweaty and clammy to the touch. In only a few minutes, she would have to shoot a bolt of lightning toward the podium. The entire Alliance was counting on her, and she couldn't fail them, even if she couldn't shake the fear throttling inside her chest. A part of her wished Bastian were here. It would have been nice to have a medic with the group. . . . And it would have been nice just to have him next to her.

Uncle Red tapped Zara's arm as if to say, *It's almost time.*

Shoving aside her doubts, Zara concentrated on the space above the double's head. She had one chance to make this shot. Maybe two at the most.

"In my years as Führer, I have tried fervently to further my great-grandfather's dream. The Empire has prospered under my rule as I've further developed our military and expanded our treasury. In the footsteps of my great-grandfather, I intend to rule the Nazi Empire for many years to come."

Zara's eyes watered. She reached deep inside her, channeling every bit of power that she could gather.

Charge, she commanded.

Yes, she felt it there, the charges pulling and pushing, the heat climbing degree by degree.

Charge!

The double's speech went on. "And so, on this night, I ask you to join me in celebrating our rule of the Eastern American Territories." He smiled as the press corps snapped his photograph.

Zara's gaze slid over her shoulder toward the fence. Where was the Alliance's diversion?

"It's seven-sixteen," Alene whispered, frowning. "I'm sure they'll be here soon. Hold on for a few more minutes."

But Zara's fingers cramped as she tried to stave off the lightning. Now that she had its attention, it begged for release, snapping its electric jaws at her hands.

Another minute passed before Zara noticed a few of the soldiers pressing their fingers against their earpieces. Their eyes skimmed over the electrified fence. Then she heard the shouts.

"Freedom, or death!" The cries multiplied by the second. There were hundreds of voices, hundreds of marching feet. Cameras flashed again, this time pointed at the fence. "Freedom, or death!"

Uncle Red touched his belt where the pistol was hidden before he squeezed Zara's knee. "You ready?"

One by one, the guests swiveled in their seats, stretching their necks toward the lawn. Murmurs rumbled through the garden as the first rebels neared the fence. Three of them broke through their comrades, holding a backpack between them. A sniper shot fired from the White House rooftop and one of the rebels staggered. Four steps later, another bullet felled the second rebel. Zara watched, utterly frozen, as the third rebel ran to the fence.

Back on the podium, the Führer pounded a fist against the wood. "What is the meaning of this?" he said. Around him, the Corps of Four edged closer, flanking the dictator.

Dodging the gunfire, the third rebel reached the fence and screamed, "Freedom, or death!" He reached for something in his pocket, triggering the backpack of C4, and that was when everything changed.

Explosions erupted where the rebel had stood, splintering the fence open and sending a heat wave across Zara's face. The guests screamed around her, toppling chairs over and scrambling for an exit.

Alene turned to Zara. "Now! Release it!"

Zara's fingers curled into her fists. *Charge!* she shouted in her head once again.

The lightning flashed to life.

A zigzag of voltage cracked the podium and a fierce white light blanketed the stage. Zara's eyes shut automatically and the lightning went wild, shooting its electric web over the first row of chairs. A man cried out, followed by a chorus of gasps. Zara pried her eyes open to find the double sprawled in front of the podium, his neck twisted at a sharp angle. The Corps of Four sprang into motion, hurrying toward the nearest doors to protect the real Führer from the attack.

"Another one!" Alene said.

Zara launched a flurry of lightning bolts toward the Corps of Four while her uncle started firing. One of Zara's bolts smacked into the Monster's thick neck, the largest member of the Corps of Four, but he merely shrugged it off due to his bulletproof skin and ran inside. But the next one hit the Mind Controller's shoulder. His body spasmed, and he fell face-first into the lawn. Puffs of smoke rose from his tuxedo jacket.

Zara blinked. Was he dead?

She stared at his crumpled form, but he didn't move. A few brave members of the press corps snapped photos or pointed their video cameras at the body, sending the footage out live.

"We have to go!" Alene yanked Zara by the wrist, snapping her out of her daze. "We can't let them find Dieter!"

21

Chaos reigned in the garden as the guests clawed and pushed each other to find cover. A few rows up from Zara, a Japanese emissary tripped in the grass, screaming as the frantic horde trampled her. A soldier managed to hurl her over his shoulders, but a mask of blood had covered the woman's face. Her body was limp.

"Stay calm!" the soldiers shouted, but they were shoved aside.

Zara caught a glimpse of Colonel Eckhart barking orders before the guards thrust him into the building. Seconds later, she lost him in the swarm of incoming rebels who were fighting their way across the White House lawn. Snipers on the roof fired a spread of shots at them, felling a rebel with each shot, but more of them flooded through the broken fence.

"This way!" Alene led Uncle Red and Zara inside into a yellow-walled solarium, perfumed with orange trees and decorated with portraits of the German countryside. Far ahead of them, three soldiers blocked the doorway that the Corps of Four had escaped through. Alene grasped Uncle Red's elbow. "Can you take them out from here?"

"I can try, but they're wearing vests like we are. I'd have to clip them each in the head and at this distance . . ." His lips pursed as he took in the soldiers. "I don't know."

"Fine, we'll go with the other plan we talked about. You ready? Make it convincing."

Uncle Red obliged. With a pained wince, he clutched at his heart. Together, the three of them stumbled toward the soldiers.

"You can't come this way!" one of the guards shouted. "Turn around!"

Alene's voice turned frantic. "Please, *mein Herr*! The ambassador is having a heart attack."

The guards wouldn't budge. "Only authorized personnel past this point."

"But the ambassador — please help!"

"I said turn around!" the Nazis barked. They stepped forward to push Alene in the other direction, but she was through with talking. She lunged forward, breaking the distance threshold that kept Zara and her uncle disguised. The guards cried out in surprise at the sight of them and reached for their guns, but Alene had already pounced.

Swinging her arm, she smashed her fist into one of their throats and wrestled the pistol out of his hand. Meanwhile, Zara shoved the other two guards onto the hard floor with a fierce gust of wind before Uncle Red finished off all three of them with shots to the forehead.

Zara stood over the bodies, her breaths labored, but there wasn't time to rest.

"Take what you can!" Alene tossed another pistol to Uncle Red and they searched the guards' belts for extra magazines. When they had plucked them dry of supplies, Alene took the lead again with Uncle Red and Zara only a few steps behind her.

They raced through a powder-blue sitting room and into another marble-paved hallway.

White columns flanked them on both sides, and a formal library opened up on their right, filled with hundreds of leather-bound volumes. At the very end of the corridor, Zara saw two members of the

Corps of Four — the Monster and the Medic. They had nearly disappeared around the corner with a handful of soldiers when Alene and Uncle Red both fired a deafening string of bullets. One of the bullets struck the Monster's neck, but it bounced off his skin like a penny hitting pavement. Another shot wedged into the Medic's shoulder, causing him to stumble and cry out. He plummeted to the floor, but the soldiers dragged him to safety before Alene could reload.

"Watch out!" Uncle Red yanked Zara aside as the soldiers reemerged, unloading their weapons down the hall. Sentinel Braun walked behind them, a bright ball of fire in her palms.

"Kill the rebels!" Braun shouted, right before she released the fireball.

Zara rolled behind one of the pillars just as the trail of fire sailed through the air where her head had been. Taking aim, Uncle Red shot off a couple rounds, taking down one of the soldiers, but Sentinel Braun had whipped behind a pillar as well, out of danger.

With gunfire spraying all around them, Uncle Red heaved Zara, Alene, and himself past a cluster of oil paintings of Neuberlin and behind a nine-foot-tall decorative oak cabinet. Bullets roared through the fine-crafted wood, but Uncle Red and Alene fired right back. While they provided her cover, Zara formed a tornado at her feet, urging it higher and higher until it towered as tall as the cabinet. Mrs. Talley's execution flashed through her mind — the burning, the screams — and the tornado spun faster. Zara launched it with a flick of the wrist, sending it tearing through the marble floor and barreling toward Sentinel Braun.

"I'll try to take out the soldiers!" Alene shouted to them. "Cover me!"

Uncle Red nodded and slammed a new magazine into his gun, firing a rapid round of shots while Alene crawled toward a pillar. "What do you want to do about Braun?" he called to Zara when he had finished.

Zara didn't have time to answer him. The cabinet exploded in a roaring tower of flames, due to a fireball from Sentinel Braun's fingertips. Uncle Red dove to his right while Zara lurched to her left, smashing her shoulder against the cold marble.

"Get up, Zara!" Uncle Red screamed, his voice drowned out in the firefight between Alene and the last soldier.

Dashing to her feet, Zara only had a second to breathe before Sentinel Braun, much closer than Zara realized, launched a massive icicle at her chest. Zara managed to muster a squall of wind to shove the ice away from her body. The icicle crashed onto the ground, breaking into a thousand pieces.

Braun was far from finished. With a grim smirk, she conjured a boiling wall of fire next, engulfing Zara in its fiery shell. Crying out, Zara shrank into a tight ball as the flames flicked against her neck, at any patch of bare skin. As the fired closed in, she blasted air from her hands to cloak her from the onslaught, but the fire raged hotter, pressing toward her inch by scorching inch.

Black smoke punctured Zara's precious shield of air. Thick and heavy, the smoke invaded her throat and seared her lungs. Her heartbeat slammed faster. She only had minutes left. Maybe seconds. Her lightning was no use to her, and now only a shrinking layer of oxygen separated her from the flames.

Oxygen. The word reverberated in Zara's skull.

Fire couldn't burn without oxygen.

A desperate plan gelled in her mind. Zara opened her hand, frantically hoping this would work.

Disperse.

As she held her last sip of breath, Zara screamed for the air to move apart. She reached for it, begging for it to spread out. At first, the air only circled around her wrists, puzzled. But then she squeezed her eyes shut to focus on this one task.

Disperse!

Slowly, very slowly, the air obeyed.

Despite the acrid smoke, Zara's eyes sprang open to find the fire dissipating. The flames died down as the air obeyed her. A sweet coolness fanned across her face, and she drank in a long deep breath.

"Unmöglich!" Sentinel Braun choked out, her eyes searching Zara. *Impossible.* Her lips pursed tight, she urged the fire to climb higher, but the flames only flickered, drowsy from the lack of oxygen.

Zara's gaze narrowed on Braun's throat. *Disperse,* she thought.

The air heeded her, and Braun soon clawed at her neck, choking for breath. Zara repeated the command yet again and her own head went dizzy — the thin air was starting to affect her, too — but she wouldn't stop.

For Mrs. Talley. "Disperse!"

Sentinel Braun dropped to her knees. Her hands glowed red, mustering one last pillar of flames, but it sizzled to nothing before it could launch from her palm. She slumped to the floor, nose first, unconscious.

At last, Zara released the air from her bidding and gulped down a big breath. Both Alene and her uncle ran to her side, and Uncle Red stopped cold when he saw Braun's body.

"Is she dead?" he asked Zara.

She shook her head, still drinking in the sweet air. "I don't think so."

Raising his pistol, Uncle Red took aim at Braun's head. His lips curled as he racked the slide. "For Nell," he said.

Then he fired.

Blood splattered over Zara's shirt, spraying across her arms and hands. A bullet hole marred Sentinel Braun's pale cheekbone, a crater in her smooth white skin.

Zara looked up at her uncle, and he wrapped an arm around her. For a moment, she let herself sink against him, despite the carnage around them, despite the carnage ahead of them.

They had defeated two sentinels. Only two more to finish off.

Uncle Red looked over Zara, searching for any signs of a wound. "Are you hurt?"

Zara coughed out the last wisps of smoke and shook her head. Despite the soreness in her throat, she wasn't injured. Not badly, at least. She had fared far better than the lifeless soldiers strewn face-down in the library. Their blood had already seeped onto the thick blue rug, spreading its redness wherever it touched.

"What did you do to the sentinel?" Alene said with her brows creased. "How come you didn't tell us you could do that?"

"I didn't know that I could," said Zara. Her mouth tasted like ash, and she coughed again.

"Well, that trick might be useful again," said Uncle Red, "but let's not discuss it here. Where do we go now, Alene?"

"Up those stairs and toward the residential wing." Alene motioned for them to follow her. "This way."

As they neared the end of the hall and rounded the corner to a carpeted staircase, rapid footfalls thundered behind them. Uncle Red dragged them up the steps and checked his pistol magazine.

"How many rounds do you have left?" Alene murmured while she did the same to her two guns.

"Five. I'm on my last magazine," he said.

"I'll handle whoever's coming. Save your bullets," Zara said. Despite a dull throb in her temples, she flexed her fingers and urged another bolt of lightning to form in her hand. By the sound of the incoming boots, they might have to face over ten soldiers at once. The footsteps drew closer, and Zara commanded the lightning to surge stronger, but then she heard voices shout in English, "Find cover! Get down!"

Zara peeked over the banister to see a surge of Alliance rebels rushing into the hallway. Rifles in hand, the ten rebels hurtled behind the pillars to shield themselves from the Nazis pursuing them. Gunfire exchanged between the forces, blasting into Zara's ears, but she had grown so used to the sound that she didn't even wince. She watched the rebels stand their ground, even though the Nazis shot off an onslaught of ammunition. The sight of that buoyed her, and she aimed her lightning at the Germans, but Alene pulled her arm back.

"Save it for the Führer!" said Alene. "We have to put the mission first."

"She's right," Uncle Red said. "We have to keep moving."

Zara hesitated — those rebels were outnumbered two to one. If she left them now, they might be dead within the hour, but she nodded at her uncle and willed the lightning to fizzle away. They had to take out the Führer at all costs.

Together, the three of them ascended another flight of stairs and reached another endless hallway, this one covered in gold paisley wallpaper. Chandelier sconces lit the elegant space, shining a warm glow on the walls, and an apple-green carpet ran underneath their shoes. Adrenaline pumped faster through Zara's blood. She had a hunch they were getting close.

"The residential wing should be close," said Alene. She squinted down the hall, as if calling up a map in her mind. "I'll scout ahead. Cover me."

While Alene prowled down the hall, Uncle Red anchored himself along one wall, his gun at the ready, and Zara conjured a lightning bolt. Her eyes alert, she scanned the corridor for any movement, her ears perked for any sound, but she saw and heard nothing. Suddenly, she felt a shudder beneath her feet. The crystal sconces swayed and the floor rumbled like an earthquake had struck the White House. Zara's gaze whipped down the hallway to find Alene, but it was too late.

The Monster swooped from around the corner, his arms outstretched, and rammed into Alene. She cried out in surprise and tried to pedal back, but the Monster slammed into her. She crashed into the wall and it cracked on impact, chunks of plaster falling with her. Alene slid to the floor, her eyes glassy.

"Alene!" Zara cried.

But Alene didn't move.

The Monster's eyes snaked toward Zara and Uncle Red. Seven feet tall and three feet thick, he released a terrifying roar, shooting spittle out of his ogre-like lips. An ice-cold fear slithered into Zara's stomach, and she reached for her uncle's arm.

The Monster charged.

Zara stood frozen, eyes wide and jaw slack. How would they ever survive this?

"Get out of the way!" Uncle Red screamed.

Breaking out of her haze, Zara seized her uncle by the shoulders and hurled them both against the wall while the Monster barreled past them. Uncle Red lifted his gun and launched three shots into the Monster's back, but the slugs ricocheted off of his skin, like pellets bouncing off rubber.

"Bullets won't work!" Zara said. They couldn't rely on her uncle's shooting skills. Not this time.

Releasing another roar, the Monster spun around and Zara ran toward him, putting as much distance as she could between herself and her uncle. A tangle of lightning bolts emerged on her palms, and she sent them flying toward the Monster. One of the bolts missed him completely while the other landed on his arm, but the Monster barely grunted.

Her lightning wouldn't work, either.

"Whatever you did to Braun, do it to him!" Uncle Red shouted behind her.

Fear stitched into every one of Zara's pores, but her uncle was right. Her new trick might be their only shot to get out alive.

The Monster thundered toward her with his massive arms open, ready to squash Zara in his crushing embrace. The fear doubled in Zara's veins, but she focused on the Monster's head.

Disperse, she commanded, begging the air to spread apart, but it wasn't enough. The Monster's face had turned a furious red, but his pace failed to slacken. Instead, he zigzagged over the carpet, jarring Zara's concentration, until he could draw in a long breath.

With nowhere else to go, Zara leapt upward to the ceiling, asking the wind to carry her, and barely escaped his clutches. She watched him hurtle past and readied a tornado in her palm, but the Monster had turned his attention elsewhere.

To Uncle Red.

"No!" Zara screamed. She dropped to the floor and took off sprinting. "Uncle Red, run!"

Uncle Red fired the rest of his magazine into the Monster's chest, but they were only pinpricks against the Monster's steely skin. His pistol clicked empty, and he stumbled back.

"Uncle Red!" Zara shouted again. She launched into the air, gliding as fast as the wind would carry her, sheer desperation propelling her forward.

Disperse! she called to the air surrounding the Monster. *Oh, God, disperse!*

That only drew the Monster's fury. Growling, he seized Uncle Red by the collar and smashed him against one wall, then the other, back and forth like a puppet. Then he tossed Uncle Red thirty feet down the hall, where Uncle Red landed with a whimper.

The blood emptied from Zara's head. She cried out her uncle's name, but he didn't answer. He lay there, limp. Broken.

Had the Monster *killed* him?

The Monster closed in on her. The wind spun on Zara's hands, fueled by the vicious anger that ripped through her body. She launched a gust toward him, but it barely slowed his approach. He captured Zara with his oven mitt hands, mashing her abdomen until her ribs threatened to pop. She struggled for breath, but it wouldn't come. He was too strong. Too big.

As her legs kicked uselessly, Zara channeled her last bits of strength on one command.

Disperse.

The air particles spread farther and farther apart. The Monster's mouth twitched, but he wouldn't release her.

Disperse! Please, disperse.

Finally, the Monster's face reddened. His lips opened, gasping for breath like a caught fish.

It was working. Zara urged the air to thin out even more until his fingers loosened around her waist. She crashed onto the carpet, gulping air into her desperate lungs, but she didn't take her eyes off of the Monster's purpling face.

"Disperse," she said aloud.

The Monster's fingers scraped against his neck, but he couldn't take even a sip of air. He fell to his knees, coughing, spluttering, until his eyes rolled into his head and he thudded next to Zara. Even then, she wouldn't let the air come rushing back. An ordinary human would never survive that long without oxygen, but the Monster was far from ordinary.

Finally, after another minute passed, Zara crawled onto her feet, her eyes sweeping the hallway for her uncle. Her heart skittered to a stop when she spotted him. "Uncle Red!"

He lay sprawled in the middle of the carpet, his eyes shut tightly, his collarbone protruding from his skin. She crumpled next to him and searched frenziedly for a pulse, almost sobbing when she found it. He was alive. But Uncle Red needed a doctor after what the Monster had put him through — and he needed one fast.

"Zara?" a voice mumbled behind her.

Zara tore her eyes from her uncle to find Alene not far from her, slumped against the opposite wall. Alene's arm lay crooked at an awful angle.

"Zara," Alene said again, wetting her dry lips. "Listen to me."

Reluctantly, Zara left Uncle Red's side. "Where are you wounded? Aside from your arm?"

"Doesn't matter. You have to find the Führer." Her teeth gritted, but she spoke through the pain. "Do you hear me?"

"I'm not going anywhere without my uncle."

"We're dead weight to you now." Alene cradled her arm. "Go."

"My uncle —"

"He can't help you anymore! Think about the mission. The whole Alliance is depending on you."

Zara shook her head. She wouldn't abandon her uncle. That wasn't in *her* plan. "Garrison could do it," she said. "He should have destroyed the control box by now."

"We don't even know if he is alive — we can't get in touch with him!"

Zara went very still. The success of this mission now fell squarely on her shoulders. She was the only one who remained uninjured. She was the one who could finish this. But she couldn't let her uncle die in front of her. Her gaze shifted from Alene to her uncle, back and forth, back and forth. A desperate idea popped into her head.

"Can you use your powers?" Zara said quickly.

Alene's eyes flashed at her. "Why?"

"I need you to disguise yourself — as a soldier, as a maid, as whatever. You have to bring my uncle to a doctor."

"Stop wasting time!"

"He could be dying! I'll find the Führer, but you have to take my uncle to a doctor. Promise me."

"I told you already —"

"*Promise* me. I'm not leaving here until you do."

"Fine, fine," Alene burst out, grimacing all over again when she moved her arm. "I'll get your uncle out, but you have to leave right now. You have to find Dieter. No matter what."

Zara helped Alene to her feet. Then, with her heart twisting in half, she ran to her uncle and gripped his hand. "Hold on, do you hear me?" She kissed his clammy cheek. "Please hold on."

Beside her, Alene crouched over Uncle Red's body and, with a narrowing of her eyes, altered his appearance to a young Nazi lieutenant. Then she glared at Zara. "Follow this hall and head to your right. The Führer's suite will be in the residential wing — the first door on your left. He should still be there if Garrison blocked the escape route to the bunker. You got that?"

"F-First door on the left."

Alene grunted while she reached into her pocket and pulled out a small handheld camcorder. "You need to tape the assassination. Otherwise this whole thing is for nothing."

With her whole body trembling, Zara nodded and took the video recorder, sticking it in her pocket. She watched Alene drag her uncle toward the stairwell and almost begged her to take her with them, but she knew she had to let them go.

Zara forced her legs forward, each step taking her deeper into the White House and closer to the Führer. She ignored the fear churning through her, the panic pounding at her heart, bursting to be let out. She had to press onward — for her uncle, for the entire Territories. And especially for her mother.

Tonight, she would make Annie St. James proud.

22

Following Alene's instructions, Zara hurried down the corridor, turned right, and found herself in front of two towering doors, more than double her height. The entrance to the residential suite. The mahogany doors were carved with delicate roses and twirls of ivy, an antique most likely, imported from Germany for some gargantuan sum. She knew they were locked before she even touched them. The Corps of Four had always been vigilant in protecting the Führer — no door was left unsecured. Although now it was the Corps of One. Only the Medic remained.

Zara pressed her hands against the doors to open them, but gunshots burst from within the suite, puncturing through both the antique doors and the lock. Ducking down, she hid behind the wall until the soldiers were forced to reload. Then, with a web of lightning on her hands, she kicked open the door and launched the bolts in a wide arc. Five guards flew backward, sprawling over the carpet. One of them struggled to rise, but Zara knocked another bolt into him. Pain hummed along her forehead — she could feel her well of energy dwindling each time she used her powers — and she knew she had to save enough strength for the Führer.

Gingerly, she stepped through the dismantled doorway to find a circular sitting room before her. The soldiers lay across the cream carpet, their uniforms smoking. She eyed them one by one, waiting for them to twitch or reach for their guns, but none of them moved.

The ticktock of a grandfather clock floated into Zara's ears, reminding her that she was losing precious time. Her gaze swept across the space, getting her bearings. Six doors spanned the arc of the room, each one tightly shut.

Zara tiptoed to the first door on her left, as Alene had told her, and readied a ball of lightning on her hand. *Better safe than sorry*, she thought as she reached for the handle.

Her fingers never met the knob.

Heavy strides thumped behind her, and Zara threw herself onto the carpet as a pistol fired into the sitting room. But she wasn't fast enough. Red-hot pain burst through her chest, right below her ribs. She gasped, and the lightning bolt flew free from her hand. A man screamed.

Zara writhed against the floor, breathless from the pain. She almost passed out from it — she would have welcomed that, even — but the blackness didn't take her. Her hands groped along her chest, but she didn't find any blood, only a puncture on her vest where the bullet had stopped.

The man screamed again, and Zara forced herself onto her knees, her cracked ribs making each breath agony. Colonel Eckhart stood by the door to the residential wing, and a blackened pistol lay by his feet. A small bolt of her lightning must have hit the gun; its metal had burned the Colonel's hand, which had ruptured with red blisters.

Zara propped herself against the wall, each breath a torture, and she tried to muster a gale-force wind to knock him off of his feet. But the wind wouldn't come.

Cradling his hand against him, Colonel Eckhart hobbled toward her. "You filthy *Mischling*!" he spat. She tried to summon another lightning bolt, but he kicked her in the ribs, and the world went white with pain. Zara curled into herself, wanting to scream, but only a hoarse whimper came out. She clenched her fists, begging for the wind or lightning to hear her.

"I should have killed you weeks ago!" He lifted a blue-and-white vase from a buffet table and raised it over his head. Zara raised a feeble hand to stop him. His intentions were clear — he didn't need a gun to kill her.

The Colonel brought the vase down, and Zara shoved her hand up to meet it, channeling every particle of air that she could. A desperate wind whooshed forward, and the Colonel flew backward, smashing into an oil painting of Reichsmarschall Baldur's wife. Colonel Eckhart brushed off the hit, fury in his piercing eyes, and he was about to smash in Zara's head with his fists when he stopped midswing.

"Father!"

Colonel Eckhart's head jerked toward the doorway. Zara's did the same.

Bastian stood in the doorway, a medical bag slung over one shoulder and a pistol cocked in his hand. The barrel was pointed at the Colonel's chest.

Zara thought she was seeing things. Bastian was supposed to be back at the factory, not here in the chaos of the White House, pointing a gun at his father. She blinked hard to chase the illusion away, but Bastian — and the gun — remained in the doorframe.

The Colonel's face flooded with relief at first, but then he snarled when he realized Bastian was pointing the gun at him. "Put that thing away!"

Bastian shook his head.

"Are you going to *shoot* me, *mein Sohn*?" Colonel Eckhart said in disbelief.

Bastian's fingers trembled, so much so he used both hands to steady the pistol. "Step away from her, Father."

"Is she the reason why you turned traitor?" His voice lowered into a growl. "This *Untermensch*?"

"Step away. I won't say it again."

Colonel Eckhart didn't budge. "My own son, the defector." He barked out a bitter laugh. "Are you really abandoning me and your mother over this *Mischling* girl?"

"You're the one who abandoned Mother to that facility!" Bastian roared. Anger overtook his features. Zara had never seen him like this before. "And Opa. You could have asked for leniency — both Mother and I begged you for it — but you let him die."

"That man was a poison to our family!" His cold eyes looked Bastian up and down. "This is his influence, isn't it?"

"So what if it is?" said Bastian defiantly.

Streaks of redness climbed up Colonel Eckhart's neck. "Look at what your precious grandfather has made you become — turning your back against your own country and now your own blood. I should have had your precious *Opa* killed years ago!"

Colonel Eckhart charged at Bastian so fast that Bastian barely realized what was happening. With his arms raised, the Colonel leapt on top of him, sending Bastian's pistol careening across the floor. They grappled, fists flying. Colonel Eckhart punched Bastian in the jaw, then in the stomach.

Despite the throbbing in her chest, Zara pushed herself up and mustered a spark of lightning, just enough to stun someone. Once Bastian shoved his father off of him, she sent the spark shooting into the Colonel's back. He cried out, his arms jerking upward, and he tumbled over. His eyes clasped shut.

Bastian stood frozen, panting hard. "Is he . . . is he dead?" He knelt by his father's body and pushed two fingers against his wrist. "There's a pulse."

Zara couldn't tell if he was relieved or disappointed. Ignoring the pain in her ribs, she stared at Bastian, still stunned to see him in front of her. "What are you doing here?" The question finally tumbled out of her. "You're supposed to be back at the factory!"

"I came with the others. They needed medics, so I volunteered." His voice was flat, and his face had emptied of color. Zara wondered how many deaths he had witnessed that night. "It's mayhem outside. There are more rebels coming, but the Nazis already sent in reinforcements. I knew I had to find you." His head jolted over his shoulder as the sound of gunshots peppered their ears. "We don't have much time."

"We? This isn't your mission!" As relieved as Zara was to see him, she didn't want him here. She had already watched her uncle get nearly killed — she couldn't lose someone else she cared about. And she cared about Bastian. It was terrifying for her to admit that, but she did. The thought of seeing him gunned down or ripped apart by some sentinel made her bones shudder. "You need to go with the others before it's too late."

He didn't move an inch. "Where is the Führer's room?"

"Bastian, go." She didn't have time to argue with him. If the reinforcements were on their way, they had minutes at the most. She shoved him toward the doorway, but it was like pushing a wall of muscle.

Bastian caught her hands and gently placed them at her sides.

"You don't want to see what I have to do," Zara pleaded.

"Yes, I do." He drew in a long, long breath. "For his sake." His head bowed and he said, *"Für dich, Opa." For you, Grandfather.*

Zara looked at him, searching his eyes. "Are you sure?"

"Where is he?" he said grimly.

There was no more time to argue. She nodded at the first door on the left. "He's in there."

Cautiously, she stepped to the door and summoned a bolt of lightning onto her palm. She wished she could coax it larger, but it was the best she could do with the ache in her ribs. She glanced at Bastian.

"On the count of three," she whispered. He nodded and braced himself against the wall next to the door while she stood opposite him. "One . . . two . . . three!"

She blasted the door open with a surge of wind, and that's when the shooting started. Instinct took over. Zara slammed to the floor and shouted for Bastian to do the same. She cradled her head as the bullets soared past her, blasting past them in a deafening roar before Zara finally heard a hollow ping. An empty magazine.

"Now, before they reload!" Bastian said urgently.

Zara flung a tornado through the door, saving her last bit of lightning for Dieter. Bastian shielded himself as chunks of plaster and glass flew into the hallway, biting against his clothes. A man's voice cried out from inside the room.

Crawling forward over the detritus, Zara peered inside the suite and saw an opulent living room, large enough to consume her entire house. Furniture lay toppled on its side, victims of her tornado: a silver lamp lay cracked on a plush rug while a glass chandelier swung wildly from side to side.

Bastian tilted his head. "Blood," he said, pointing to a bright red smear on the cream carpet.

Zara held her breath and got to her feet, stepping silently into the suite. She followed the blood trail behind a mahogany-trimmed sofa and stopped cold when she saw the body.

"It's the Medic," she murmured to Bastian.

Lying on one side, the Medic sprawled over the carpet with a sharp chunk of wood jammed into his neck. His limp fingers had curled around the wood, maybe in an attempt to heal himself, but he had bled out too quickly.

Bastian searched for a pulse. "He's dead." He craned his neck over the rest of the suite. "Did the Führer escape?"

The safe room, Zara thought. The blood rushed out of her head. If the Führer had made it to the elevator and the safe room, then this whole night would have been for nothing. She hurried around the suite, yanking each door open: the bathroom, the laundry, the linen closet. Garrison had mentioned that the route to the safe room was hidden inside a closet — was this the one? She thrust her hands through the sheets and towels until she bumped into a fingerprint pad on the wall.

A red button flashed on the pad, along with an angry ERROR message.

Garrison had done it. He had snuck into the White House basement, discovered the elevator that connected the safe room to this closet, and destroyed the elevator's control box, effectively preventing Dieter's escape. She whispered a thank-you to Garrison, hoping he had gotten out of the building by now, and looked back at Bastian. "Dieter didn't make it out. He must be in here somewhere."

"Then we better find him soon."

They stalked through a wood-paneled library and saw the main sleeping area ahead, where the Führer must be waiting for them, only footsteps away. Zara's heartbeat launched like a rocket.

"In there," Zara mouthed to Bastian, who had come up behind her. She conjured one more lightning bolt, wishing it would burn hotter, and glanced inside the bedroom.

Dieter was crouched next to a grand four-poster bed, which was neatly made with silk pillows and down blankets. He stumbled toward Zara with a thin cry, his hands outstretched to strangle her.

The lightning leapt from Zara's hand. Dieter was thrown backward, his entire body twitching from the direct hit. When he stopped shaking, he clawed at his chest and struggled for breath, his watery eyes narrowing at Zara and Bastian. Hatred seethed inside his sunken pupils. His lips puckered to spit at them, but the spittle merely dribbled down his chin.

Zara stared right back. Here he was, the leader of the Empire. The great Führer himself. For years, she had mopped the floors under his portrait at the academy, under those round apple cheeks and that smear of a mustache.

But this husk of a man looked nothing like that portrait now. His corpse-white skin hung loosely off his face, and his eyes had retreated into their sharp-angled sockets. He looked as if Death had laid claim to him already. A dying skeleton.

"You must think yourself very clever," the Führer rasped in German, "but my soldiers will hunt you down. They'll tear you apart piece by piece."

Faint shouts carried into Zara's ears while piercing helicopter lights roamed beyond the windows. She yanked the camcorder from her pocket and shoved it into Bastian's hands. "Start taping."

"Why?" he said, taken aback.

"We have to, for the Alliance broadcast." If it were up to her, they would kill the Führer and leave right afterward, but the Alliance needed this footage for the mission to succeed. If the Nazis had one stunt double for the Führer, they would try to use another to hide his death — unless the Alliance had proof that the true Dieter was dead.

Zara waited for Bastian to point the video camera at her and Dieter. He motioned for her to start, but she only stared at the lens, wishing Garrison was here, because he would know what to say. The shouts rose in volume down the hallway.

"Citizens of the Territories!" Zara said, the first thing she could think of. "We, the Revolutionary Alliance, speak to you tonight from the White House."

The Führer tried to crawl away, but she stepped in front of him, her boots stepping onto his feeble fingers. He wailed, but she didn't move. Her mind flashed with images of her mother and Mrs. Talley and Molly, who had given their lives to Dieter's regime. Their courage sustained her for what she had to do next.

"We've suffered under the Führer's oppressive rule for decades, but tonight we claim our freedom." Zara didn't know where these words were coming from, but she didn't question them.

The Führer looked up at her, wheezing. "You will never get away with this. Your little Alliance will crumble under the strength of Germany!"

"Dieter Hitler." She pointed at his head and summoned a spark of lightning, channeling everything inside of her to coax it larger. It shone brightly in the dim room, lighting the Führer's sick countenance. "You will be punished for your crimes against us."

"You dirty, sullied *Untermensch —*"

Zara released the lightning, and it rammed into Dieter's chest, where it traveled ravenously over his frail frame. Dieter's limbs convulsed from the strike, and he clutched tightly at his heart, choking on his breath. The wheezing stopped, and Zara knew he was dead. She blinked at his body.

She had killed the Führer, leader of the Nazi Empire.

Her heart felt cold.

"Turn off the camera," she said to Bastian.

Footfalls pounded into the residential wing, peppered with yelling voices. *German* voices. Zara's gaze leapt toward the sound. She would have to wait to process what she had done. Right now, they needed to get out of the White House.

Bastian shoved the video camera into his pants pocket. "What do we do?" he cried.

She yanked him toward the nearest window and wrapped her arms around him. "Don't let go!" she said before blasting a window open with a gale-force wind. As the soldiers flooded into the room, she launched Bastian and herself skyward as fast as the air would take them.

They catapulted above the White House, above all of Neuberlin, until the shrine to Führer Adolf was only a bright smudge below them. Even then, Zara urged them higher, until they skimmed the lowest drifting clouds, into a current so cold that their breath frosted as soon as it left their lips. Bastian's hands clutched around her like a life vest.

"Is anyone following us?" she shouted against the wind. "A helicopter? A sentinel?"

Too cold to say a word, Bastian shook his head.

She pointed them westward, ignoring the chattering of her teeth. Her ribs ached with every movement, but Zara pushed them onward; soon they had left the city behind.

There was no time to rest, no place to stop.

Not for traitors like them.

Not for Zara, killer of the Führer, the *Mischling* — the kami — who had slain the most powerful man in the world.

23

The next three days blurred into one exhausting pattern: run, rest, eat whatever they could forage, then get on the move again. Or else the Nazis would hunt them down.

Right after they had left the White House, Zara had used the wind to carry them over Dominic's cigar factory, hoping to land and find a few friendly faces, but she only saw police lights blinking around the building. Their safe house had been compromised.

So they had to keep going.

Their new destination was an Alliance location in Wardensville, West Virginia. To find the small town, Bastian had broken into a car late one night and stolen a map out of its glove box. During the day, Zara and Bastian took turns sleeping and searched for water and food, stealing strawberries from a farm or snatching half-eaten sandwiches from a trash bin. At night, they hurried along the side roads, their ears always perked for the chop of helicopter wings or an incoming car. They were exhausted, hungry, and sweaty, but at least they remained one step ahead of the Germans.

Zara hadn't dared to fly again after that first night. With every sentinel and soldier searching for them, she felt too vulnerable in the skies, especially after the Nazis had released their fighter jets. So they kept to the roads, even though it would take them days to cross the hundred miles between Neuberlin and the Alliance headquarters. They didn't know where else they could go. Despite the grueling pace, Bastian hadn't complained, even though Zara noticed the weariness in his eyes and heard the growl of his hungry stomach. Maybe he was too exhausted to protest.

Four days in, they hid themselves in the Appalachian wilderness as a troop of sentinels circled over the forests. Zara only wanted to stay a couple of hours before heading out, but her ribs still throbbed — they had been badly bruised, according to Bastian's assessment — and fatigue swiftly overtook her.

She awoke in the darkness, the moon hanging in the clear night sky. Around her, crickets sang and locusts chirped. She heard no aircrafts and saw no searchlights, and Zara let her senses relax, if only for a minute. But she couldn't shut off her mind. The same thoughts invaded her head every time she had a second to breathe. Thoughts of Dieter. Of his lifeless face. Lifeless because of *her*.

She had killed the most powerful man in the world, and Zara's chest felt heavy at the warring emotions inside of her. She didn't exactly regret what she had done. No, the Führer had to die; there was no question about that. But she thought she would feel different somehow. Elated. Triumphant. Instead, Zara could only think about what lay ahead of them. Once the Alliance got ahold of her assassination tape, everyone in the Territories and beyond would know what she had done. They would know her name — and thinking about that made her a little sick to her stomach.

Zara turned over to find herself face-to-face with Bastian. He had huddled closer to her in his sleep, his breaths slow and deep. As she watched his chest rise and fall, she nudged aside her thoughts of the Führer. They had to get to safety first. That was the most important thing right now, and she would have to deal with her splintered thoughts later.

Bastian groaned, and Zara rested her hand on his shoulder. Only a few weeks ago, she remembered tensing whenever he neared her, but now his face hovered so close to her own and she didn't pull away. She didn't want to pull away. And that made her wonder what Bastian would want — would he mind their closeness? Her hand on his arm?

It doesn't matter, a voice clucked inside her. Here they were, on the run from the Nazis, both of them dirty and hungry and tired. They still had twenty miles to go before they reached Alliance headquarters, so all of this wondering about Bastian should have been the last thing on her mind. But here in the stillness, with the Nazis far away and with Bastian so close, Zara wondered about it anyway.

Bastian stirred and groaned in his sleep. "Mother," he said in German. "Mother, run!"

"Bastian." She shook his shoulder. "Bastian, wake up."

His eyes fluttered open and he blinked from Zara to the treetops and back again. The peacefulness of deep sleep had disappeared completely from his face. "How long have I been out?"

"I have no idea. I fell asleep, too." She stretched her sore back. "You should try to get more rest."

"I don't think I can now."

"It was only a nightmare. I'm sure your mother's fine." Zara thought about all of the times she had awakened Uncle Red from his own dreams. She clung to hope that he was alive, that he and Alene had escaped. If they hadn't . . . The panic started to build in her chest, so she buried those questions deep inside her, just as she had done with her thoughts of killing the Führer. One of these days she would have to sort through all of those memories, but not tonight. It would be far too much for her right now.

"The Nazis were chasing her in my dream," Bastian said as he sat up. He rubbed his eyes, but the fear had rooted inside of them. "Because of me. Because of what I've done. If they hurt her —"

"They won't."

His tone sharpened and he sprang to his feet. "We don't know that for sure."

"She's going to be all right, Bastian," Zara said, standing to meet him.

"You don't know that!" he burst out. His chest heaved. "What if they kill her for raising a traitor? It would all be my fault."

Zara stilled. He had never snapped at her like this before, not once. She felt an overwhelming helplessness well up inside her. "I don't think the Nazis would kill your mom. If they did, they would have to kill your father, too, right? And they let him attend the gala."

His head hung low. "Maybe." The anger had already retreated from his face. "*Scheiße*, I'm sorry. These last few days . . ."

She couldn't blame him for lashing out. They had been on the run for a while, surviving on snatches of sleep. And now he looked so small against the fifty-foot trees surrounding them, like a frightened child. Without thinking, Zara leaned forward and wrapped her arms around him, because she didn't know what to say and she was so tired of running day after day, hour after hour.

Slowly, Bastian's hands settled around her waist, and she tucked her head into the curve of his neck. She felt his tears fall on the top of her head, and soon she found herself crying, too. All of the emotions she had bottled up — the worry for her uncle, the fear of getting caught — poured out of her in a torrent.

"It's okay," she heard Bastian whisper to her. "It's okay, Zara."

He held her, rocking her, until her eyes dried, until his shirt was wet from her tears. That was when Zara pulled back from him, embarrassed.

"I'm sorry, your shirt —"

"Is only a shirt. And it's pretty wrecked already." He glanced downward, taking in the dirt stains and rips on his T-shirt. Then, in spite of everything that had happened to them, he gave her a small smile. "You can buy me a new one later."

She smiled back wanly and punched him in the shoulder, but his hands remained fastened around her. They were standing so close, their faces lingering inches apart. Bastian reached out and tucked her hair behind her ear.

"Zara, I . . ."

Her heartbeat skyrocketed. She couldn't find her voice.

Bastian's chin tilted down, and his lips brushed against hers, shyly, nervously. Zara leaned her mouth into his, softly at first, tasting his breath, tasting him. Goose bumps tickled over her skin as his fingers brushed across her neck, then trailed down her back. He pulled her closer, and Zara froze, startled at first, but she took his lead and sank into him.

A thrill shot through her, shivering down into her toes. One hand wove through his hair and the other curled around the back of his neck. For a few precious seconds, the exhaustion flew from her body. She anchored herself to this kiss, to him.

Bastian pulled back his head suddenly, and Zara wondered what she had done wrong. He blinked at their feet. "We're . . . floating."

Zara looked down to find them hovering three feet in the air. She must have summoned the wind without even realizing it. "I'm sorry!" She was about to bring them back to the ground, but Bastian caught her hand.

"I don't mind," he said, leaning back down toward her mouth.

But the chop of helicopter wings broke them apart, sending them sprawling to the ground as Zara lost focus. With her head still filled with their kiss, she pushed through the haze to locate the helicopter. She found its lights in the distance, circling over a trail they had passed, and her body tightened like a bowstring.

"We better get going," Bastian said, crawling up beside her. "In case they come toward us."

Zara nodded, and he helped her to her feet. Bastian's hand lingered on hers, and she didn't let go of it.

"We'll keep heading west. The sun set over that ridge." She tried to focus on their escape route, but she wanted to stay in the shadow of these trees. She could forget about the Nazis and their helicopters if she only shut her eyes.

"Lead the way," said Bastian. At last, he dropped his hand against his side, and Zara stepped in front of him. She forced her feet forward and shook the remaining haziness from her head. They had to keep moving if they wanted to survive.

They started their slow march through the brush, and Zara didn't let herself look back.

When they finally reached the tiny town of Wardensville, they were both starving and caked with grime. Their map was now tattered and torn, but it had led them here, where the Alliance headquarters were located.

Dawn broke over the horizon as they scaled the hill that led to an old Victorian hotel bearing the address that Garrison had told Zara so many nights before. She wanted to spring up the hill and call out for her uncle, but the last few days had sapped the life from her bones.

The hotel had seen fairer days. Its violet paint had faded to a sickly lavender, and some of the windowpanes hung crookedly off their hinges. A leaf-thick forest surrounded the building on all sides. When they reached the front porch, Zara read the sign that greeted them: WELCOME TO THE HOTEL LIBERTY, EST. 1875.

For a second, she hesitated. They had avoided civilization since the assassination, and she was struck with the sudden fear that the Nazis had discovered the bunker and were setting a trap. But then she felt Bastian's hand at the small of her back. Since their kiss, he had been doing that more and more. She knew most of it was out of necessity — taking her hand when they crossed a muddy creek or pulling her boots off at night when she was too tired to do it herself — but there were other times when she felt his hand on her shoulder or his arm curling around her before they gave in to their exhaustion. She never pulled away. Out in the woods on the run, Bastian's touch became her anchor whenever the fear jolted her awake or the hunger pains rooted deep in her belly.

"I'll go first," said Bastian.

"No, we'll go together." They had done everything together since leaving the White House. She didn't see why they had to stop now.

They approached the steps, but a young man stepped out onto the porch, motioning for them to stop. He looked over their ragged clothes, their hungry faces. "I'm sorry, but the hotel is closed for renovations."

"Please!" Zara croaked. Her thirsty throat screamed for water, and she racked her memories for what Garrison had said to her before the White House attack. He had said to her to say something when she arrived here. What was it? "The . . . the birds will chime . . . at midnight?"

Relief flooded the man's face and he ushered them inside. "I thought I recognized you from the television reports on Channel Seven, but I had to make sure. Standard procedure."

"I'm on TV?" Zara breathed.

"The Nazis got a picture of you from the White House security footage. It's all over the radio broadcasts, too, but —" His voice trailed off. "That's more than I should've said. The others will fill you in and . . . Can I shake your hand, Ms. St. James?"

Zara stared at him, then at his hand. No one had ever asked this question before — the Greenfield *Kleinbauern* didn't even want to touch a kami like her. She raised her own hand weakly, and the young man grasped on to it and shook it hard. "What was on the television reports?"

"Yes, what have you heard out of Neuberlin?" Bastian said.

"They'll explain everything in the debrief. I'm sorry, but I'm not authorized to say much else." Then the man hurried to the dusty receptionist's desk, where he accessed a hidden keypad and punched in a long string of numbers. A trapdoor hissed open by his feet, revealing a metal ladder into the secret Alliance bunker below.

"Clark! We have company!" he shouted. He motioned at Zara. "You can head down now. Watch your step."

Zara climbed down the steep ladder and stumbled into a narrow corridor that resembled a submarine — metal walls, flickering lights, and steel floors that echoed with every boot step. She braced herself against the cold wall, her head woozy from thirst and hunger. A woman ran up to her, introducing herself as Margaret Clark, and took Zara by the arm.

"Careful now," said Clark. "What's your name?" Recognition flared in the woman's eyes when she saw Zara's face. "Zara St. James! You made it out? We've been waiting for days for you."

"Is my uncle here, too? Redmond St. James?"

"I'll have to check the roster, but let's get you to the infirmary first." Clark's gaze flickered over to Bastian. "We'll have both of you checked out and fed a square meal. I'll find Murdock, too. I know he'll want to speak —"

Zara didn't hear the rest of what Clark was saying. Despite the blisters on her feet, she took off down the hall, shouting for her uncle. Dozens of faces popped out of the metal doors, but none of them were Uncle Red.

"Zara, wait!" Bastian shouted behind her.

She ignored him, too. "Uncle Red!" she cried. A tremor shook her thin shoulders. He had to be here somewhere. Alene had to have gotten him out.

But what if she hadn't?

"Uncle Red!" Her voice was breaking apart, but then her tired gaze fixed on a man running toward her, his face obscured by the dim lights. He sprinted toward her at full speed, completely barefoot, his shoulder and upper arm wrapped in bandages, and then he was hugging her with his good arm.

"Zara! Oh, God!"

It was him. It was Uncle Red. He engulfed her in an embrace, rocking her back and forth like when she was little and had skinned her knee.

"You're okay," she said into his shoulder over and over again. She buried her face against him, so relieved to find him alive.

"Alene brought me here. I've been so worried." His hands gripped her shoulders, making sure that she was real. "That might be the last mission you ever go on."

Zara laughed through her tears. "Yes, sir."

Uncle Red looked past her shoulder and extended a hand toward Bastian. "We've been worried about you, too. Welcome back."

"Did Alene make it, too?" Zara said. "Did Garrison?"

The smile slid from Uncle Red's face. "Let's get you two to the infirmary first, and Murdock will tell you everything."

"They're okay, aren't they?"

Uncle Red only wrapped his arm around her. "What matters is that *you're* okay. Right now, that is enough."

Zara knew he was avoiding her question, but she was too tired to press him on it. Her uncle was alive. She and Bastian had made it to safety. That was all that mattered for now.

"Let's get you to the infirmary, okay?" Uncle Red said gently, keeping his arm around her. "I'll show you the way."

After her and Bastian's medical checkup, they were given a meal of boiled carrots and potatoes and allowed hours of drowsy sleep before they were fully debriefed.

Zara and Bastian were spared no details.

Right after the raid on the White House, Neuberlin had collapsed into chaos. Riots overtook the city as the factory workers and day laborers, thousands upon thousands of them, ransacked the streets and set fire to government buildings, inspired by the Alliance's attack. Murdock — the new head of the Alliance — broadcasted the guerilla battles as well as the raid on the White House on Channel Thirteen, a channel well-known for its scandalous soap operas and game show reruns. It wasn't Channel Seven by a long stretch — security at the news channel had tightened significantly after the Fort Goering debacle — but it was the best the Alliance could do. Despite the smaller viewership, the video had spread like an oil slick. It had poured from one channel to the next, playing on live television and on the radio.

Operation Burning Eagle had been a total success, and now its effects were spreading across the Territories. Uprisings had popped up in all major cities, from Boston to Atlanta and to the factories of Chicago. The riots gained even more fervor at the news of the Soviets' advance on Berlin — Comrade Volkov had sent his troops through the borderlands, and they were now fighting the Germans in Nazi Poland.

With Germany under attack and Neuberlin in flames, Reichsmarschall Baldur had fled to Heidelberg (formerly Philadelphia), and tried to regroup there, but a group of rebels had followed him and bombed his convoy. Baldur was now dead, and his staff hurried to control the Territories without him. Nazi troops had been deployed across the country, and thousands had been arrested already. And just recently, a fat bounty had been placed on the head of Dieter's killer. A million-reichsmark reward.

On Zara's head.

After Zara had fallen asleep in the bunker, the Alliance had taken the assassination footage and arranged another broadcast on Channel Thirteen. The Nazis had pulled the feed once they caught wind of it, but the damage had been done and was already spreading. Now, there was a bounty out on Zara, along with her accomplices: Uncle Red, Alene, Bastian. Initially, there had been one placed on Garrison, too, but it was rescinded after his arrest. Zara had gone to bed as just another *Kleinbauer* and had arisen as the face of the Alliance.

"Any questions?" Murdock asked her and Bastian when he had finished his report.

"Garrison was arrested?" Zara whispered, her face draining of color.

"He was caught on the way to the bunker," Murdock said grimly. "We're doing our best to break him out, though."

"I want to help if I can."

"That's not possible, I'm afraid. Not with that reward on your head. But I'll keep you updated," said Murdock.

"What happened to Johann, Dieter's son?" Bastian asked.

"Disappeared. We think he's in hiding with his mother in Germany proper somewhere, biding their time until Johann comes of age."

Bastian then asked how he could track down his mother, but Zara could only stare at her hands, the hands that had ended the Führer's life. *The face of the Alliance?* For so long, she had yearned to be a part, any part, of the Revolutionary Alliance, but now she found herself at its very center. She didn't know what to think about that, except to cringe at the thought of her likeness splayed across TV screens and printed on every newspaper.

In the days following, she walked around the bunker in a daze while every rebel asked to shake her hand or wanted to discuss the details of the assassination. She busied herself with the never-ending tasks that filled the bunker. Recruitment levels had skyrocketed, and Murdock was quick to order more guerilla attacks, more bombings, more destruction. The Nazis may have had the weapons and their sentinels, but they were divided on two war fronts, and the Alliance now had the manpower advantage. The rebels chewed at the legs of the great Empire like tiny snakes. A lone serpent was easily crushed, but a horde of them was deadly.

Garrison had been right all along — the Alliance merely needed a catalyst to ignite a revolution. That was why it pained Zara that he wasn't here to witness it. After the White House mission, he and hundreds of other rebels were still missing. Zara often thought of him, along with Kristy and her mother. She hoped they had made it to a safe house somewhere, but there was no way of knowing it with communication so spotty.

But two weeks after the assassination, the Alliance finally discovered what had happened to Garrison. The Nazis broadcast his execution on Channel Seven, decrying him as a rebel spy and beating him on live television. When they had their fill of kicking him, the Germans dragged Garrison to his feet and tied him to a wooden post — but he didn't flinch once. And he didn't close his eyes when the firing squad took their places. He stared at them instead, his chin tipped high, his face defiant until the end.

Mercifully, it had been a quick death. Zara was grateful for that when she saw the footage. Her uncle had told her to look away when the guns fired, but she kept her eyes open, like Garrison had in his very last moments. She felt like she owed that to him somehow.

Once Garrison's body crumpled, Zara finally buried her face against her uncle's shoulder. The Alliance may have started a revolution, but it had lost one of its brightest members. A stream of tears slid down her cheeks, for Garrison, for the others who died with him.

With the war only beginning, Zara knew there would be many more to come.

24

It was Alene's idea to have a commemoration for the fallen rebels. Late one evening, almost three weeks after the Führer's assassination, she gathered everyone into the cafeteria to drink to those they had lost. Two hundred people trickled in for the event, nearly all stationed at the Alliance headquarters. They each grabbed a bottle of beer or a cup of cheap wine, and Zara quickly claimed three of the cups: one for her, one for her uncle, and one for Bastian, even though she didn't see him in the cramped cafeteria. As usual, the infirmary kept him busy around the clock.

Ever since they had arrived at the bunker, Bastian had thrown himself into the infirmary, clocking fourteen- to sixteen-hour days to treat everything from head colds to broken bones to festered bullet wounds. In mere days, his fame had spread throughout the bunker: the son of a Nazi colonel, now an Alliance rebel. Many of them had found reasons to pass by the infirmary to get a good look at him.

But Zara rarely saw Bastian. She caught only glimpses of him in the cafeteria as he assembled a plate of fried potatoes and headed back to his patients — and that made her wonder if he was avoiding her. After everything they had been through at the White House, she hadn't expected him to treat her like just another recruit. Perhaps he was absorbed in thoughts of his mother. Or perhaps he was regretting his and Zara's kiss, the thought of which made her whole face burn. Whatever it was, she and Bastian hadn't spoken in days, aside from a mutual hello if they passed each other in the bunker's dark halls. And that stung.

Maybe it's better this way, Zara told herself. Yes, they had survived the White House attack together, but that didn't change their pasts. She had grown up in *his* world, the farm girl born to serve his Nazi kin, who would be never more than an *Untermensch*. And now he was living in *her* world, an Aryan-blooded golden boy among the *Kleinbauern*, who would always speak with his German-tinged accent. No matter where they went, one of them would always be considered *other* — and maybe they could never bridge that gap. As friends, possibly. As something more, though? Zara didn't know. And she wasn't even sure if she wanted something more, though the thought of it made her pulse quicken.

In the cafeteria, Alene stood on one of the tables and waited for everyone to quiet down. "I know we're all busy, so I'll make this quick, but I wanted to take the time to honor those who aren't with us anymore." She raised her bottle of cheap beer. "To the fallen! We will never forget."

The rebels lifted their drinks in return. A few people murmured, "Hear, hear," while others said the names of the deceased.

"To Garrison."

"To my sister."

Zara added softly, "For Mrs. Talley."

Next to her, Uncle Red murmured, "For you, Annie."

Alene raised her glass higher. "Freedom, or death!" she shouted, right before she downed her drink.

That drew a louder "Hear, hear" and the chime of clinking glasses. Zara brought the cup of wine to her lips, but she halted midway when she saw Bastian enter the room. His gaze searched the rebels until it arrived at Zara. She swallowed the contents of her glass and glanced down at the sticky floor. He crisscrossed toward her anyway.

"I thought I might find you here," he said.

Zara thrust a cup at him. "Thirsty?"

"No, I better not. Not tonight." He fidgeted with the collar of his white medical jacket, which the Alliance had insisted he wear. It was a tad too big around the shoulders, but it suited him.

A stiff silence bloomed between them. Zara noticed how Bastian kept tucking his curls behind his ears — his hair had grown past the nape of his neck now — and how he didn't quite meet her eyes for some reason. It reminded her of when he first spoke to her at the academy, when he had wanted to join the Alliance but didn't know how to ask her about it. She wondered if there was something on his mind, although she had no clue what it might be.

"I recently spoke with Murdock," Bastian said finally. He had to raise his voice to compete with the drinking crowd.

Murdock? Zara had seen the two of them whispering to one another these last few days, their heads bowed and their voices low. "About anything in particular?"

He jabbed his thumb toward the door. "Would you mind if we went someplace quieter? We could take a walk outside."

At first, Zara wanted to stay planted in the cafeteria. *Now* he wanted to talk to her? After avoiding her for days? But another part of her — the part that won out — didn't want to say no.

So they slipped out of the cafeteria, Zara following Bastian, and crept up the metal ladder that led from the bunker to the hotel aboveground. Bastian guided her outside into the quiet symphony of the Shenandoah night. Crickets chirped and an owl hooted. The first fireflies of the season flashed on and off, on and off, like Christmas lights.

A shiver breathed across Zara's arms. She shouldn't be out here. *They* shouldn't be out here. Technically, they weren't supposed to go outside without authorization, but with everyone drinking at the commemoration, there was nobody to stop them.

As they walked over the hotel's overgrown lawn, Bastian turned to Zara, his hair almost silver in the moonlight. The pale light softened the circles underneath his eyes and the hollowness that had worn into his cheekbones. Guilt wormed through Zara's heart at the sight of his gauntness. It couldn't have been easy for Bastian to adjust to his new life here. The food rations. The meager quarters. The constant fear the Nazis had discovered them. Maybe Bastian wasn't avoiding her after all. Maybe he was simply trying to scrape by.

Bastian shoved his hands into his pockets, rocking back and forth on his feet. "My father has been promoted. Murdock told me tonight."

"He's a *general* now?" Zara exclaimed.

"Apparently. I thought the Nazis would have stripped him of rank after the Fort Goering attack, but they rewarded him for attempting to protect the Führer." A bitter note crept into his voice.

Zara wasn't sure why he had brought her outside to talk about this, but she didn't want to go back to the bunker just yet. She hadn't seen the sky or stars in days, and the fresh air tasted sweet on her tongue. "So I guess it's General Eckhart now?"

"I suppose so. Murdock said that he'll be going back to Germany. The Nazis want him to prepare more troops for the Soviet advance."

Good riddance, Zara wanted to say, although she wished Colonel Eckhart had been stripped of his rank completely. "What will happen to your mom? Will she go with him?"

"Murdock and I have been discussing that, too." He retucked a curl of his that had sprung free from behind his ear. "We're going to go get her. My father put her in a mental facility in Neuberlin, and that's no better than a death sentence."

"A mission?" Now the puzzle pieces locked into place in Zara's head. Bastian must have wanted to talk to her about breaking his mother out of the hospital. The Nazis didn't euthanize the Aryan mentally ill, but the patients of these facilities were usually neglected and mistreated until they withered away. Which didn't seem to bother Bastian's father. "I'll go with you. I'm sure we can find a place for her here at the bunker."

"Murdock already sent out a team." Bastian stared down at his worn boots, a pair he never could have worn back at the academy. Too old and too scuffed. "And my mother won't be coming to the bunker. She'll be going somewhere safe, away from the fighting."

"Where?"

"Iceland, we hope. To a safe house there." He kept his gaze glued to his boots. "The team should be arriving tonight with my mother. Then I'll be accompanying them to Iceland to make sure my mother gets settled. There's a freight ship that will take us there."

Zara wondered why he hadn't mentioned any of this to her. "How long will you be gone? A few weeks?"

"Longer than that." He still wouldn't look at her, and that made Zara's stomach fill with dread. "After my mother makes it to the safe house, I'll be heading for Brussels."

"Brussels?" Zara said, not sure if she had heard him correctly. He couldn't have meant Brussels in Nazi-controlled Belgium.

Finally, their gazes met. "I'm joining the Widerstand, Zara."

Seconds passed before the words sunk into her. Her lips parted, but she didn't know what to say. This had to be a joke. The *Widerstand*?

"Everything happened so quickly," Bastian stammered out.

"Murdock asked me last week to act as a liaison to the Widerstand, so I've been talking with one of their leaders. We spoke for a while about my *Opa* and how I had joined the Alliance, and then they sent me a telegram three nights ago. They asked me to join them. And I've . . . I've accepted. I'll be leaving tonight."

The wine turned in Zara's stomach, and her head fogged at this rush of information. So this wasn't a joke. Bastian really was joining the Widerstand, and he really was going to Brussels. He was going to leave the Territories behind.

He was going to leave her behind.

"Why didn't you tell me sooner?" she burst out. She wanted to shove him but forced her arms to remain at her sides. "You've known for days and you didn't say a word?"

"I never meant to keep it from you intentionally," he said. "The Widerstand discovered that my father is a general in the Nazi army, and all of a sudden they were offering me passage aboard a transport ship. I told them no at first. I couldn't leave my mother in the Territories. But then they offered her a place at one of their safe houses in Iceland if I agreed to what they asked."

"Agreed to what?" Zara demanded. Hurt burst through her, wave after wave.

"They want me to give radio shows, maybe appear in broadcasts. I'm a general's son, turned defector. They want to use my name."

"Do you know how much danger you're putting yourself in?" Fear clutched at Zara's throat, now mingled with fury. He had no idea what he was getting himself into. "The Nazis are already hunting you down, and now you're giving them another reason to find you!"

"I know that, but I have to do this. I have to get my mother out of Neuberlin. If the Nazis take her, they can use her as a pawn to get to me. They could torture her. . . ." He grimaced saying those words. "The Widerstand can offer her safety on neutral ground. I couldn't refuse that. Wouldn't you do the same if it were your uncle?"

Zara hated his answer because it made too much sense. Of course she would do the same thing if her uncle were in danger — but that didn't excuse him from keeping all of this from her. "What about the Alliance? You begged me for weeks about joining and now — finally — you're a part of us, and you're just going to leave?"

"The Alliance will get along without me." He added softly, "And they have you."

He was trying to be nice, but Zara didn't want to hear it. "You should've told me sooner."

"I — I didn't want to disappoint you." His face reddened with each word he spoke. "I was afraid you'd think less of me. That you'd think I was giving up."

He *was* giving up in a way, but deep down Zara understood why he had decided to join the Widerstand, even though it cut her in half to admit it. They had gone through so much together, and now he was leaving. She was so tired of getting left behind.

"If the Nazis found you . . . If they arrested you . . ." She couldn't say the rest. She couldn't even think about it. Her anger shattered apart, leaving only sadness and the knowledge that this might be the last time she ever saw him.

"I know the risks. They're the same that you take every day," Bastian said, his voice gentle. He tucked a stray piece of hair behind her ear. "You're the bravest person I know, Zara."

"I'm not the one who will be the Widerstand's poster child."

A slow smile spread across his lips. "Says the girl who's the Alliance's poster child." He ran his fingers through his curls. "I hope — I hope you can understand my decision. Maybe not today, but someday."

"I do understand," she whispered, even though his decision made her chest ache.

Bastian pulled her into his arms, and she smelled soap and earth and a tinge of ammonia. "One day, when all of the fighting is over, I hope to see you again," he said into her ear.

Zara didn't know how long that would be. Months? Years? There was a chance that the Nazis could win this war; then that "someday" would never come. She had nearly lost Uncle Red in this revolution — what if she lost Bastian, too? The seams of her heart split inside her. She didn't want him to leave, but she couldn't ask him to stay, either. This was the world they lived in now — a world pushing them an ocean apart.

"You're really going, huh?" she said, leaning away from him to stare upward, trying to memorize the lines of his face, the flecks of gold in his eyes.

In response, he pulled her in tighter and she wrapped her arms around his broad back. Zara wasn't sure how long they remained like this. The only thing she could think about was how he was safe with her right now, safe from the bombs and the bullets that would chase him until the Nazis or the resistance claimed victory. But victory loomed so far ahead of them. Finally, Zara's arms fell painfully against her sides.

"When do you have to leave?" she asked.

"In a few hours." He reached for her hand, curling his fingers around hers. "What will I do without you?"

"Win," she replied simply.

Bastian smiled, his dimples deepening. "Win. I plan on it." His head tilted to one side. "Then I'll come back."

Despite the hurt, Zara returned his smile. "I'll hold you to it, Eckhart."

"You promise?"

A spark of hope entered her eyes. "Promise."

25

The days passed, blurring into a week and then another, until the spring stretched into the hot haze of summer. Every morning, Zara awoke to the tap-tap of footsteps from the new recruits, who filled the hallways with their chatter. Inspired by the assassination — and especially by Zara — they streamed into the bunker every night. Most of them had spent their lives in hard labor, toiling on tobacco plantations or sweating in cramped factories, and they had never held a gun before, much less fired one. But they were determined, and that determination paid off. After a few weeks' training, they were ready for deployment into the big cities — New York, Heidelberg, Neuberlin — where the fighting surged the strongest. Hundreds of rebels fell to Nazi ammunition every day, but that was the one resource the Alliance now had plenty of: manpower.

The revolution had marched into a full-out war.

While the fighting raged on, Zara hardly slept at night, not when the radio messages surged into headquarters every hour. As the video of the Führer's assassination spread from town to town and from home to home, thousands of laborers had taken to the streets. In larger cities, the *Kleinbauern* snatched any weapon they could find — axes, shovels, illegal guns — and clashed with the Empire en masse, overturning cars and setting fire to Nazi buildings. The war had spread to the smaller townships as well, where farmers and workhands banded together to raid German homes and pilfer German businesses. For the first time since the war, the Alliance had ignited a fire that wouldn't stop spreading.

"We need more weapons," Murdock said at one of the Alliance's nightly meetings. He was a serious man, around the same age as Uncle Red, who had spent his life building railroads before joining the Alliance. "Redmond, what's the report on our munitions campaign?"

"We've launched a raid on Camp Zimmermann for rifles and pistols, and another on Fort Hauser for heavy artillery and tanks," Uncle Red replied. They were sitting around a round oak table nestled in the bunker's main meeting room. Twelve chairs circled the table, with Murdock and Alene sitting at the head and ten other rebels fanned around them, including Uncle Red in his new role, the weapons coordinator. "I'm waiting to hear back about the Zimmermann mission, but Fort Hauser was another success."

"Make sure those weapons get up to New York. The rebels need everything we can give them."

"Yes, sir," said Uncle Red. From across the table, Zara flashed him a smile. Maybe it was unprofessional to smile at a serious meeting like this one, but her uncle had done a bang-up job so far. For weeks, he had been organizing weapons raids and hiding the goods in fruit crates and livestock trucks before dispersing them to where they needed to go. She was proud of him.

Murdock moved on to tactical strategies next before he hit the heaviest topic on the agenda: the Alliance's next big strike. So far, they had organized fifty new chapters and orchestrated the death of Reichsmarschall Baldur, slowly chipping away at the Nazis' foothold in the Territories, but they needed to strike even harder, broader, to crush the Germans to dust.

"We're in a lucky situation right now," Murdock continued. "With the Soviets now occupying the borderlands and moving closer toward Germany each week, the Nazis are facing a war on two fronts without any help from their allies. The Japanese are facing a mass rebellion in China, while the Italians are stuck in their own muck. The great Nazi Empire is at its weakest point right now, and that's why we need to set our sights on Heidelberg."

Murmurs rippled across the table, followed by nods. After the Führer had fallen, most senior Nazi officials had fled to Heidelberg, hoping to regroup and rebuild their regime. The Alliance would have to stamp them out if they wanted to scatter the German leadership even further.

"Will your forces be ready in two weeks?" Murdock said, directing his question straight at Zara.

Zara steadied the wobble in her voice. From the corner of her eye, she saw her uncle giving her an encouraging nod. "We'll be training day and night until then, sir."

"Good. How many soldiers do you have now?"

"Fifteen. Another Anomaly arrived last night from the Hudson Valley."

"Prepare them well, St. James. We're going to need every last one if we want to take out Heidelberg."

"Yes, sir."

The meeting soon moved onto the Reds and how they had recently crossed into Ukraine, heading closer and closer to Berlin, but Zara's thoughts had drifted to her recruits. Her very own troop of Anomalies. After Bastian left, she had been itching to get back out on the front, but Murdock thought it was too risky with the hefty reward on her head, not to mention the posters of her face plastered throughout the Territories. Murdock then laid out his plan for her: to train and lead their new Anomaly recruits. After the revolution had broken out, they had come out of hiding and sought out the Alliance, oftentimes getting transported from chapter to chapter until they reached this bunker. Murdock had gone to great lengths to bring them here, and now he expected Zara to make soldiers out of them.

It wasn't easy work — she knew that now. Zara had been training them for over a month, but the Anomalies were just getting a handle on their abilities. Most of them had spent their lives fighting their power, too afraid of catching the Nazis' attention; but here at the bunker Zara commanded them to practice their skills for hours each day. And she was starting to see results. Marcus Reilly could teleport between rooms now without getting stuck in a wall. Jess Toscano, a tiny girl of only fourteen, could heal broken bones, which was a big leap from when she first arrived and could barely touch a paper cut. So far, the troops' roster of powers was impressive: super-strength, chameleon skin, weather manipulation, and the most prized of all, earthquake summoning. There were only fifteen of them compared to the hundreds of Nazi sentinels, but Zara had faith in her little troop.

Half an hour later, the meeting concluded. Murdock left the room to speak with more advisers while Alene hurried to radio her chapters. She nodded at Zara as she passed, but she left it at that. She hadn't said much since Garrison's passing, and Zara hadn't pressed it. She figured Alene needed time to heal, as they all did.

With the room nearly empty, Uncle Red gathered his paperwork, and Zara followed him out of the door. Due to their new positions, she only caught snatches of her uncle here and there, but she was happy to see him thriving at his work. Every day, she noticed him standing a little taller, his back a little straighter. This was the Redmond St. James that her mother would have recognized.

Uncle Red tapped his pen against his notepad. "Are you busy?" he asked. "I could use a hand in the weapons bay."

"I was going to grab a shower before the Anomalies finished training, but maybe after that?"

"No, no, I'll manage. I'll see you at dinner, then?"

"You know I don't skip meals."

That made him smile, and Zara smiled back. She could never erase Mission Metzger or her mother's passing, but Uncle Red was finally showing glimpses of his old self: the smiles, the jokes, the fire that burned inside him to fight the Empire. She liked this side of him.

"I'll meet you at eight-thirty. Don't be late," he said.

Of course, Uncle Red would always be Uncle Red.

Parting ways, Zara headed to her room to find her towel. Two of her soldiers, the two youngest, darted past her. "Hey, no running in the halls!" she called out.

The two girls, one fourteen and one fifteen, halted and mumbled quick apologies. "Sorry, Ms. St. James."

Zara sighed. She wished they would call her Zara like her uncle did, but nearly everyone at the bunker addressed her this formally. Uncle Red told her that she better get used to it. Now that every man, woman, and child in the Territories could recognize her, she would never be just Zara again. She was the face of the Alliance, the Anomaly who had killed the Führer himself. Although thinking about all of that made Zara uneasy. She was just a cleaning girl turned rebel who had to eat and sleep like everyone else.

"Where were you running off to anyway?" Zara asked.

"Alene told us we could go upstairs for a few minutes if we were really quiet," said Jess, the healer. She glanced up at Zara and nibbled her lip. "You want to come with us?"

Zara bit her own lip. She really *did* need to shower, and she had a hundred more tasks on her plate, but heading up to the hotel was a treat in the dingy bunker. Only a few soldiers were allowed up there at a time, in case the Nazis were scouting out the area.

Her shower could wait.

With the girls running ahead, Zara followed them up the bunker ladder and into the hotel foyer, which had long collected a thick layer of dust over its damask furniture and uneven floors. Jess sneezed while they padded toward the window. Outside, the sun had already set, which allowed a dusting of stars to shine across the moonless sky.

"Never thought I'd be so happy to look out a window," Jess said with a sigh. Sometimes she reminded Zara of Bastian, with her gentle hands and her soft heart. She couldn't help but think that, maybe in another world, Jess and Bastian could have been friends.

Zara's fingers drifted into her left pocket, where she kept the first telegram that Bastian had sent her after he left. It was a brief message, but he told her that he and his mother had arrived in Iceland safely and that he would soon depart for Brussels. The Widerstand had already asked him to pen an essay for their underground paper and had set up a radio interview upon his arrival. He was doing well, he said, excited yet nervous. At the end of the message, he had written simply: *Remember that night by the stream?* That little sentence still made Zara flush, even weeks later. Their night by the stream had been the night of their kiss.

She had written him back, of course, but hadn't yet received a reply. She kept badgering the comms team if they had heard anything from the Widerstand, but the answer was always the same: *Not yet. It's going to be hard to get in touch with them.*

Patience. She needed patience.

Zara hated being patient.

A loud pop-pop-pop burst beyond the window, and Zara froze. She was about to yank the girls into the bunker and alert everyone that the Nazis had discovered their hiding spot, but then she saw the radiant colors spreading above the tree line, the little bursts of silver and red and ribbons of green.

"Fireworks!" the girls said. "Somebody in town must've found some!"

Zara relaxed as more lights sprouted above them. Maybe the citizens of Wardensville were in a festive mood. Zara herself hadn't seen fireworks in years, not since she was little and her mother had lit a few for them. It had been on an evening much like this one, with a clear sky and a quiet night and their eyes so bright.

July 4. Suddenly, Zara remembered the current date. The old Independence Day.

A smile spread over her lips.

Huddled against the window, she watched the fireworks pop and wane, filling her eyes with their exploding color. She wished her mom and Mrs. Talley were here, watching alongside her. Then her mind drifted to Bastian, who was so far away but who could be staring up at the very same stars, half a world apart.

Finally, Zara thought about this new world springing up around her feet, a world without Führers or *Heil Hitler*s, a world where fireworks would reign in the skies instead of sentinels and gunfire. Where a German boy and a half-Japanese *Kleinbauer* could stand next to each other, hand in hand, without their pasts splitting them to pieces.

Zara yearned for such a world.

And she would keep fighting until she found it.

ACKNOWLEDGMENTS

My first thank-you goes to the readers of *The Only Thing to Fear*. I've wanted to become an author since I was seven years old, so it has been a dream come true to have this book published and to have found readers like you.

A million thanks must go to Jim McCarthy, my doggedly persistent and incredibly hilarious agent. He was determined to sell this book — and sell it he did! I thank my lucky stars every day that he pulled me out of the slush pile and never gave up on me. Every writer needs a Jim by her side.

Next up, I never could have gotten here without the brilliance of Jody Corbett, my editor at Scholastic. *The Only Thing to Fear* was merely a shell of a novel when it first reached Jody's desk, but she read it, saw potential in it, and helped me mold it into something I'm proud of. Jody, I owe you an entire orchard of honeycrisp apples.

I'd also like to thank the entire team at Scholastic for their hard work and support. This is a publishing house that I've admired since elementary school, and I'm still a little speechless to be a part of the amazing Scholastic family.

To Andrea Coulter, my earthquake buddy and Olive Garden aficionado, thank you for being such a wonderful friend and sharp-eyed critique partner. To Ellen Oh, I thank the Writing Gods every day for putting you in my life. You're the big sister I never had.

A big group hug to Jessica Spotswood and Robin Talley, my friends and fellow Jim McCarthy acolytes. I wouldn't have survived the last four years without you cheering me on every step of the way. And another hug to

Miranda Kenneally, who is all-around awesome and one of the most generous people I have ever met.

To the Sisukas — Debra Rook, Kathleen Fox, Rebecca Petruck, and Cindy Cipriano — I'm so glad that we met at the SCBWI Carolinas retreat back in 2009. You guys are the best. To Dr. Paul Kerry, thank you for taking time out of your busy schedule to help me with my German vocabulary. Any mistakes are mine.

And now for the mushy stuff . . .

Thank you, Mom and Dad, for taking me to the library when I was little and buying me a ridiculous amount of books. To my brother, Ryan, I hope you enjoy your big sister's novel. It's not Redwall or A Song of Ice and Fire, but I think it'll be up your alley. To my sister, Kristy, thank you for reading all of my novels and for always asking me questions about them. You don't know how much your enthusiasm has meant to me.

Much thanks to my mother-in-law, Donna Richmond, for her support and for always asking, "When can I read that book of yours?" And thank you to my sister-in-law, Aimee Richmond Rhoads. Like Zara said, the ache of missing you never goes away.

To my little daughter, Aimee Rose, you're a bit too young to read Mommy's first novel, but I can't wait to share it with you one day. Until then, I hope you don't mind our weekly trips to the library.

Lastly, to my husband, Justin, how can I put into words the depths of my heart? Thank you for loving me, for supporting me in this crazy dream of mine. When we first got married, you turned to me and said, "Hey, why don't you try writing full time for a while?" I'm still not sure what I've done to deserve you, but I'm thankful for you every day, for every minute — even when you eat my leftovers and refuse to use your blinkers. But you know that I love you anyway.